I0587576

TOMORROW

IS

YESTERDAY

KASTUŚ AKUŁA

CONTENTS

PREFACE TO 2025 EDITION

In 1968, when Kastuś Akuła first published *Tomorrow is Yesterday*, he offered something rare in the English-speaking world: a Belarusian account of WWII told without Soviet censors, Soviet mythmaking, or Soviet heroes. His Belarus was not the monolithic "partisan republic" of official history, nor a minor province on someone else's map. It was a homeland caught between two empires, each calling itself a liberator, and each killing without mercy.

We are bringing this novel back into print in 2025, the centenary year of Akuła's birth. In the hundred years since he was born in the village of Veratei, Belarusians have seen the collapse of empires, the churn of war, the violence of dictatorship, and the long reach of exile. They have also endured the quieter oppression of being misrepresented, or left out entirely, from the stories told by their neighbours. Akuła's voice refused that erasure.

Born Aleś Kachan in 1925, he grew up in a rural Belarus where the borders, language of instruction, and ruling authorities changed frequently. His mother died in 1939; his father was arrested after WWII and died in a Soviet camp. As a teenager under German occupation, Akuła trained briefly as a teacher, then attended the Vilnius Belarusian Gymnasium. His first poems appeared in the wartime Belarusian press.

Arrested and sent to a Minsk camp during WWII, he was eventually released, joined the *Belarusian Krajova Abarona* in 1943, and was evacuated west with its officer school. He saw battle in Alsace, fought alongside the

French Resistance, and later joined the 2nd Polish Corps of the British Eighth Army. After the war, he completed British officer training, then emigrated to Canada, working first on farms before moving to Toronto. There, he founded the first Belarusian Canadian diaspora organization that still exists today.

Akuła was as active politically as he was culturally. In 1967, at Expo in Montreal, he publicly denounced the visiting Soviet delegation, scattering anti-Soviet leaflets and shouting, "Death to Moscow's killers! Freedom for Belarusians! Long live independent Belarus!" He founded the newspaper *Belaruski Emigrant* and the veterans' journal *Zvažaj*. Through all of it, he wrote.

Tomorrow is Yesterday was his second book and his first novel — and his only one written in English. It is a war story, but not the kind most readers are used to. By the time the Germans arrived, much of Belarus had already spent over two decades under a brutal Soviet regime, enduring civil war, repression, famine, and tyranny. For many Belarusians, whose image of Germany came from the very different experience of WWI, any alternative to the Soviets seemed to hold promise. But the war that followed was not only a clash of empires — in Belarus it was also a civil war, with Belarusians resisting both occupiers and, at times, fighting one another, falling prey to both sides.

Akuła does not grant his characters the comfort of simple heroism. We see them forced into impossible choices — where survival may require compromise, and refusing to compromise can cost everything. His war is not a morality tale; it is a record of how people navigate the space between annihilation and dishonour.

The novel's roots reach deeper than the 20th century. Akuła invokes the Kalinowski Uprising of 1863, drawing a line from 19th-century insurgents to the Belarusian resistance of his own lifetime. That line, we might add in 2025, is still unbroken. Belarus remains under authoritarian rule, its language, culture, and political self-determination are still under pressure. To read *Tomorrow is Yesterday* now is to see not only the past, but also its reflection in the present.

Akuła's style is part of that experience. His English is the English of a mid-century émigré writing in a second language — direct, sometimes archaic, always his own. Sentences can come as blunt as rifle fire; metaphors may draw from a rural Belarus that has since vanished. For this Grunwald edition, the text has been lightly edited for clarity and readability, but the voice remains as raw and distinctive as when it first appeared.

This is not a comfortable book. It is not meant to be. For readers in 1968, it broke the Soviet monopoly on the story of Belarus in WWII. For readers in 2025, it shows how long that shadow still falls — and how the struggle for freedom and self-determination, from Kalinowski's insurgents to today's prisoners of conscience, continues today.

Read it as a novel, and you will find drama, survival, and the stubborn spark of endurance. Read it as testimony, and you will hear the voice of a man who lived through two tyrannies and carried his homeland with him into exile. Whichever way you approach it, it is part of a story that is still unfolding.

TOMORROW IS YESTERDAY

To My Countrymen in Bondage
Who Will Rise Again

1

THE ARREST

Late that morning, Mary Karaway arrived in the city full of hope. She intended to find a job, settle in, and then hunt down the murderer of her mother and children.

But things did not work out that way. Twelve hours after her arrival, she faced a police desk, ignorant of which law of her newly adopted country she had broken. She was some six thousand miles away from her home, which had been turned by the war into a pile of ashes. She knew not a single friendly soul in this strange, huge city. Her knowledge of the language was limited to a few dozen words. The mess she was in, she thought, and the mess was not of her own making...

At a glance Mary differed little from the two streetwalkers facing the police officer in front of her. That beaten look almost passed for a trademark of the least fortunate members of the world's oldest profession, incessantly harassed by various protective bodies of an allegedly pious society. The difference between Mary and the streetwalkers was discernible in their poise and behavior. While the two in front had an air of familiar nonchalance about them – as if they were changing streetcars on the journey from one adventure to the next – Mary looked around like a rabbit that was scared to death, expecting to be torn to shreds by a ferocious dog.

The women were chatting to each other while one of them answered the officer's questions. Evidently they felt quite at home here. Had Mary been less preoccupied with her own predicament, she would certainly have concluded that the ladies were hardly novices.

Mary Karaway was a shapely blonde of medium size. The somewhat large cheap print dress she was wearing did no justice to her well proportioned figure. Her naturally waved, sun-bleached hair cried for attention. Wrinkles radiated from her large, expressive, frightened blue eyes. Her lips showed no trace of make-up, and the sun-coloured cheeks enhanced her delicate, natural beauty. Her frantic, furtive glances at the people in front of her and at the policewoman hovering close by betrayed a desperation born of uncertainty.

She clutched her worn brown handbag in her right hand, and held a gray jacket across her left arm. She shifted from one foot to the other – these were probably the sorest feet in the city. All afternoon and well into the evening she had searched for a man whose address her uncle had given her. But where his house was supposed to be, new apartments had been built. Thus the single link – the stepping stone by which she intended to join the huge and dynamically growing population of Toronto – had disappeared.

Mary had not given up at once. Discouraged, but refusing to admit failure, she ate a meal in a restaurant and then resumed combing the neighbourhood. When she was unable to learn anything about her uncle's friend, she assumed there must be some people of Slavic origin in the city who could help her. Even the sound of her native language could have raised her sagging spirits.

She was out of luck here too because the few people on crowded sidewalks, around beer parlours, theatres, and restaurants, responded negatively when she asked them if anyone spoke Byelorussian. Some looked at her suspiciously, sized her up with their eyes; others simply ignored her. Never before had she felt so forlorn and dejected. Her attempts to reach them, to ask for assistance, failed miserably. A whole world was turbulent inside her. She was a world apart in this sea of easy-going

Canadians.

She rejoined the human race swiftly when, dead tired, her feet sore from walking, her head buzzing with the noises of the big city, she sat to rest on a park bench. Two drunks sauntered across the green lawn from the sidewalk and, without saying a word, sat down close to her. One of them looked her over. Reeking of beer and tobacco, he stuttered, "Looking for fun, sister?"

Puzzled, Mary tried to figure out what the man wanted.

"Hey, this is a new one! She won't even answer." His companion laughed. "Try again, Harry."

The man named Harry moved closer, polluting the crisp spring air with his filthy breath. "I said, lady, do you want to have some fun?"

Before she could react, the other fellow nudged Harry and muttered a warning. "There's a damn copper behind us." Harry and his friend got up and quickly walked away.

Presently a tall man in a black uniform faced Mary accusingly. He barked some questions to her. When she could produce no satisfactory answers, the policeman took her to the cruiser, where she joined the other two on their way to the station. Now, for the first time in this country, she realized she must have run afoul of some law. Once again she was face to face with the authorities, and this reminded her of the police state that had wrecked her life.

Her attention was caught by the curly red hair and the square jaw of the police officer behind the desk. She had an uneasy foreboding. What will they do to me? Lock me up? Is this just the beginning – the arrival that I had pictured in such rosy colours?

The policeman's questions were brief and to the point. Frustrated by her inability to answer them, Mary mumbled incoherent answers, hectically showing them her passport. The man stared at her with mildly curious eyes.

"This is not the way to start here, sister," he commented in an acid tone. "Take her away, Pat." He motioned to the police woman.

Looking at the other two behind bars, Mary had the impression they felt quite at home there. Obviously no recruits to the game, whatever it was. Their nonchalance affected Mary in an adverse way; instead of relaxing and joining them and laughing at the world, she withdrew into herself even more. This was probably due to her slowly dawning realization that for the first time in her life she was being locked up with common prostitutes. Moreover, according to the police, she was herself a prostitute. This repulsive idea made her involuntarily shrink from her two cellmates.

"Aw, come on sister, cheer up. They won't bite you. Tomorrow you'll be out again. You'll see. What's the matter with you? Are you fresh at this game?"

One of the women was trying to reason with Mary, appraising her with skillful eyes.

"Even if you are fresh, you'll get experience in no time, sister. That's right, in no time at all. I told you, there's nothing to worry about. As they say, these are occupational hazards. Ugh! Hazards, my eye! These jackals in the city hall want our dough, so they go out and nab us. But I'm telling you, one day you'll get smart and smell these stinking coppers from a distance. Honest to God, you will. Then they won't catch you. Of course, if you get loaded once in a while."

She kept prattling on, reeking so strongly of whisky that Mary moved away from her.

"Quit bothering her, Susan," interrupted the other woman. "Don't you see she's not interested? Maybe she doesn't know the language, like the cop said."

"Well, in this business you don't have to. Just spread the goods and grab the dough."

2

MERCY IN THE NIGHT

"This is quite a start," Mary thought, while the other two chattered to each other. "I'm in jail with two prostitutes, away from anybody I know, in a foreign country, with no knowledge of the language, customs, laws, people, no place to call my own. So this is the way I'm starting my life here."

"Somewhere in this city the murderer of my children and my mother walks the streets, probably posing as a respectable citizen, perhaps a father himself by now. Am I on the right track? What track? In a jail cell?"

Suddenly, Mary had to stifle her incipient laughter. She sensed she would suddenly explode in a macabre tremor, laughing at herself, at this God-forsaken world, and at the thing they called justice. If she did not watch herself, she would rock with laughter until every fiber of her body yearned for respite. She could not, she must not. If she did, they would lock her up in the insane asylum and then, she knew, she really would be at the end of her rope.

As recollections flooded her mind, bitter memories took over. A terrible war raged. Remnants of the Red Army congested the roads, took cover in the forests and an avalanche of Germans swept them clean. A week earlier, the mailman handed her the dreaded official letter. It curtly announced that her young husband, one Valodzia Karaway, was missing in action. "Missing" was the key word. Perhaps he was killed or taken prisoner. She kept nursing hope that one day Val would return and together they would resume their life where they had left off.

Mary never knew her father, and once her mother told

her that Mary had never laid eyes on her father. He had
perished somewhere in the trenches of the First World
War.

Now there were two small children to look after. Until
recently she taught at the village school. Somehow the
family managed to live on Mary's meager teacher's salary,
the pittance her husband and mother earned on the
collective farm. Now Val was gone, perhaps for good.

Their village of Shuly, a half mile off the highway,
nestled on the edge of a forest. During the long nights and
cloudy days the highway was clogged by the retreating
Red Army. On clear days, low-flying German planes
paralyzed it. The villagers were tense, expecting the
unknown. They had their full share of Russian
introduced collectives, and any change would be
welcome. Centuries old, the national adage once again
rang true:

Daddy, daddy, the devil knocks at the door!
Never worry, little one – if it's not a Muscovite.

The villagers of Shuly had drunk their bitter cup to the
dregs. The retreat of the Russians resurrected their hopes
for a better future. After all, there is God in heaven who
somehow must compensate them for the hardships they
had endured.

No smiles crossed the faces of the villagers. Their own
kin had been mobilized into the army to defend the hated
colonial regime and Holy Mother Russia, the source of
their misfortunes and privation. Anxiety was written on
the harrowed faces of the senior villagers. They
reminisced about the time "a way back" when the
Germans had occupied part of their country during the
First World War. Based on those reminiscences, they

attempted to build an image of the advancing Germans, who might tomorrow and forever after be their masters.

In the late afternoon the skies cleared, and the sun smiled on the war-torn land. The highway was so congested that a prompt dispersal in case of an air attack was unthinkable. True to their reputation for combining punctuality and surprises in the blitzkrieg, German fighters appeared in the West, strafing and pounding the roadway with light bombs. One after the other, the planes dived upon their defenceless prey. What half an hour earlier had been an orderly, retreating army now became a panicky mass of burning equipment, dismembered limbs, and writhing bodies. The sea of men, horses and equipment now attempted to take cover in the woods and bushes adjacent to the highway. The fighter planes swooped around, hunting the unfortunate men out. Some circled as far as Mary's village, and the people, horrified by the terrible carnage on the highway, kept under cover.

Darkness brought an uneasy calm over the countryside. The suspense increased. Hardly a villager ventured out to the highway, lest one might be taken for a disguised German parachutist and executed on the spot. That night few villagers slept soundly in their beds.

Mary's children went to bed late. She bent over them in semidarkness and whispered her prayers. Still numb with the shock of the day's events, Mary perched on the bed and stroked the curly blonde hair of her son Valodzia. The six-year old boy was her pride and joy. Three-month old Alenka slept soundly in the crib, suspended by the birch-tree pole from the ceiling.

Who could fathom the depths of this lonely mother's heart? For the millionth time she called out to her husband Valodzia, whom she believed must still be alive somewhere. She loved him so much she was afraid to think what she would do if he never returned.

A faint knock on the front door! Mary and her mother froze. Who was out there at this late hour? The knock was repeated, louder and more insistent. Immediately thereafter there was a thud as if a heavy sack of potatoes had fallen on the verandah.

"Mary, my dear, go out and see who it is," her mother said, anxiously.

Mary tiptoed to the front door. She stopped and listened. The whole world seemed to have disappeared. A dog barked in the distance. Then a low guttural groan reached her ears from whatever was outside. Mary unlatched the door and opened it just wide enough to peek out. When her eyes grew accustomed to the darkness, she could make out a prostrate figure in uniform. Holding her breath, Mary strained her eyes even further.

"Who is it, Mary?" mother inquired.

"There's a man here. A soldier, I think."

After a moment's silence, her mother's voice came again,

"Well, let him in. What are you waiting for?"

"He's lying down, wounded maybe..."

Mary recognized the Soviet uniform but could hardly discern the man's face in the darkness. Then her mother approached from behind and said, "Let me see, Mary."

As they bent and examined the mysterious bulk by their doorstep, the figure stirred, and a faint whisper called out, "Help me."

"What are we going to do?" Mary asked.

"Well, in the first place we can't stand here with our hands down, that's for sure," said her mother, her voice tinted with urgency. "Let's take him inside."

They grabbed one arm each and attempted to raise the man to his feet, to prop him up against the wall. He groaned again and his mouth was wide open. In the heat of this activity, Mary was prompt to note that the soldier was young and handsome. His eyes opened, then closed again. As they tried to stand him on his feet, he groaned louder and louder.

"Look," said mother, "'the left leg is wounded above the knee." Mary examined the torn and burned trousers, the sticky flesh. She drew her bloodied hand away.

"Mother, try to hold him below the armpits, I'll grab the legs."

With a great effort, they dragged him inside and paused, contemplating what to do next. The man's breath was heavy.

"Let's lay him on your bed, Mary," mother commanded.

They dragged him beyond the partition and laid him down. "Now light the lamp. Put it in the corner and shade it. We have to be careful. Germans may be around."

Tiptoeing around the bedroom, Mary lighted the small kerosene lamp and drew the window blinds down. The two women stood at the foot of the wooden bed, mutely staring at the figure clad in green. He could not have been more than thirty five years old, his face pale and handsome, his trousers burned above the left knee, the raw flesh an ugly mess.

The wounds seemed to be extensive. Without a word, Mary fetched a basin, filled it with cold water from the pail that stood by the big brick stove on the birch-tree stump, and brought a clean towel. Her deft hands removed the sticky trousers, washed away the clots of blood, and the raw flesh was fully exposed. Even a child could tell at a glance it was a bad burn.

"Look, what a wound, and burned too!" Mary exclaimed, hesitating what to do next. "He must have lost lots of blood. What are we going to do, mother? This man should be in a hospital."

"I'll tell you what, dear. Never mind a hospital. He needs first aid, and we have to do the best we can and rely on God's mercy. I'll tell you what. You run over and fetch

Nina. She knows all kinds of herbs, and I'm sure she can help. Let's hope the wound is clear of shrapnel. If not, well... run along, girl, there's no time to waste."

Mother's deeply furrowed face projected both compassion for the man's life and extreme urgency. The soldier opened his eyes wide and attempted to utter something. The women froze, listening. Lips moved, and out came a faint whisper, "Water..."

Mary brought a copper cup filled with cool water. They propped the man's head higher on the pillow. Opening his misty eyes, he drank a little, drew in a deep breath, closed his eyes, and lay peacefully. Mary donned the old gray jacket, tied an outworn kerchief under her chin, and without another word left the house.

The old woman Nina lived near the village just inside the forest. In the area she was widely known and respected as an outstanding shaptukha, almost a sorcerer. Nina had the ability to heal infections, poisonous snake bites, and other minor maladies with herbs and their liquids, although some villagers would swear they watched Nina administer the remedy to the infirm in a totally incomprehensible language. Her utterings and whispers, maintained those in the know, had a great healing power. How it was done, whether by summoning mysterious spirits or employing the tricks of superstition, nobody knew for sure.

As far back as Mary could recall, Nina had appeared to her to be as old and as mysterious as she did today. She never really aged. Her small hut, with its tiny blind windows, its hunch-backed thatched roof, just inside the forest, was a puzzle in itself to the youngsters of the village. Mary approached the dwelling with forebodings. She made her way through the woods cautiously, lest ghosts or other unknown spirits be disturbed in their lairs and swoop down on this messenger of mercy.

It took no time at all to arouse the old woman. But Mary

had to make quite an effort to explain to the old shaptukha the nature of her business, for the recluse was hard of hearing. As soon as she understood what had happened, Nina fetched her old linen bag, with its herbs and ointments, and hobbled back to Mary's house. The old woman walked slowly in silence. Her eyes downcast, a bit hunch-backed, her medicine bag suspended on a stick across her right shoulder, the woman trotted in small careful steps alongside Mary. "Now, my little daughter, keep close to me, for I cannot see right, I cannot see right," she implored Mary in her low guttural voice. From time to time Mary held the old one's elbow and gently steered her along the path.

The sickle of the half moon rose in the East, its bronze face now and then disappearing behind the dark clouds. The sleeping countryside lay quiet, except for an occasional barking dog. Chants and noise came from the highway, which had apparently come alive again after that terrible afternoon slaughter. The old shaptukha walking in small steps beside her, the bronze sickle in the dark sky, the sinister nocturnal forest, the traffic on the road, and the novelty of today's events... all this seemed so unreal as to be almost unbelievable. Perhaps this old Nina was an evil witch leading Mary – an orphaned girl – to some devil's feast to be roasted on the fire. Mary had an active imagination. In all the tales she heard, all the witches – and there was an abundance of them – had the yellow mask-like face of this old shaptukha.

The nightingale's low-pitched trill from bearded willow trees some distance to the left on the banks of the creek, pricked Mary back into reality. The bird appeared to be quite oblivious of the unusual events now being staged in its vicinity. The incorrigible singer! How would it comprehend that its song now sounded hollow in a woman's heart? The voice attuned to love now sounded a discord in the echo of the war. In Mary's house, an unknown man lay fighting for his life. Mary would like to imagine that it was her own Val and that she was the one on whom his recovery hinged. Perhaps her husband too was alive, sheltered and looked after by someone only God knows where.

Mary and the shaptukha entered the house. They heard subdued voices. Apparently the soldier had regained consciousness. They approached the bed. Nina laid the linen bag on the bed's edge and proceeded to exchange a few words with Mary 's mother.

"The children woke up," Mary's mother said. "I had a hard time soothing them. The boy kept asking for you. What kept you so long?"

Without answering, Mary looked at the children who slept peacefully, tucked under their covers, and said, "Was it really that long, mother? I hurried so."

Now Mary came close to the soldier's bed and gazed at the man. His gray eyes were now half open. There was something peculiar and probing in the well-outlined features of his face. Mary felt the eyes looked at her and through her, with a brutality all their own. She recalled she had seen eyes like that somewhere – and she could not recollect whose they were – and that they belonged to a brute rather than a man.

"So you are Mary. Your mother told me about you and your Valodzia," the man's even voice said in Russian.

"You are Russian?" Mary asked.

"Yes. Ouch!" he cried out in pain, his face contorted, as Nina worked on the wound.

"Aksinya, bring the lamp over, I can't see well," the shaptukha asked Mary's mother.

Mary fetched the lamp and held it close to the old woman. Silently their eyes followed her wrinkled thin fingers. To the raw flesh she applied some dark aromatic ointment, then laid huge soft leaves on top of the wound, and asked Aksinya for material with which to bandage the wound.

"I say he's been lucky," Nina commented "Whatever it was, it burned the flesh, no damage to the bone. It'll take some time to heal, but he's young and strong and he'll be all right."

The soldier stirred uneasily as Mary held his leg and Nina wrapped the cotton around it. Mary noticed a wide, egg-shaped brown birthmark on the outside just above the kneecap.

"How long, Nina? Can you tell?" Aksinya inquired.

The shaptukha did not reply at once. She proceeded to gather belongings, meditatingly looked at the man on the bed and then at Aksinya, and said in her low voice, "I can't exactly say; maybe two months or more... bad burns like his take an awful long time to heal."

The two Karaway women froze in silence, exchanging glances. The alarm clock ticked away on the home-made wardrobe by the wall.

"My God, what will happen when the Germans come," Aksinya's anxious voice exclaimed. "They may take him away before he recovers"

"You have to hide him," Nina said.

"What can we do, two helpless women? Where can we hide him?"

"I'm sure you can think of something," the shaptukha retorted. She washed her hands, Mary assisting her with the soap and towel. Fetching her medicine bag, she said to Mary, "My dear, maybe you can help me to get back. It's dark and I can't find my way alone."

"Certainly, grandmother, certainly."

As the two women disappeared into the forest, Aksinya was pensive and sat at the bedside. She stared at the closed eye-lids of the soldier with an anxiety and apprehension she could not explain. This was contrary to her usual self. All she had done was her Christian duty; she was sure anybody would do the same in these

3
THE NEW MASTERS

Early the next morning the Germans came. Without any opposition, German tank units and motorized infantry proceeded peacefully down the dusty road. It was an impressive show by any standard.

The village folk ventured out to the highway and stood quietly by the roadside, their mouths agape, as the Wehrmacht advanced. These alien people had beaten what was alleged to be the mightiest army on earth. What would they bring with them?

Their uncertainty as to the Germans' reaction to their presence by the highway disappeared, the villagers relaxed, and smiles appeared on some faces. A few courageous souls waved their hands at the passing armed procession, and the dusty, sweaty occupants of the tanks and lorries responded favourably.

Beneath this show of good faith, deep down in the hearts of the villagers there were mixed feelings. Who could tell what to expect? The knowledgeable old folks commented in a guarded fashion. Suspicion gnawed at their hearts. During their lifetime, they had sustained the hardships of the First World War and had licked their wounds for a decade or more afterwards. Byelorussia, their country, had regained independence, but not for long. The tug of war between foreign predators resumed, and shortly after the war their country was partitioned and recolonized by Moscow and Warsaw. The burden of colonial oppression bore so heavy on everyone that any change was most welcome. The older villagers figured they lived in an imported hell and theirs was a dead-end road on a downward spiral.

Mary Karaway and her mother faced the new day with trepidation. What would the Germans do if they came and found a Red Army man in their house? They imperilled both the soldier and themselves. One does not kick out a man just because he is a foreigner, not in this country anyway. Yet they must do something. The soldier needed time to convalesce, and Mary's was no hospital bed. As they stood chatting in subdued voices outside in the warm sun, Mary holding Alenka to her breast, Aksinya said to her daughter, "The poor fellow told me he's from Leningrad. Just married and had to go into the army. Someplace, his wife is worrying about him as you worry about your dear Valodzia. This terrible war, my God!"

"Did he tell you his name?" Mary asked.

"Something like Kol-, let me recall...Kolpakoff, I think. That's right. 'Vanya Kolpakoff', he said."

"Do you like him, mother?"

"Like him? I haven't thought about it. I'm sure I don't dislike him. Do you?"

"I'm not sure. As he stared closely at me last night I had a strange feeling. I'm not sure..."

"Go on," her mother urged her.

"Oh, I don't know...I felt as if those eyes were not looking at me but through me. Funny, isn't it? Perhaps I'm mistaken. The man is sick now. But somehow my sixth sense warns me...Really, I don't know, mother."

"Strange you say that. I had the same impression. But the man is harmless and needs help. Whatever he was or is, we must help him, Mary. Maybe God sent him to us. Think about your own Valodzia."

"Of course, you are right, mother. Do you think any neighbours know about him?"

"How can they? He came in quite late and nobody as much as mentioned anything to me this morning. Except for Nina..."

"I suppose we have to call her again to change the dressing, eh?"

"We have to."

"Did you give him anything to eat last night?"

"No. He was in no condition, but today he had some food."

Two days later, Germans appeared in the village. The squad of infantry – with a young, blonde, blue-eyed lieutenant in command – drove up in front of the school, stirring everyone from his dwelling. Even before the civilian who came with him spoke broken Byelorussian through the loudspeaker, the villagers approached the school-yard in groups and singly, their faces all expectation.

A line of armed infantrymen kept them at a distance from the officer, who surveyed the unfamiliar peasant weather-beaten faces from the school's verandah. He then proceeded to rattle away the first order of the new authorities, the civilian interpreter conveying this to the gathered crowd. From the lieutenant's gibberish, the peasants gathered that one mighty benevolent and noble-hearted fellow named Adolf Hitler, for the golden future of Europe, undertook to liberate all oppressed peoples, Byelorussians among them, from Judeo-Bolshevism, and now was rapidly accomplishing his unselfish task. Soon the first fruit of Adolf's outstanding generosity for Byelorussian peasants would be the liquidation of the hated collectives. Everyone able and willing to work would be awarded free land.

At this bit of news, the faces in the tense crowd brightened and voices of unreserved approval were heard. The lieutenant called for order and continued. In return for the *Fuehrer*'s generosity, the liberated people must help uphold the new order, help Germans liquidate the remnants of the hated Judeo-Bolshevism. All known communists must be speedily turned over to the local German authorities, who would deal with them according to the new laws. All weapons, radios, typewriters, and other miscellaneous articles must be turned over to the Germans; Red Army deserters must on no account be sheltered but reported to the local German military commandant. To sum it up, the Germans expected the fullest co-operation. Anyone disobeying these orders would be summarily executed.

The Wehrmacht lieutenant ended his reading by announcing that tomorrow or the day after a skeleton local administration would be set up to help the busy Germans in implementing the *Fuehrer*'s blessings. To assist the Germans, and for the citizens' own protection, a police force would also be formed.

After this the Germans speedily departed, presumably to shine the *Fuehrer*'s light, and bestow his blessings on the folks of the next collectivized village.

The order that the Wehrmacht officer had read was pinned to the door of the school building. Everybody's attention was focussed on this neatly printed piece of paper. Underneath the spread-winged eagle and the swastika the text followed in German and Byelorussian. It presented to the villagers the unfamiliar face of the new master, whose features must be minutely scrutinized and considered with the greatest possible attention in every detail. The peasants crowded around it, craned their necks, commented on every word and paragraph. The paramount topic of interest was the item about the liquidation of the collectives and the awarding of free land to everybody who desired to work it himself.

Slow and cautious in their deliberations, reluctant to jump to any conclusions, the peasants took their time discussing the great news. No one seemed eager to go home. The daily chores could wait. Now it was time to think and try to figure out what tomorrow might bring.

Mary stayed home with little Alenka and Valodzia. Aksinya had neither the time nor the courage to linger with the crowd. The wounded soldier in their bedroom now became as menacing as life itself, a Damocles' sword that had to be speedily removed before it plunged down on their lives.

Vanya Kolpakoff ate, slept and rested well. He seemed interested in the new rules and regulations of the Germans, and suggested himself that for the benefit of all concerned he should be removed from the house to a better hiding place. That was when the *lasnichowka* was first mentioned as a possible hideout.

The *lasnichowka* was the residence of the game-keeper, the state-appointed warden of the forest. The house was about a mile away, deep inside the woods. Because of the nature of the Soviet regime, the dwelling itself was an object of hate for the local residents. It harbored a state functionary, who together with his dogs prevented people from making use of the wealth of their woods. Always encumbered by privations and material shortages, the residents needed timber for firewood and for building material. They also needed the various kinds of wild berries and mushrooms of which Byelorussian forests possess an abundance of riches. On top of it all, Byelorussians love forests and the wonders of nature as much as Englishmen love the sea.

The Soviet colonial regime never paid any attention to the interests and needs of the common people. This meant that they had to steal "state property", which included anything and everything in the woods, even berries and mushrooms. The unfortunates who were caught at this were always dealt with very severely. To add insult to injury, a *lasnik* or forest warden, was almost always a Russian, a foreigner in this colonized country. This fact alone was reason enough to treat such an official with suspicion and distrust. He was a foreign bureaucrat who guarded the gates to what the residents rightly considered the richest part of their own land. As if all this had not been enough, the warden was usually corrupt himself: he would pilfer and sell timber to the highest bidder.

To make a long story short, one dry summer day two years ago, the *lasnik's* house went up in smoke. Only a small barn remained intact some distance away from the burned-down house among the birch trees. The state authorities never apprehended the arsonist. Guardedly, as long years of oppression had taught them, many people nevertheless hinted that they were happy about the fire, although the hated official merely moved to another *lasnichowka.*

The abandoned barn now appeared to Mary and her mother as a possible shelter for the soldier in their care. The following night Mary travelled to the next village, where her older married cousin lived, and asked his assistance in removing the soldier from the house. Together they built a rather primitive stretcher, and, in the dark of the night, carried Kolpakoff to the barn in the *lasnichowka.* They put him in the hayloft, which was as comfortable as any bed. The roof of the barn, they felt, was strong enough to provide protection from rain or snow. Everybody, including the soldier, was satisfied with this arrangement. Mary promised to bring him food once a day, possibly after dark to avoid the prying eyes of the neighbours.

4

ATTACK IN THE HAYLOFT

Five weeks had now gone by since the night Vanya Kolpakoff knocked on their door. Late every night Mary would sneak out to take some food to the soldier in the *lasnichowka*. She had to be very cautious to keep her activities secret. Rumours abounded of other wounded or healthy deserters in the area. However, rumours and gossip running rampant through the countryside never filled anyone's stomach. The people of Shuly kept themselves busy with the implementation of the New Order. They partitioned the collective land into private plots and started tending them.

The location of the village provided the people with ringside seats to the process of history. Trainloads of miscellaneous army equipment and supplies as well as reserves of men passed regularly on the railway, just beyond the highway, towards the East. From the opposite direction came hospital trains filled with the wounded.

Along the highway moved thousands of boots as well as bare feet. Long gray columns of Soviet prisoners of war – lean, hungry, exhausted, well-clad or in tatters, wounded or healthy, – passed Westward. European and Asiatic Russians, Byelorussians, Ukrainians, Armenians, Uzbeks and Tadzhiks, Georgians and Cossacks, Kalmuks and Buryats – all the nationalities from the lands colonized by Moscow were amply represented in this uniformed sea of humanity.

They refused to spill their blood for the protection of the Kremlin despot any longer, but escaping Scyllas they found themselves in the deathly embrace of Charybdis.

Guarded by well-armed, well-fed men and huge Alsatian dogs those who were unable to continue on their journey to Golgotha, who were exhausted or infirm, were being shot on the spot. The native population was mobilized to dig holes and bury them.

The natives have never previously witnessed such bestial brutality on their front doorstep. Stalin's dreaded executioners snatched their victims from their beds in the middle of the night, but these so-called liberators did not even make the most elementary efforts to camouflage their crimes. Even the oldest citizens of Shuly, no matter how keenly they searched their memories, were unable to recall past when people would have been sent to their graves so swiftly, inhumanly and openly in front of all who cared to watch.

Being aware of her responsibility for her convalescent word, Mary prayed that the day would soon dawn when the soldier would recover sufficiently to depart. Her own children needed her motherly care and attention, and in the coming fall the schools might reopen. She hoped to be offered a chance to resume her previous job. Of course nobody knew for certain what the new masters intended to do in the realm of education. The now-distant battlefront afforded a dubious measure of security, and Stalin's promised counter-punch did not seem to materialize.

One day Mary made a trip to Haradok, a county seat town some ten kilometers distant, to visit her good friend, the teacher Yustyna Murashka. The friendship between the two originated in the Miensk Pedagogical Institute where they both studied before the war, and was later reinforced by the close proximity of the schools in which they worked. Now Yustyna lived closer to the center of the activities, and was therefore better known than Mary in her distant village.

Yustyna related – and this was supposed to come from

reliable sources – that in September the schools would reopen with instruction in both Byelorussian and German, and that some people were already busy drafting the blueprints of the new educational system. Mary herself would certainly be recalled to resume her pre-war vocation, Yustyna assured her.

Now for the thousandth time Mary thought over the details she had learned from Yustyna. Her own and her family's future depended on it.

One day she fetched a home-made osier basket and ventured out to the woods, ostensibly to pick mushrooms. Her purpose was to see Kolpakoff in the daylight and ascertain his real condition of health. At night Mary could not be sure whether the soldier was completely recovered or not. He certainly acted fit and sound. At times when Mary approached him more closely to take a good look at his healing wound, he would grab her by the hand and try to pull her into the hayloft. She had some narrow escapes. The man was hungry for sex and the other day Mary mentioned this to her mother.

"Well," Aksinya said with a twinkle in her eyes, "you can congratulate yourself: you must have fed him well if he acts like a fenced-in bull. Why don't you take a look at him in daylight? Perhaps what he needs now is a girlfriend, not a nurse." Mother paused, reflected, and then grew serious. "Mary, be careful. Times being what they are, we certainly don't want a deserter in the house."

Mother's warning was wise. She knew her daughter, and knew that if she allowed herself to be seduced by Kolpakoff, their life might become complicated beyond reckoning. "Don't worry, mother," Mary assured her. "I'm not a little girl any more."

As Mary came to the clearing in the forest, she was confronted by a quite different view from the one she was accustomed to seeing at night. Vegetation overgrew the heap of rubble where the game keeper's house had once stood. The moulding still held fast to the rectangular boulders that once formed the foundation of the house. The fire must have burned undisturbed for no log-stumps were visible. The rusty skeletons of two iron beds and a fair-sized pot-bellied stove, toppled on its side, testified mutely to this place having once been a human dwelling. Only a wagtail bird jerked its feathers as it perched on top of the tilted iron bed, appraising the newcomer with curious eyes.

With a brief glance, Mary surveyed the clearing and, wondering about the uninterrupted processes of nature, proceeded to the barn. Like an orphan, abandoned and forlorn, the barn took refuge in the shade of the long, overhanging branches of a birch-tree. Built of dry sturdy pine logs, inside it was partitioned in two: the horse stable and the feed storage compartment. The latter housed a hayloft.

Mary cautiously crossed the threshold and stared at the empty pile of hay. She intended to surprise the man; instead, she was surprised facing the disorderly abandoned bedding, wondering where the occupant of this temporary dwelling might be. She did not have to wonder for long. Through the multi-voiced sounds of the forest she rather felt than heard or saw the emergence of a shadow immediately behind her in the doorway. Before she could take another step inside or turn around, the all-too-familiar voice greeted her: "Welcome, my dear guardian angel!" Abruptly, she turned around.

The man stood in the doorway, with a sizable birch tree stump in the shape of a human head under his left arm and an open jack-knife in his right hand. Earlier he had asked the teacher to bring him a sharp knife so he could do some wood-carvings.

"So you saw me coming?" Mary said, placing her basket on the dirt floor and closely examining her ward in the light of day.

"Certainly," smiled Kolpakoff. "You know I cannot be caught napping by anybody. The military rule: never allow your enemy a chance to surprise you, you know."

The enigmatic flicker of a smile fluttered across his face. The extensive growth of his hair and beard underlined his robust countenance. His complexion appeared sun-tanned. He looked well-rested. Mary wondered exactly when this invalid began sunbathing. At night she invariably found him in the hayloft, and assumed that the man hardly ever left it, except for the calls of nature. It appeared that the invigorating air, and the enchanting tunes of the birds of the forest may be better tonics for physical and spiritual recovery than anything a medical practitioner could prescribe.

"Am I your enemy?" Mary questioned him, her eyes glued to the soldier's face.

"Mary, my dear angel! Did I imply that? You are the most beautiful and certainly the most merciful of all flesh and blood angels one could ever want to admire and possess."

There was something pristine and brutal in his face. Mary could hardly describe it, but it made her feel uncomfortable. The man wore her own Valodzia's civilian clothing. The blue shirt, unbuttoned at the neck, displayed a dark hairy chest. His self-assurance, his solid stance, certainly did not call to mind the feeble, wounded invalid who needed a nurse's care.

Mary could not help wondering what was going on under that inscrutable mask. What his face concealed, his dark gray eyes seemed to display openly. Mary had seen that look before and it made her anxious. She had no doubt that it was a look of sexual desire, made stronger by the weeks of his enforced seclusion in the forest.

Mary had glimpsed the same, only less intense, desire in the eyes of the village boys, who sometimes accosted her on the street, with this single subject in mind, trying desperately to pinch or touch her. The urge displayed in

Kolpakoff's eyes heralded the easily predictable onslaught of the aggressive male.

Now Mary tried to keep her head. She sensed that Vanya was not the type who squandered time on lengthy overtures and preliminaries. A number of times, when she brought him food in the darkness of the evening, he attempted at once to reach for the jackpot and Mary barely managed to repulse his advances. Presently Vanya's eyes, softened by an all-too-obvious haze, began to caress her lightly clad, exquisitely proportioned body, impudently trying to disrobe her. The somewhat tight-fitting dress (a left-over from her not-so-distant immature years) concealed less than it displayed. Mary's natural beauty fitted remarkably into the blooming and serenading nature all around them. The situation was ready-made for love. Any man in Kolpakoff's shoes would have certainly found it almost as impossible to curb his natural desires.

The man continued talking. "Mary, what a wonderful surprise for me. How good to see you in the daylight. You can't imagine what it does to me. All alone here, I often dreamt you were an angel sent by heaven to nurse me"

His eyes displayed alacrity, Kolpakoff threw the birch log away. The jack-knife described a swift arc in the air, as it half-buried its sharp, shiny blade in the pine log of the wall. Kolpakoff advanced one step, his animal senses unbridled, oblivious to everything else around him, his eyes devouring the exquisite beauty in front of him.

"Please, Mary, please. Be good to me. I won't hurt you. I want you desperately."

Mary glanced over her shoulder for an avenue of retreat. There was no time to waste. She felt like a bird in a cage when a hand reaches for it. As she pushed against the door to the stable, Kolpakoff said: "It's bolted on the other side. It's useless to resist, Mary. Why do you want to play hard to get? You can't escape from me now." He kept advancing. To avoid him, Mary lurched and jumped for the front door. The steel grip of his hands tightened around her waist and lifted her off her feet; she was being carried to the hayloft. The grizzled beard jerked in agitation as the muffled feverish voice implored: "Let me, Mary. I won't hurt you."

The woman, gasping for breath, yelled: "Let me go, you beast!"

His hand busy reaching for her undergarment, Kolpakoff's thin lips opened between moustache and beard and sought her lips. Struggling and writhing in his tight grip, she fiercely sank her teeth into his right hand. The soldier cried out in pain and released her. As she jumped away she could hear a loud tearing sound splitting with the hem of her dress. Mary stood by the door and said in raging fury: "You dog! I looked after you, fed you, tended your wounds, so now this is your gratitude. You want me to prostitute myself. Well, you won't have me, not on your life! I have a husband..."

"Oh no, you don't. Your husband is dead, dead!" yelled Kolpakoff in rage. "Do you understand? He's dead!"

"Don't say that! He's not dead. He can't be. He'll come home one day," Mary pleaded with the man, who was now all out to hurt her, in revenge for his unsatisfied desires.

"He's alive, he can't be dead, not my dear Valodzia..." The forest echoed her cries of anguish. Mary was usually a calm, even-tempered person. This man, however, had touched the sorest point of her heart, trying to extinguish the tiniest spark of her hopes. He upset the precarious balance of her spirit after he failed to possess her body.

What rankled her most was that the ungrateful wretch should resort to violence after all she had done for him. The woman seethed with indignation. Still, deep down, she viewed the opportunity of succumbing to her own pent-up desires with some trepidation. For in her physical nature she was a thoroughbred peasant mare.

Any man, whose sexual fancies she would be willing to reciprocate, would discover the rewards of her sexual abandon.

"You ungrateful creature," she continued to admonish the miserable Kolpakoff in the hayloft, "you must leave right now. I don't want ever to see you again. Do you hear me?"

"You'll see plenty of me, Mary, I promise you," she heard his voice as she fetched the basket and left.

At home, her mother instantly noticed Mary's agitation.

"What is it, my little daughter?" she inquired, examining her face minutely. "What happened?"

"Nothing, mother, nothing at all," Mary avoided her mother's eyes, choking back her tears.

"Look at me, Mary," her mother insisted. "Your eyes show that something has happened. You'd never make a good liar. Your dress is torn. Why?"

"Kolpakoff tried to rape me," Mary said calmly and quietly.

"He what? Oh my God! Did he really? "

"Forget it, mother. Nothing happened."

"Nothing, eh? He tried to molest you, tore your dress, and that's nothing, eh? Well! Is that his gratitude for all we've done for him?"

They both fell silent, but the glances they exchanged told more than words could.

"Mother, remember the first night you asked him where he came from?"

"Yes?"

"What did he tell you then?"

"He mentioned Leningrad, I think."

"Are you sure, mother? This is important. Please try to remember."

"Sure I'm sure. But why is it so important?'

"We were talking the other night. I asked him the same question. I don't know why I did it, but I did."

"And?"

"He told me he comes from Rostow-on-the Don. This made me think. There's a possibility he lived in both cities, but he may have lived in neither."

"But why should he lie?" her mother asked after contemplating what Mary had said.

"How should I know? It seems odd to me, I can't explain it," Mary answered with vexation, still under the influence of the man's assault in the barn. Her left thigh was sore, but she felt there would be time enough to look at it later.

"You talked with him a number of times, Mary. I'm not sure you told me everything. Was there anything in your conversations that made you suspicious?"

"Let me think...Mostly he asked me about the Germans: what they did, what their intentions were, as if I knew anything about them myself. But it seems quite natural that in his position he should be on the alert against the Germans. There was something else that struck me as strange coming from him...Let me think...Oh, yes, I've got it: a couple of times he inquired whether the Germans organized any military units, recruiting local men. Strange."

"Did he ever give any hints to you about what he intended to do?"

"Not exactly. I had the impression he hadn't decided what to do himself, he was just waiting for the air to clear. But how do we know anything he told us has any truth in it?"

"We don't," Aksinya said, anxiety showing on her round, wrinkled face. "The sooner he leaves, the better for us. One hears about people being executed by the Germans for sheltering Red Army deserters. God knows, there's no smoke without fire."

"Today I told him leave immediately, that I never wanted to see him again. I think he got the message,"

Mary recalled. "We're not going to feed him any more, mother, so he'll have no choice but leave."

"Good idea, my little daughter," mother assented. "But is he healthy enough to walk? Are you sure he's quite all right?"

"That he is, mother, that he certainly is," Mary asserted. "You should have seen the way he jumped at me. If that wasn't a healthy man's action, then my name isn't Karaway. He's all right, mother. I wonder why he didn't let us discover that sooner. Perhaps he just wanted to take it easy a bit longer while he was looking for the right moment to seduce me..."

Three days later, in broad daylight, Mary went again to the now-so-familiar barn. She looked around and listened carefully, but found no trace of Kolpakoff, or any bedding or clothing. The women heaved a deep sigh of relief. Gone was the ever-present fear of being found out. Their only reward for helping the soldier was the awareness of a small Christian duty fulfilled.

5

TORTURE IN THE CLASSROOM

The second year of war brought new life to the huge Byelorussian forests; an activity not resembling anything they had known in the past. Specially trained operation groups and equipment kept arriving by parachute from what was now called the Big Land. The nuclei of the initial guerilla units were constantly augmented by Red Army deserters and escapees from prisoner-of-war camps. Since recruitment among the local population yielded only paltry results, some "persuasive" methods were employed. The youth in the forested zones were ordered to join or else. Some did. The Germans soon realized that if they were to effectively control the occupied land, they should abandon their beloved motto: "No foreigner will carry arms if a German is to be his master." First units of the so-called *Schutzpolizei* were organized. They failed to attract the morally healthy, for Byelorussians looked upon the new master with distrust and adopted a wait-and-see attitude. The ranks of police were filled with different riff-raff, of predominantly Russian and Polish origin. Many command posts were secured by Volga-Germans, Hitler's preferred blood brothers.

The natives in the forested areas soon felt the pinch of the two giants, locked in the struggle for life or death. Unwilling to choose between the two predators, defenceless, they soon became easy prey for both sides. The draconian rule – "Those that are not with us are against us" – applied indiscriminately by both sides to the local population, brought pillage, murder, rape, fire, and wholesale slaughter. The law of the jungle reigned in the extreme. Later, much too late, facing inevitable extermination, the natives realized their survival hinged on their eventual participation in the total war. Answering the call of Byelorussian patriots, who realized what was coming, many joined the Byelorussian *Samaakhova* for their own self-protection, and, on the eve of German withdrawal, they swelled the ranks of the Byelorussian Home Defence, the BKA.

At first, however, both Red guerillas and German auxiliary units, being unable to gain the loyalty and collaboration of the natives, tried to intimidate or exterminate them. The human dregs, serving either side, considered their uniforms as licences for murder, pillage and rape. Never before did they enjoy such an abundant harvest in their lives.

Mary Karaway's village, situated as it was on the edge of the huge forest, in close proximity to the main highway and the railroad, proved especially vulnerable to both warring forces. At night, Red partisans passed here to blow up the railroad tracks or ambush German units on the road; during the day the Germans dropped in to penetrate the woods and exact their vengeance on anybody suspected of harbouring their adversaries. The population found itself in the jaws of an ever-tightening trap of steel. Every peasant lived on borrowed time.

One cloudy autumn day, Mary was busy instructing the children in her classroom. The second and the fourth grades came in the morning, the first and third in the afternoon. To look after two grades at the same time, eight hours a day, was no easy task. It required total devotion, which Mary, who loved her work and children, possessed in abundance.

Shortly before noon, a loud commotion was heard outside the classroom, before the door flew open with a loud bang. The teacher and the class froze. A grizzled, bearded man in civilian garb, an ominous looking submachine-gun in his right hand, a Red Star on his tilted cap, paused in the doorway. His dark, narrow, piercing eyes savoured the suspense registered on the frightened little faces in the classroom. A man with an owlish face and another with a boyish look craned their necks from behind the grizzled, bearded one. Mary sat petrified on the bench, the pencil in her trembling hand suspended above the workbook. As the intruders entered, a commotion started in the classroom. Some children shrieked; others shrank back in their seats.

"Quiet, everybody quiet! Behave yourselves and no harm will come to anyone!" ordered the man with the Star. His narrow, dark eyes, impressive beard and peremptory attitude inspired awe and brought immediate compliance.

He turned around and looked at the wall above the door. There below the crucifixion figure hung an emblem, Byelorussian Pahonia. Recently Mary had taken Hitler's portrait down just in case something like this should happen. The partisan hesitated for a split second. Then a rapid burst of fire from the sub-machine gun thundered in the classroom, as he sprayed the image of the Great Lithuanian Knight on a white horse in pursuit of the enemy. The other two stood motionless, watching Mary and the children, smirks hovering around their lips. The salvo threw the children into panic. Some yelled, others jumped for the corner. Mary still stood rooted to the same spot, unable to decide how to act in the face of these armed men.

"Now all of you will be seated as you were," the bearded one ordered. "You," he pointed the gun at Mary, "you teach here?"

Choked with fear Mary could not say a word.

"Speak, woman, speak!"

"Yes," stuttered Mary.

"Your name is Mary Karaway?"

"That's my name," replied Mary.

"Don't you think I know it, you bitch?" he spat. All pupils sat quiet and tense, their eyes following every move of his grizzle-bearded warrior.

"What kind of Soviet woman are you poisoning young children with this fascist stuff?" he raised his voice again at the frightened Mary. The teacher paled, but still found her voice: "I didn't think reading, writing and arithmetic had any political affiliation". She instantly began to wonder whether she had said too much.

"You didn't think, eh? Who asked you for your opinion. Did you hear this, boys? She didn't think...ugh!" he mocked her and laughed, his companions assisting him heartily. Presently his narrow lips drew close together. Swiftly, as a cat jumping on its prey, he approached Mary. His angry face a foot away from hers, Mary sniffed the repulsive reek of *samahonka* or home-made vodka.

"You shall speak and think when I order you to, do you hear?" he thundered. He withdrew from Mary, calmly faced the class, and spoke: "Now all you kids, do you know who we are?"

No replies came.

"Come on, speak up. We won't bite you."

"You are partisans," some children said.

"That is quite correct," grizzled beard said, his face aglow. "Now all of you listen carefully. You will now run home as fast as your legs will carry you and tell your parents to be here within the next half hour. Is that clear?"

A murmur of assent followed.

"Hold it a minute. Make it clear to your folks this is an order. If any of them fail to appear here within the next half hour, we will have a talk with them. Is that understood?"

Within the next two minutes the classroom was empty. "Now you," the man barked at Mary, "take that nationalist bandit from the wall."

Without delay Mary took a chair and raised herself to reach for the bullet-ridden Emblem. The man spat fiercely, circling around her, examining her body shamelessly.

"Not bad, eh boys?" he winked at the other two. "I bet she's quite a piece...in bed. Too bad we have no time to spare."

Shocked and pale with fright, Mary took off the Emblem; as she stepped off the chair the bearded man patted her on the lower back unceremoniously. "I bet she's not bad at all " he grimaced again as the other two giggled.

In the ominous silence, Mary's heart throbbed violently, as if it was about to burst out of her chest. Through the window she saw some armed men. Apparently they had planned the visit and took proper precautions. For all she knew the whole village might be surrounded.

"Now put that in the wastebasket where it belongs," ordered the man. Mary promptly complied. "Now move over to the wall. You boys pull up a chair for me."

Mary walked to the wall and stopped, staring blankly in front of herself. The partisan with the boyish face fetched a chair for the leader, who stretched on it comfortably, admiring the tips of his bespattered boots.

"Turn around," he ordered so quietly that Mary almost did not hear it. She was facing him now, her back to the wall, the leader's two adjutants on both sides of her.

"Now about education," the man continued calmly and quietly. "I like education myself, especially if it's the proper kind. And education has to be proper, don't you agree, teacher?"

Mary did not answer. She was walking a tightrope, and this creature who resembled a caveman held a gun at her temple. The realization that the village folk would soon assemble here consoled her and reinforced her courage.

These forest men could not possibly harm her in front of everybody, although one never knew...The purpose of their visit here seemed to be clear enough: they considered the school in their jurisdiction and preferred the instruction to be done according to the Soviet curriculum. She heard it had happened in other villages.

"Now let's proceed with lesson number one," continued the partisan leader, boring her through with his dark, piercing eyes. "You listen carefully and answer me only when I ask you. Is that clear?"

"Yes," said Mary. She disliked the sinister edge in the partisan's voice.

"Tell us, teacher, who your father is," came the first question.

Mary eyed each of them silently.

"Now go ahead, you fascist bitch," he spat fiercely. "Don't keep us waiting. You wouldn't want me to employ this persuader to help you, would you?" He affectionately patted his sub-machine gun.

"I don't remember my father," Mary replied almost inaudibly.

"She doesn't remember her father... Do you hear, comrades? Well, it's about time we refreshed your memory." He nodded his head. The man with the boyish face sprang, grabbed Mary's hand, and drew the woman to the leader, who caught her by the hair and slapped her face savagely, then abruptly pushed her back to the wall. Mary glimpsed some stars in a variety of colours, her head spun, her nose bled. She struggled to keep herself on her feet.

"Now then," the bearded man continued evenly," let's try again: who is your father?"

"I told you... "

"Artiom!" hissed the partisan, "help her to remember. She was a *kamsamolka* at one time. How could she have forgotten?"

The owl face jumped at the woman and twisted her arm behind her back so savagely that Mary cried out in pain. She squirmed with an ugly grimace on her bloodied face.

"Let's hear it again, you fascist bitch!" yelled the leader. Mary could not bear being tortured. She would say anything to pacify the bearded man.

"My father is – "

"Come, come, who is he?"

"Comrade Stalin," the woman pronounced in a hoarse whisper.

The grip on her left arm slackened.

"Stalin is no comrade of yours, you fascist scum!" the angry voice thundered. "You have disgraced the great father Stalin and our socialist fatherland. Stalin has no mercy for scum like you."

With the swiftness of a panther, he jumped on the woman, hitting her with all the force he had. Mary reeled, gasped for air, then lost consciousness.

When she came to, she found herself prostrate on the floor. All her body and face hurt terribly. There was an uneasy hum in the room; the village folks were assembling. "Go on, get moving! We haven't got all day!" the voice by the door prompted them.

Hands lifted Mary from the floor. Hazily, she saw her mother's tear-stained face, but Mary had no strength left even to cry. As Aksinya wiped the blood off her daughter's face, villagers watched them in silence. They seated Mary on the front bench.

The man with the Star leaned on the table, his eyes travelling the width of the classroom. "Citizens of Shuly. I'll make my speech brief and sweet. You see the teacher of your children in front of you. She dared to refuse to co-operate with us, and we had to use some gentle persuasion."

His quiet voice fooled no one.

"First of all, I must warn you that this is a lesson for

everybody. We shall tolerate no resistance, but we mean no harm to those who co-operate with us. Starting tomorrow, you will send your children to school just as before. They'll get proper learning here, I'm sure. The only difference will be that they'll learn what our Soviet authorities want them to and won't be subjected to any more of German fascist or Byelorussian nationalist propaganda. Mary Karaway knows the Soviet programme well, and I'm sure she will comply as well as the rest of you. Any questions?"

The stony silence continued.

"I take it your silence means agreement. That's just fine. Don't keep your kids away from school. That won't do. Is that understood?"

Again no reaction.

"Now that we have so speedily dispensed with this important subject, before I close the meeting I'd like to remind you that we came here to stay. That means we'll be around. Let nobody try to fool us. Now the meeting is closed."

That afternoon, long after partisans left, the *Schutzpolizei* from Haradok came in. They questioned a number of people, trying to unearth some information about the partisan unit which paid them a visit in the morning. They learned little. People were too scared to talk. Everybody felt trapped by the steel jaws of the opposing forces and there seemed to be no escape.

The *Schutzpolizei* drank some *samahonka*, ate fried salt pork and eggs, and withdrew shortly before sundown. Mary, her face swollen, some of her teeth loose, stayed in bed at home. The next day, and for a couple of weeks, the school stood empty.

6
THE MURDER

Partisan and German zones of control were fluid and ill-defined. The penetration of opposing forces overlapped, and adversaries' paths frequently crossed. One could seldom know who the master was today and what tomorrow would bring. It depended on many factors. The people living in the fringe zones were fair game, subject to pillage, rape, and reprisals. The news of the razing of whole villages, their inhabitants burnt alive, ran through the country like wildfire. Many unit commanders of both sides became so widely known by their barbarous deeds that a mere mention of their names struck fear in the hearts of the unfortunate peasants.

Late in the fall, news reached Shuly that in the *Schutzpolizei* unit operating in the area there was a Volga-German named Bergdorf, allegedly an extremely blood-thirsty man. Two days ago, in broad daylight, he shot a number of suspected partisan collaborators in the village of Lastawka, three miles distant; before that the same unit effected indiscriminate reprisals on peaceful people in a locality five miles away.

According to the stories about Bergdorf, his actions weren't necessitated by military considerations. Bergdorf was pictured as a man who made it his practice to avoid partisans in open confrontations, but who was adept at pillaging and raping the population he was supposed to protect.

Bergdorf's boys certainly must have appreciated the tastes of their boss, which invariably included mass orgies with the local girls, executions, looting, and burning. As the war progressed, people stopped wondering how such things were possible in a country occupied by the nation that supposedly valued law and order, however predatory, as the main pillars of its existence.

Neither Stalin nor Hitler had any use for the local population, except as a reservoir of slave labour. Both dictators viewed this unfortunate country as one fit only for future colonization. They acted accordingly. Local authorities ruled their dominions with lead and fire and acted as supreme dispensers of life and death to the natives.

The people of Shuly blessed every hour that passed, and dreaded the one approaching. The setting sun might herald a visit from the forest's masters; the dawn could bring in the Germans or their helpers. Lately, the partisans became so bold as to appear in broad daylight, as on the day they chose to express their dissatisfaction with Mary's school.

The snow blanketed the fields, orchards, forest, and gardens. Finally and abruptly winter came to Shuly. Now the villagers cocked their ears to catch the muffled sounds of horses' hooves, to register the barely audible whiz of smoothly gliding sleighs, and the occasional chatter of approaching intruders. Any village dog barking in the stillness of the night might herald the arrival of hated pillagers and executioners.

Late one night, the dim light in Aksinya's house flickered as it struggled for survival on the home-made wick, immersed in a tin can half-filled with precious kerosene. Mary nursed Alenka, who had a bad cold and cried, coughed, and interfered with Valodzka's sleep. Her mother swept the wooden floor, then proceeded to ready the firewood for tomorrow. It had to be brought in from outside.

As Aksinya went out, she heard sounds from the road

which branched off the main highway North. In the pale moonglow she caught sight of two sleighs approaching the village. Soon barking dogs telegraphed the news all over the village. Aksinya instantly forgot the original purpose of her trip outside, and ran through the back door into the house to warn her daughter.

"Partisans, Mary," she whispered, her voice pregnant with fear, her hand still holding the door handle. The woman hesitated what to do next. It did not occur to her that the *Schutzpolizei* could drop in at this late hour.

"Where, mother?" Mary asked.

"Right outside. I saw them, two full loads, possibly more. My God, have mercy on us, protect us from evil hands." She crossed herself and began chanting prayers, gluing her eyes to the icons above the table in the corner. Mary cast an anxious glance toward the door, then continued soothing and rocking Alenka. Come what may, she reasoned, there's little one can do about it.

Heavy, muffled steps sounded on the verandah, and presently the door flew open. Mary peeked from behind the partition to see who the intruders were. She stared in disbelief. The face of the man in front was more than familiar. How could it possibly be? Her mother turned around and blinked her eyes to make sure she was seeing right. The man in the police uniform entered the room as if he were the master of the house; two more men immediately followed behind him. Aksinya could not hold herself any longer. She ran to the man to welcome him. With an automatic weapon dangling on his ann, he just stood there, swaying easily on his feet.

"Vanya, my dear," greeted Aksinya, "is it really you?"

His answer took her breath away.

"Do you know my name, old woman?"

"Sure, sure, you are Vanya Kolpakoff, the one we... "

"My name is Bergdorf," he announced brusquely, brushing the woman aside like a persistent fly.

Aksinya froze in her tracks. Was this the man they nursed back to health, or she was not seeing right? She felt the suspense unbearable. With anxiety in her voice, she proceeded: "Vanya, my dear. What does it matter what you call yourself today? To us you are a friend we helped."

"Shut up, you damned old fool!" roared the sergeant. "Stop prattling and tell me: where's that darling daughter of yours?"

So speaking he looked across the room. Aksinya, perplexed, eyed him closely. Clad in a mouse-coloured uniform, the sergeant's insignia on his shoulder bands, he did look totally different from that feeble, wounded, and bleeding creature they dragged from their verandah into their house. The man looked drunk and dangerous. Aksinya could find no justification for his belligerent attitude in her mind. The bushy dark hair showing under his pilot's cap, the thin military moustache, standing with arms akimbo, a Schmeisser gun slung over his right shoulder, the peremptory voice expecting instant compliance – was this the man transformed from that weakling? Is this the man they described as the scourge of the countryside?

Behind the partition Mary stood, holding Alenka in her arms and shivering in fear. For a fleeting instant she regretted she had fought off the man's advances in *lasnichowka*. Now his bloodshot eyes – if she could see right from here – were searching for her.

Aksinya ignored the sergeant's direct question and with a great effort endeavoured to pacify him. She approached the man boldly and, taking him by the arm, attempted to steer him to the table.

"Vanya, my dear son. I am so glad you have come. Please do us a great favour, be our guest, sit down please. You, too," she invited the other two armed men at the door, who apparently were very much interested in what their boss was going to do next. Unceremoniously, Bergdorf pushed the woman aside, and Aksinya swayed, almost losing her balance.

"You damned old bitch," the policeman roared, "I asked you a question: where is your daughter? I have an account to settle with her."

Without any further ado, he proceeded into the bedroom where Mary stood, clasping little Alenka to her breast.

"Ah, so here you are, my angel of mercy!" he exclaimed with undisguised joy. "Aren't you glad to see me? I told you you'd see plenty of me, and here I am. Remember, this isn't the *lasnichowka*. I am the master here."

The teacher never had a chance. As he walked in, he grabbed her by the arm right away. A scuffle developed. The brute wrestled the baby free and threw it to the floor. Heart-breaking shrieks filled the bedroom.

"Vanya, leave her alone! Vanya!" Aksinya cried. She clawed his left arm and attempted to pull the brute away from her daughter. Mary, her terror intensified by the ear-splitting shrieks of her small daughter, clutched the man by the arm as he mercilessly kicked the squirming bundle on the floor with his heavy boot. Aksinya held the policeman by the coat-tails. The man spun around with violent ferocity, and both women rolled away from him. The next instant the tiny bedroom thundered with a flash of lightning. Mary swayed on her feet as the world slowly receded into the darkness.

7
AWAKENING

Mary attempted to open her eyes. The lids seemed as heavy as lead. With an effort she opened and closed them again. The first dizzy sensation of coming back to life proved enough to exhaust her again. Her misty eyes slowly scanned the log-supported, frost-covered ceiling, where frozen earth protruded between the axe-hewn boards.

The gray light seeped inside from somewhere over her head. Twined ivy lined the walls, and two wooden posts supported the roof in the middle. It was a dug-out the size of a large living room. Four beds stood on one side, four on the other, a narrow aisle in between. Across the aisle a man lay on the bed heavily covered. Mary could not see his face.

Her subconscious mind wrestled with the problems of awakening. Everything seemed to be so unreal, so different from the surroundings in which she lived previously, that she receded back into uneasy slumber. When she woke up again later, the same features she subconsciously registered in her hazy mind earlier now stood out clearly all around her.

She lay covered with a heavy quilt. As she tried to move her limbs, she discovered a pain in her left side. It was bandaged below her ribs. Cautiously her right hand explored under the quilt covers. Heavy dressing bulged out over her stomach. Her legs moved freely without any hindrance. After this discovery, Mary's mind wandered further. The blackout proved to be hard to penetrate. There was an uneasy struggle in the room, her Alenka screaming, and then... the flash of thunderous lightning... Mary felt the shrieks of her children resurrected in all their terrifying agony.

Her chest heaved uneasily. The sharp pangs of pain in her left side completely awakened her. She lay motionless and listened. The voices she could hear before from outside subsided, with the sound of steps receding in the distance. Her sixth sense told her someone was right outside the dug-out. Who was it? Was it friend or foe? What was she doing here? Where were her mother and children? Speculating on probabilities, she came up with one possible answer: the Red guerillas. What did happen that night? How long had she been here?

The next time Mary awoke the first thing her gaze encountered was the hunchbacked figure of a woman sitting on the bench in the corner. A small kerosene lamp stood in front of the woman. She kept looking at some papers, her face heavily outlined as if seen by a moonlight. Her head wrapped up in a heavy babushka kerchief, she presented a picture of serenity. This seemed so unreal that Mary blinked her eyes, trying to chase the dream away. It was not a dream. Mary's parched lips and dry throat prompted her to reveal a sign of life. "Water," she whispered weakly.

The figure by the table moved, got up, and approached Mary. The woman stared intently at the teacher.

"So you have awakened. Lay still and don't talk. I'll bring you some water and call the doctor. He told me to call him as soon as you came to."

The gentle voice soothed Mary.

"Where am I? Who are you? Where are my mother and children?" she whispered.

The woman's face, wide in the cheekbones, displayed motherly sympathy. The lips moved: "I told you to lie still and don't talk. Heaven knows we almost gave you up for dead. Just wait till I bring you some water."

She turned around and left. Some time later she reappeared, followed by a heavy-set man with a growth of beard and a benevolent face. Without a word she brought a tin cup of cool water to Mary's lips, propping her head higher on the pillow. As Mary sipped the water slowly, the woman said: "My name is Prudnikava. I am a medical nurse here. This is our doctor, Posnik. He'd like to examine you."

Prudnikava stepped aside, and Posnik stepped forward. The man was in his early forties. He checked Mary's pulse, and fumbled with the bandages under her quilt cover.

"How do you feel?" the doctor's voice was gentle.

"I really don't know, Doctor," Mary responded in a small voice.

"The pulse is still too high," the Doctor continued, looking at his wrist watch. "You must avoid any kind of exertions, even talk. Just lie still."

"Doctor, what happened?"

"We pulled two bullets out of you. You lost so much blood, there was little hope you would pull through... How is her temperature, Prudnikava?"

"Still too high. I checked two hours ago. Do you want me to check now?"

Mary broke in: "And where, Doctor... where am I?"

"You are among friends. You mustn't worry," the Doctor explained curtly.

"Partisans?" Mary gasped.

"Yes. They've saved your life. Unfortunately... "

"Where are my mother and children?" Mary groped for the Doctor's hand, prepared for the worst.

"I said you mustn't get excited. You haven't quite passed the danger point yet. If you co-operate you may pull through."

The fact that he evaded a direct answer to her question, and the expression of sympathy in the Doctor's fatherly eyes, were more eloquent than the man's words. Mary knew. The terrible realization threw her completely off balance. Hot and cold waves surged through her weak body, assaulting her brain. Her lips moved but no sound came. Instead she felt invisible pliers squeezing out two hot tears from her swollen eyes. She closed them.

The next morning loud noises awoke her. All beds in the dug-out were filled. The man who was her sole companion across the aisle had disappeared. The doctor, Prudnikava, and another woman, whom Mary had not seen yesterday, spoke in undertones two beds away from her. From snatches of their subdued conversation, Mary gathered that they were talking about the problems of accommodation of the wounded. There must have been a heavy encounter with the Germans.

The younger woman silhouetted against the door, her handsome profile and blonde hair looking remarkably fresh, wearing a green pilot's cap with a Red star, listened attentively to the doctor, occasionally nodding in agreement. "Who is this girl?" Mary searched her memory. "Haven't I seen her somewhere before?"

And suddenly from the past the image of one creature emerged, who happened to be the last person she would have wanted to meet anywhere.

8

THE VULGAR BEAUTY

With a twist of good humor, one Byelorussian folk tale relates how the Creator, moulding the animal and bird kingdoms, ran short of accessories. It was then that the Heavenly Master promptly invented and for the first time applied the law of compensation. Thus, for its deficiency in mental faculties, the bull was compensated by powerful horns; for its lack of courage and strength, the hare got fast-running legs; and that incomparable singer of the forest, the nightingale, being short-changed on looks, came away rewarded with an exquisite voice.

When, in the labyrinths of life, one scrutinizes the various types of human beings, the so-called normal people included, one is invariably drawn to the assumption that the Creator applied the same law when moulding humans, the Biblical version notwithstanding. Adam examines daily and attempts to assess various assets and shortcomings of Eve. Keen and dedicated students of this art are sometimes amply rewarded for their zeal. Among the flowers of the female jungle they may encounter what is properly called a perfect example: a girl in whom the disparity between physical and spiritual assets happens to be especially pronounced.

Mary Karaway met one such person while in high school, although it never occurred to her to practice the tricky and intricate art of an amateur connoisseur of humans. Engrossed in the daily task of mastering various branches of knowledge, she paid little attention at first to one Larisa Voynik, a girl student in the ninth grade of high school. As time passed, however, she had to take notice, for it was she who became personally affected by the other girl's various defects of character.

At a superficial glance, one could not help but be impressed by Lara's looks. She was remarkably well-developed for her age of sixteen, and even an austere student frock seemed to underline her blossoming beauty. The observer could hazard a guess that the girl represented one of those hard-to-find samples vegetating sometimes among the weeds of backwoods villages in that predominantly agricultural country. Many discriminating painters would find Lara a fitting subject to be immortalized for posterity.

Her remarkably well-proportioned figure was enhanced by her beautifully moulded, blonde-haired, blue-eyed face. Any cosmetician would pay dearly to try his art on Lara's face; the features, as if made to order, were all there, needing only the creative touch of a master to present them to the world in their full glory. Soviet society, where women lived like oxen of burden – bricklayers, steel workers, collective farmers, and the like – allowed no room in its centralized industry for the production of any cosmetics for the fair sex. Female students were even forbidden to use lipstick. Thus the beauty Lara possessed was entirely unartificial, all her wholesome own.

One is naturally disposed to expect that beautiful creatures act and behave beautifully. In Lara's case, one was bound to be instantly disappointed, for she was amoral to a degree that she did not even bother hiding the defects of her character. Modesty – an essential pillar to support the visual masterpiece – was totally absent in her. The girl was aggressive and inconsiderate, base and presumptuous. Whatever inherent virtues she may have had, they apparently had little chance of developing in the state children's home.

Brought up by Soviet society, she practically became the

embodiment of the numerous ethical aberrations of that society. Family warmth or Christian morality was never allowed to mould or improve her character. Thus, in Lara's case, the classical Marxist dogma that a human being is made by his environment may have been used to prove the baseness of the Soviet environment.

One looking at Lara, in or out of school, would almost have felt compelled to approach her and advise her in a paternal manner: "Look, girl, stop being so vulgar. You are exquisitely beautiful, but your behaviour and your filthy tongue would spoil it all. Restrain yourself, act like a modest charming girl, and everyone will adore you."

When Lara spoke and acted in daily life, her face, which in repose seemed alluringly and angelically innocent, acquired an unpardonable vulgarity. No wonder that her fellow male students constantly attempted to pull her into the gutter the way they would pull a beautiful tramp, which they considered her to be. The stories went around that while still in high school she dispensed her favours to various men. How much truth there was in these stories would be hard to say, but one may call to mind the universally accepted proverb that there is no smoke without fire.

Lara took it for granted she could command any boy's attention by the slightest hint; herein, as it appeared later, lay the seeds of her conflict with Mary. The boys, lured by her looks, were later repulsed by her ill temper, her manners and behaviour, and almost as a rule preferred the company of Mary. One of the most attractive girls in the crowd, Mary was also modest and unassuming, precisely the qualities Lara lacked. She was also a hard worker in school and topped everyone in her class.

Lara could not profit by any objective comparison. Infested as she was by false values, nourished by the abominable monstrosities of Soviet ethics, where parents, elders, and God Himself became sinister outcasts only to be persecuted, spied, and spat upon, she could not comprehend that anyone as beautiful as Mary could also possess healthy morals. This front must be false, Lara thought. There must be some muck she could rake. She must discredit the girl, no matter what.

One day Mary realized that she must be the target of gossip. Some boys, formerly respectful, now hardly concealed that meaningful, caressing, hungry look in their eyes; others were even bold enough to openly proposition her. Lara openly taunted her in front of other students; her loaded questions producing puzzled looks and generating distrust.

At first Mary was puzzled. In her own behaviour she could find no grounds to justify the vile gossip. She decided to dig deeper, and try to find the source of those unfounded calumnies. Her job was easy enough; all threads led to the same skein, Lara Voynik.

Mary's friends advised her to report Lara's malicious smears to the school *Kamsamol* or Communist Youth executive. In theory, at least, this body was supposed to be the guardian of the morals of Communist Youth. Prudently the girl dissented, for she refused to be dragged into the mire.

Mary Karaway thus failed to take up Lara's challenge and did her best, no matter how difficult at times, to ignore Lara's malicious remarks. To bring about an explosion in this charged situation one needed a fuse, and it appeared on the scene in the person of one Viktar Viasiolka, the son of a high-ranking railroad official, who had just been transferred to the city. Viktar was one of those boys one can justifiably call a worldly type, versatile, amiable, and dashingly handsome. To make the circle complete, he had a good sense of humor and enough prudence to please everybody. In short, he was the type who would be chosen – if such a custom existed in Soviet schools – as the student most likely to succeed in the class.

Lara instantly took notice of the newcomer; the girl decided he was a prize specimen that should not be allowed to slip through her fingers. Encountering Mary, she warned her: "You'd better keep away from Viktar. He's my boy and don't you dare get in my way."

"Don't you worry," replied Mary with perhaps a hint of condescension, "you may keep him. What's more, if he comes to me, I'll promptly send him back to you."

9

THE RED PICNIC

Meanwhile, the local party and *Kamsamol* zealots hatched a new idea. Maintaining that sun, water, and fresh air rightfully belonged to the peasants and proletarians, they declared that henceforth these media of nature should work for the people's health and advance proletarian culture, just as in the past the impoverished, abused, and exploited masses toiled for the material enrichment of their bourgeois overlords.

To have healthy and cultured minds, people must first of all have healthy bodies. For this purpose the sun, the water, and the fresh air must be harnessed. And so the ingenious undertaking called "Culture for the Masses" was conceived in the minds of the local party leaders.

A joint meeting of party and *Kamsamol* executives of Haradok was held one June evening. The party secretary, a selfish and thoroughly vain careerist, who would do anything to get credit and advance himself on the bureaucratic ladder, outlined his plan with the proper amount of pomposity, supposedly motivated by his unselfish interest in the rapid progress of the socialist culture among the masses.

After expounding and substantiating his concepts of wide range cultural work among the unreceptive local Byelorussian masses, he outlined his plans for a campaign in detail. The gigantic, mass undertaking, called "Culture for the Masses", which would parallel what in the Western world is known as an annual picnic, would take place next Sunday. Party and *Kamsamol* members would organize a massive advertising campaign to prod the people, particularly the youth, to join whole-heartedly in this cultural rest.

The place where this proposed gigantic assembly would take place, happened to be right in the town's vicinity; about a mile out where the river circled a large blooming meadow on all sides, surrounded by an attractive wooded area. The program itself presented a few problems. To launch the picnic, there had to be a speech of course, which the party secretary himself undertook to deliver. The youthful agitbrigade – a troupe of assorted homegrown talent organized recently to propagate the various assets and alleged blessings of Russian colonial rule through recitals, songs, and dances – would furnish the main attraction. The party secretary dwelt in glowing terms on other details too numerous to mention.

The idea pleased everybody. With a few minor changes, it was enthusiastically approved. The members of *Kamsamol* and the local Communist Pioneers were charged with undertaking a two-day promotional campaign.

For two successive evenings, the youngsters plastered town fences, doors, walls, and telephone poles with huge posters. They marched through town streets with lighted torches, chanting slogans and generally arousing a hubbub the like of which the town had never heard before in its long history.

Just before noon on Sunday, a column of school students and local trade-union members proceeded to the designated picnic site, their numerous posters proclaiming: "Culture for the Masses", "Work and Rest Culturally", "Thanks to Great Stalin for a Happy Childhood", and "Long May the Sun of Stalin's Constitution Shine". The huge, solemn-looking image of the Kremlin's despot, unimpressed by the sunny wonders of Byelorussian spring, swayed in the muscular hands of some youngsters at the front of the line.

All over side roads and paths, people moved to the designated site. It soon became apparent that the official body, which initiated this Soviet picnic, could not control so many arrivals. Even before the planned programme got under way, sunbathers took off their clothing, splashed around in the clear, cool waters of the river, rollicked in the meadow, enjoying their silly pranks like dogs finally loose from the grip of the leash.

The party and *Kamsamol* leadership gathered on a newly erected platform, exchanging smug glances and chuckling at what they considered genuine enthusiasm for their terribly original undertaking. Presently the hoarse voice of a red-nosed, middle-aged announcer, who had apparently last night fought another losing bout with vodka, attempted to focus public attention to the programme that was about to start. A few gaping people, more for reasons of appearances than curiosity, approached the platform around which students and some trade-union members were ordered to stand, while the majority remained scattered across the choice spots of the meadow. Unperturbed, the party secretary, like a virile, puffed-up male turkey about to approach a hen, launched into his inaugural speech.

Duly acknowledging the benign character and inexhaustible wisdom of that "great teacher and benefactor of the people, Father Stalin", he proceeded into the well-charted waters of the blessings of the Soviet regime. Only in a socialist country, maintained the pompous little man, only in the U.S.S.R. were there opportunities for the people to rest culturally. Yet to embrace and cherish the fruits of genuine Soviet culture, which was about to dawn on the Communist-blessed proletarians of Haradok and the local collective farmers, people must have healthy bodies, for – as one great Marxist sage put it, "Healthy spirits dwell in healthy bodies". Therefore, local Party organs, and the speaker most of all, shall spare no effort to bring culture to the masses. This first huge rally was only the beginning.

If the party secretary had terminated his prepared speech right at this point, the history of the whole day might have been recorded differently. He was not one to gauge the price of overtaxing his listeners' thin patience. In the familiar vein he continued, the stereotyped, pious jingoisms of repugnant propaganda now tainting the nourishing fragrance of bird-cherry shrubs, obstructing the larks' heavenly hymns to the glory of the Creator, and the joyful chirping of other birds in the forest.

Those closest to the platform pretended to listen to this disharmony of nature in solemn silence, wishing that this Party-tuned street organ would promptly terminate his familiar and detestable prattle so they could partake of the blessings of the golden spring day. As if in answer to those secret wishes, nature itself gave a generous helping hand: the huge poster-picture of Stalin, driven superficially into the soil, was swayed by a stronger spurt of breeze, tilted, and fell to the ground.

Among the listeners around the platform this event provoked a ripple of laughter, arrested promptly by the realization of possible unpleasant consequences for this unguarded display of their disregard for the despot-idol. Heads on the platform turned around, the speaker stopped, his tightly clenched fist ready to underline a point suspended in mid-air. Confusedly he watched the commotion behind. Presently the brush-moustached, ruddy image of the dictator reappeared above the embarrassed group of dignitaries. The party secretary, endeavouring to regain his dignified composure, resumed his address. If anything, his voice now became shrill and admonishing; his previous self-assurance and pomposity disappeared, and his dark brown eyes seemed to fix those immediately in front of him, as if searching out those audacious enough to laugh at such a catastrophic incident. Stuttering, he concluded the address with stereotyped Communist slogans, accompanied by loud handclapping of the comrades immediately behind, and a faint response from the general audience.

After a short intermission, the agitbrigade took over. With the air of an oft-divorced matron facing the justice of peace with a new spouse on her arm, they dished out their outworn propaganda "art". One by one, or in groups of two or three, as inconspicuously as humanly possible, people drifted away from this attraction of the festivities; they formed groups and attended to the food and drink they had brought along with them. When the shrill finale on "the Blessings of Stalin's Constitution" finally heralded the welcome end, people breathed with relief. After a short intermission, the youth band started playing a foxtrot, and now the meadow around the platform became really crowded with swinging couples, some of them already intoxicated. By this time the afternoon was well advanced.

10

THE DUEL

Vibrant, fresh, beautiful, and desirable Lara changed many hands. She lacked no attention from her horde of admirers, many of whom attempted to steer her into the adjacent woods, ostensibly to explore nature. Lara enjoyed herself with abandon, totally unbecoming for a student of the local high school. On purpose, no doubt, the boys treated her with a few generous drinks of vodka. But when in the course of intoxicated hilarity she was asked about the whereabouts of Viktar and, momentarily puzzled, she gazed around, her expression changed, acquiring a vulgar look.

"I bet that no-good whore dragged him into the woods somewhere," she spat fiercely. "Let's go find them, eh, boys? I'll fix that scheming wench real proper this time!"

No further encouragement was needed. This was the signal so eagerly awaited. The show or the showdown ahead would certainly beat the one just terminated by the agitbrigade.

In the shade of the giant oak-tree, half reclining on their elbows, in no way concealed by any foliage from the prying eyes of others nearby, Viktar and Mary laughed. Clad in one of those almost-standard flowered cheap dresses that afforded so little choice to Soviet woman shoppers, Mary nevertheless seemed to be extremely charming to Viktar. He liked her most of all for her genuine modesty, her almost total absence of self-conceit so apparent in that other assertive girl of whom he tired so promptly. Moreover, she was bright and clever enough – a commodity so rare among teenage girls – to sustain a stimulating conversation, and to heartily enjoy good jokes of which Viktar seemed to have plenty for every occasion.

Mary liked the boy's looks. He was something exceptional among the usually dull school crowd. He told her many things of interest about the distant places he had seen on his journeys across the land he called "our limitless grandma". His father's high-ranking job on the railway as stocks and yards inspector afforded him the opportunities to travel.

Mary suspected Viktar knew numerous girls sexually, although he never directly approached her solely with this object in mind. She attempted neither to attract nor to discourage him, though the idea of taking up Lara's challenge often tempted what little self-conscious vanity she possessed.

There was one thing about Viktar that intrigued and scared her. Among his many stories, anecdotes, and puns, quite a number contained acidly virulent, hard-punching satire aimed at the omnipotent power in the land: the Communist Party. Mary never dared to seek out the origins of Viktar's audaciousness. The frank, undisguised openness with which he communicated various anti-regime barbs to her sometimes made her suspect he was baiting her into revealing her own feelings and ideas on the subject, provided she had any, which circumstance caused her no small amount of concern. She felt safer with him alone than in the crowd, lest some dangerous joke slipped from his tongue. In a crowd, however, Viktar allowed himself no such unbridled liberties, but kept his tongue on a leash.

Sitting now under the oak-tree, Viktar had just delivered the punch line of one of his hard-hitting limericks, and they both giggled heartily.

"And did you hear this one?" continued the boy, obviously glad to have so charming and responsive a listener, "about a backwoods party official who for the first time in his life had been given the opportunity to address a crowd of liberated Western Byelorussians? You know about those poor blood brothers of ours who were choking to death in the yoke of Polish lords?... Finally our glorious sun dawned on them...Well, this fellow at some celebration or other climbed the platform, puffed up his rather impressive chest and with all the aplomb of a manure-pitcher babbled for some time gesticulating so vigorously that his arms got sore; then, after delivering various trite slogans, he decided not to miss the golden opportunity and add one of his own: "Citizens of Valovichy!" he yelled at top of his lungs, "join the common march to the world revolution! Eight billion oppressed peasants and workers eagerly await your assistance to liberate themselves from the capitalist yoke!"

"People applauded him as they did other speakers, and only a few of them caught the absurdity of what he said. Satisfied with his debut as Cicero the fellow stepped off the platform, where upon one of his friends grabbed his hand and shook it violently, saying: 'You've given more than an address!' 'What do you mean? the party official asked, puzzled. 'Why,' laughed his friend, 'with one twist of your tongue you've increased the world's population by some six billion.'"

Mary laughed again. Just at that moment the noisy group of their school chums emerged from among the trees, with Lara in front. At this sight, annoyance crossed Viktar's handsome, suntanned face, while Mary remained absolutely calm, though puzzled. It was easy to discern at the first glance that Lara, leading this group with somewhat unusual bravado, as well as a few of the others, appeared intoxicated.

Viktar and Mary sat up, eyeing these unexpected visitors. Lara abruptly stopped a few feet away from Mary and, looking contemptuously at her, yelled: "You dirty bitch! I told you to keep away from my boy, and you wouldn't listen...I'll teach you!"

Mary had no time to dwell on the appearance of this crimson-faced, alcohol-saturated girl. Lara jumped rapidly, attempting to grab Mary by the throat. Instantly reacting to this sudden, unprovoked assault, Mary rolled sideways, trying to free herself.

As if stung by a poisonous snake, Viktar jumped and joined the others, cheering and jeering in the ring formed around the school's most attractive classmates. Someone attempted to interfere but another hand restrained him. Catcalls, whistles, and shrieks of delight accompanied the struggle. Unashamedly the boys admired various areas of the girls' exposed anatomy. A hand shook Viktar's shoulder and a girl's voice pleaded: "Viktar, separate them. You are the reason for all this; how can you stand here laughing?"

Not even turning his head, so as not to miss a second of this unexpected show, the boy replied: "Why should I? It's just a kids' tussle. They won't kill themselves." No doubt the fight appealed to his so imaginative mind. Right then he must have been savouring and committing to memory several juicy details so that in the future they would enrich the treasury of his anecdotes.

From their performance it appeared the girls were almost evenly matched in strength, though uneven in their experience. Propelled by a force of hate, Lara spent herself in erratic moves, while Mary – although now agitated and angry – still seemed to possess some presence of mind. They rolled on the grass, the ring of spectators following them. After a prolonged tussle, which somewhat sapped her reserves of physical strength, Mary freed herself and was about to deliver a hard blow when her opponent, ferocious as a Gypsy woman, tore away to the side and caught Mary's hair.

The tumultuous noise resounded through the woods,

competing with that of the youth band on the platform. The picnickers sensed that something unusual was taking place, and many rushed to the scene. The ring around the combatants swelled and tightened.

Presently Lara aimed with her fingernails at Mary's face. Realizing the imminent danger not a moment too soon, Mary grabbed Lara's wrist and twisted hard. Her other hand squeezed the thumb of Lara's hand that held her hair. Lara's hold relaxed. Violently pushing her opponent away, Mary rose to her knees and swung sharply. A succession of hard blows dazed Lara completely. Like an experienced boxer, Mary kept punching, keeping her opponent off balance. Lara's bleeding nose spotted her pinky dress, smeared her face. Now she resembled a ferocious bitch, gasping for breath and unable to deliver the punishment to the party intended.

Presently a peremptory voice rose above the din. The crowd parted and two youths of impressive size appeared inside the ring. The secretary of the Haradok *Kamsamol* executive, Anton Nizhnik, demanded in an authoritative voice: "What's going on here? Have you girls been fighting? Of all the things in the world...this tops them all!"

Now on her feet, Mary stared down at the self-appointed darling of the school boys. Her blood-smeared face, contorted by a mixture of anger and humiliation, her hair dishevelled, Lara lay panting on the grass. "You bitch!" she whined with her remaining strength, "I'll get you no matter where and when."

This threat evoked no sympathy from the crowd. Mary gazed about aimlessly, her hair in disarray, one sleeve of her dress torn. There's no sight more repulsive than that of a teenage girl, degraded, humiliated, and physically beaten, screaming for retribution. Lara, the sweet angel, was gone; the eyes of the spectators beheld a base, amoral animal. Even her most tolerant school chums searched their hearts in vain for sympathy; they could find none where little existed before.

Viktar approached Mary and took her by the hand. Turning sharply around, the girl looked at him closely, as if seeing him for the first time. Viktar was taken aback by what he saw in those lovely blue eyes, filled with reproach and contempt. "You," she stuttered, unable to continue. "Keep away from me!" This warning in a threatening hoarse whisper made the boy realize he had lost a reliable friend.

"You girls better come with us, we have to investigate this," Nizhnik ordered, looking at both of them in turn. "What a shame! *Kamsamol* members behaving like a... Come on..."

"The Culture for the Masses" rally turned out to be a complete fiasco. The party secretary's vision of reaping a rich harvest for his successful cultural campaign, initiative· and perseverance, was shattered into splinters. Now both he, the Communist Party, the *Kamsamol* executive, and the Haradok high school authorities looked for scapegoats. The boy who carried the picture-poster of Stalin and left it unattended behind the platform at so august a moment turned out to be the son of a sub-kulak. His father, before they made him join the collective, was the proud owner of two cows, a horse, and a sizeable plot of land, and was thus considered by the regime as too wealthy and a class enemy.

The boy was promptly kicked out from the school. His future was doomed by what they called a "wolf's ticket". Thus he joined that large class of unreliables for whom advancement in the Moscow colonial world was blocked by their class origins or a chance mistake.

In a so-called "social trial" in the school's auditorium, packed solidly by students, their parents, Party, *Kamsamol*, and school governing bodies, Lara and Mary had to expiate their sins. The trivial and self-conceited among those present nourished the unsavory details about the two girls, mostly Lara, on this public laundry day.

Numerous courageous souls lent Mary their support, testifying about her good character and behaviour. The girl, although self-consciously blushing from a deep sense of shame, was gratified to learn she possessed many valuable friends. The youth who caused the girls to fight, Viktar Viasiolka, acted as the undaunted hero of the day. Although reluctant to commit himself, under the prompting of the Party's moral judges, he lent his assistance to Mary. Thus Lara suffered another and more terrible defeat than on that Sunday in the forest.

Both girls were reprimanded, Lara sentenced to a probationary period of one year in which to correct her behaviour. They should have saved their breath. It was the last time they saw her before that great cataclysm, called the Second World War. Nobody seemed to know where she had gone, although there were rumours that she was doing well in Viciebsk. With her looks and lack of scruples, one need not have wondered.

11
LARA THE DEMON

Of all the possible places, in this partisan dug-out, the girl with a Red Star on her pilot cap was none other than Mary's one-time school chum, Lara. What was she doing here? In what capacity? A nurse? Is she somebody important, being on such familiar terms with the Doctor and Prudnikava?

"My God, please help me," Mary broke out in cold sweat.

She tried to stifle her incipient cough, but the effect increased her pains, and she emitted a low groan. The doctor approached her, followed by the two women. Mary closed her eyes and held her breath. The seconds, terrible seconds – opening a new chapter in her life, she knew – ticked away. The voice, Lara's voice, spoke: "When did you bring this woman here?"

"About three days ago, I believe," the Doctor replied. "She was saved by our ambush in Shuly. Her two children and mother were killed by fascist Polizei, her house burned."

Silence. And then it came: 'Why, so we meet again, Mary, so we meet again." The voice was that of an executioner gloating over her soon-to-be victim. Mary tried to control her heaving breast, keeping her eyes closed, for she had no desire to see Lara's triumphant face in front of her.

"Do you know her?" the Doctor asked.

"Know her? Like my own self. We went to high school together. Do I ever know her?" she forcefully underlined the word "her" with her voice full of vengeance. "I shall not beat about the bush, doctor," she continued. "This woman doesn't deserve to be here. Do you know, doctor, that she has been teaching school in Shuly, poisoning Soviet children with fascist propaganda? So this is how they rewarded her...I say it serves you right. Now open your eyes, you bitch! Come on, open your eyes!" she ordered. "Or are you afraid to look decent people in the face? Come on, you filthy bitch!" she bent over Mary's bed and pressed the sick woman's stomach with her thumb.

"Larisa Siamionawna, you mustn't!" the Doctor interjected, a shade of annoyance on his fatherly face. "She needs complete rest."

"Come on, doctor, why have mercy for the enemy?"

"It's my duty," the doctor attempted to explain.

"I know your duty," Lara interrupted him. "But you must have grown soft. Don't you ever forget that fascists have no mercy for us. Do you think they'd care for you if you were wounded?" Lara's prodding her stomach was so painful for her that Mary opened her eyes. Through the mist she saw the trio. The doctor's compassionate face and the puzzled face of Prudnikava starkly contrasted with the malicious expression of the robust, blonde Lara. If anything, she had grown more mature and beautiful. The delicately curved lips were framed by the chin, its hint of sharpness barely indicating the cruelty of her character.

To Mary she presented a demon with an angel's face. Now she found herself at mercy of this abominable creature, from whom no mercy could be expected. There she stood in front of Mary, her gaze searching, tormenting the teacher.

"How is she doing, Doctor?"

"Given proper time and care, she should pull through.."

"We are certainly going to give her proper care as long as I have any say around here. Proper care now, Doctor, and after she recovers, especially after," the silky voice gloated. "Prudnikava, you take good care of her, you hear?"

"Yes, Larisa Siamionawna, I will."

"I don't want her to die, not yet," the demon's voice stressed the last two words as they moved away.

From one hell into another. Mary shuddered to think of tomorrow. Why did they have to save her? Why didn't they kill her right away?

After two weeks, Mary was on the road to recovery. Prudnikava told her they had pulled two bullets out of her. The teacher blessed God in her prayers, for the constant shifting of the partisan unit afforded little opportunity for peaceful rest.

Gradually, as her strength returned, Mary was assigned to some household duties in the kitchen or in the field hospital. During this time she came to know many people. The partisans, as she observed, were a miserable lot. They were peasants forcibly recruited by the hard-core guerillas. They displayed no enthusiasm to fight Germans or their allies, for they knew that the Red victory would bring back the hated collectives and their serfdom. Nevertheless, they realized the situation presented no reasonable alternative. Germans and their auxiliary units were now raping the country. There was no room for the third force. They simply dragged their feet, whether in action or in guard duties. As long as they carried weapons, they realized, at least they would not be caught barehanded and deported to slave labour camps in Germany. It was better to be a slave with one's feet on native soil than elsewhere.

There was no rigid discipline in the unit. The criminal element seemed to interpret well the tacit acquiescence in their actions by their leaders; nightly sorties into the villages for pillage and rape, labelled reconnaissance, fooled no one. Presumably in tune with Stalin's plans to exterminate the unreliable element, they served the dictator's purpose well, for in his book Byelorussians were highly unreliable. Almost as a rule Russians, parachuted in from the Big Land, held all major commanding positions.

Cautiously, so as not to arouse any suspicions, Mary gathered up the pieces of the puzzle about Lara. Chance remarks overheard and her own casual questions presented an ugly picture. Lara was now the protege and lover of their unit commander Karpatin. As Mary suspected all along, she stayed single; she appeared to be a boss in her own right, dabbling in Party work, screening new involuntary recruits, drifters, and enemy deserters. As a diversion, Mary learned, Lara just enjoyed taking part in small so-called punitive expeditions, where the chances of unrestrained vengeance against the helpless natives far outweighed risks and dangers involved.

Late that winter, Mary was given a clean bill of health. Physically she felt all right; emotionally she was a broken woman. Least of all, she knew not what to do with herself. With her family alive, she would certainly have attempted to escape. As it was, she was all alone, no one to turn to, nobody to confide in, and no purpose to live for. Puzzled and disturbed by Lara's intentions toward her, she even became apathetic to the girl-demon's threat. Whatever she might do, what was the difference? When late one winter night she was pulled out of bed and told to report to Lara, she took the message stoically and resignedly walked to the main camp.

The command post loomed ahead of her in the bleak winter night. She was led into a fair-sized room and was confronted by the woman. Lara sat pensively on the bench behind a small table, the petrol lamp suspended from the beam in the low ceiling illuminating her blonde hair. The inseparable pilot's cap bearing a Red Star pinned atop her hair, clad in green uniform, she looked every inch the boss she was supposed to be. Mary became totally preoccupied by the girl at the table. She watched

Lara puffing on a cigarette, in no way acknowledging her presence. Finally she turned sharply to Mary and spoke without any preamble:

"Do you know what I am and what I can do to you?"

"I heard about you," Mary replied.

"What did you hear, good or bad?"

"All kinds."

"And what do you think I'm going to do to you? You were a smart girl once: morality, compassion, and all that hogwash... Now, bright girl, figure out what I'm going to do to you."

Mary did not answer.

"I've asked you a question, you bitch," Lara hissed, venom in her eyes. "You're supposed to answer it."

With these words, she jumped up from behind the table, and slapped both Mary's cheeks with wide-open palms. The teacher stood her ground not reacting to this outburst. She always suspected that in some way Lara was sick; this appeared to be a mild demonstration of that mental disorder.

Lara reached for a shelf in the wall, took down a bottle full of gray liquid, and poured herself more than half a glass. The smell of home-made vodka penetrated the room. The girl drank the liquor in one huge gulp, wiped her mouth with one sweep of her palm, and sat down at the table staring stonily in front of her. Then the torrent came: "You lousy, filthy bitch. You expect mercy from us.. . You should be crushed like a worm, with no pity... But that would be too good for you. You don't deserve that kind of treatment," she jabbed her finger at Mary, "And that's why I've been so patient with you. In fact, I've been too patient. For weeks you've been eating our bread, using our shelter as if you were one of the decent people who spill blood for our noble cause. You imbecile, you scum, you're the lowest of the low!"

Stoically, Mary watched the girl hurl herself into a

tantrum. She was a bigger moral wreck, Mary thought, than she had presumed her to be. What made her so? Jealousy? Desire for revenge? Her own vanity?

Lara continued: "I think that you're not worth spending a bullet on. I promise to you that you won't die easily."

"Shoot me now. Why this nonsensical sermon? Get it over with," Mary retorted.

"Oh no, my dear friend!" Lara came from behind the table and approached her so close that Mary felt the hot reek of *samahonka*. "I know you'd prefer it this way, but that would be too easy for you. You see," she smiled gloatingly, "you haven't yet learned how to beg for death. There's too much pride in you... I'll get you off that high ladder of yours; you and your high morals. You stink inside, don't you see? I never forgot Haradok. I knew your so-called morality! Inside you were rotten through and through. And you have proved it. When the fascists took over you went right on poisoning our children with their so-called education, you stinking Christian..."

"You are one to talk about children," Mary shot back. "How many did you raise?"

"You keep your filthy mouth shut while I'm talking to you, you fascist bitch!" yelled Lara and slapped Mary hard across her face.

"I'm not afraid of you, Lara. Don't yell at me. I have nothing to lose."

"Oh, yes, you have. I'll see how heroic you're going to be when the time comes to dispose of you. Don't rush me. I can promise you one thing: you'll come to me crawling, licking my boots for mercy, begging for the prompt death."

She poured herself another drink and gulped it down in a single swallow. Exhaling deeply on a newly lighted cigarette, she scrutinized Mary from a distance, evaluating the effect her diatribe had made on the teacher. Now her face acquired that vulgar, ghoulish expression.

"I'm not impressed, Lara. What are you trying to prove? That you are better than me, because – you know this well – you have degraded yourself beyond redemption?"

Mary's words seemed to have pierced the tender veneer of Lara's self-esteem right through to the core. Gritting her teeth, the demon came close, too close for comfort, and to Mary she hissed like a poisonous serpent: "I should not answer your question... but I will. First of all, I don't give a hoot whether you're impressed or not." She grabbed Mary by the collar and held her tightly. Mary held herself back from spitting into the girl's face.

"Secondly, there's nothing I need to prove to scum like you. Do you hear, you bitch? Nothing whatsoever. My sole concern with you is that I administer a proper punishment. And that I promise you, I will! You see, you are now in my complete possession, Mary darling!"

Fiercely, the girl-demon spat in Mary's face and continued her shrill laughing.

Mary wiped the saliva off her cheek and proceeded to watch the creature in front of her. In her memory reappeared that other girl – so deceptive at times in her looks – with whom she duelled that Sunday afternoon in the forest. The eyes filled by incorrigible hate and humiliation, the truly base animal, her camouflage completely discarded...

Lara calmed herself, sat behind the table, and detachedly watched the woman in front of her, as if unable to decide what to do next. Her voice sounded well-controlled when she finally spoke again: "There's a piece of news which should comfort you, Mary," Lara paused, her mask inscrutable. "Interested?"

"Go on," Mary whispered, regarding the woman suspiciously.

"Yesterday your fascist masters burned Shuly to the ground... All the people, locked up in the village school, were roasted alive."

The news stunned Mary like a thunderbolt. Speechless at first, struggling to digest this bit of terrible news, she yelled in protest: "You are lying! It cannot be, you are lying!"

Mary had no relative left in Shuly. While in the partisans' captivity, she sometimes inquired of the village folk and learned the village remained intact, except that their house was burned after the slaughter of her family by Kolpakoff-Bergdorf. Now this terrible piece of news, which Lara obviously expected to shock her to the bone, visibly upset her. Mary recalled her own family's ordeal, imagined the whole population of the village locked up in the school where she had taught; her own students, their desperate helpless mothers screaming for help that never came, fire consuming writhing, living bodies. What horrible torture that must have been. Her stomach turned, and another spring snapped in her heart, another world tottered into abyss. And this monster in front of her, detachedly announcing this unheard of tragedy, realizing the effect it produced on Mary...

"Why should I lie?" Lara continued. "It's hard to see your masters for what they really are – inhuman monsters – isn't it, Mary darling? Now you know."

Lara looked at the big golden wrist watch, and Mary was too busy adjusting herself to the idea that Shuly had turned into ashes to wonder where and how the girl had acquired the watch.

"Sciapan!" Lara called. The man's voice responded behind the door instantly. "Come in here."

A tall, well-built man in his twenties appeared in the doorway. "Yes, what is it, Comrade Larisa Siamionawna?"

"Is everybody ready?"

"All waiting for you."

"I won't be a minute. Take this woman with you. She's going to have a ride with us to witness how traitors are punished."

Without a word, the man pulled Mary by the hand. They walked some distance silently. Two sleighs, each harnessed with a pair of horses, four men beside them, waited in the clearing.

"Is she coming?" one of them asked Sciapan.

"She'll be right along."

"And what do we want her for?" the man pointed at Mary. "She's useless burden."

"Lara's orders."

Soon Lara appeared clad in a warm sheep-skin, knee-length coat, with a wide leather belt around her waist, breeches, warm leather gloves, and a sub-machine gun hoisted across her right shoulder.

"Let's go," she ordered, jumping into the front sleigh and fetching the reins. "You, Sciapan, put the teacher on the back sleigh, and take proper care of her."

12
THE EXECUTION

In the semi-darkness, the horses started with a trot. With three men armed with automatic rifles beside her, Mary sat on the straw-laden sleigh in the rear. She watched the snow-covered silhouettes of the partisan dug-outs they were presently passing. The camp seemed to be asleep, except for an occasional sentry. Some recognized and greeted Lara. Bits of a tune from a mouth organ reached Mary's ears.

They cleared the last trees of the forest, and the front pair of horses, urged by Lara, took to a gallop. The rear pair took up the chase. Hunched in their sleighs, they sped through the open countryside, the dull thud of horses' hooves, accompanied by the freezing wind, howling at their ears. Into the darkness they raced, Lara constantly urging her horses to greater effort. Nobody spoke.

Still in shock of the news learned from Lara, Mary sat despondent, holding onto the rail. By now she had become acutely aware of the purpose of the mission. She was being taken along to witness murder, plunder, and God knows what.

They passed a place that Mary had judged sometime ago to be the village. The huge brick stoves with their untoppled chimneys starkly stood out amid the snow-covered rubble. Here and there remnants of dwellings were not completely consumed by fire. Mary wondered what had happened to the people. Probably burnt alive, as was then the common practice.

"Kalinawka," Sciapan said, as if answering Mary's

curiosity. "The fascists slaughtered the population and burnt everybody and everything shortly after Christmas." The skeletons of brick stoves and chimneys, receding in the distance, looked like bony fingers, pointing to heaven, crying for vengeance.

After another half hour of reckless driving through the night, Lara slowed down and stopped by a cluster of trees on a hillside. The group got off and stared in one direction. Across a small valley, half a mile distant, was a farmer's homestead perched on a hillside astride the main body of the village. It must have belonged to someone with authority, perhaps a Party member.

"So that's where the scoundrel lives, eh?" one partisan said.

"He took over the collective's chairman's property. Must be really good at licking fascist backsides,' Lara spat.

"Shall we go in at once or reconnoitre first, Larisa Siamionawna?" other partisan asked.

"Misha and Patapich," Lara addressed two men, " you two go in and see if it's safe. Don't go through the whole village, be as inconspicuous as possible, watch the dogs. Try to make it on the double; we'll wait for you here."

The two men disappeared into gray darkness. The three men and two women, immobile and watchful, listened for sounds from the village. Then they heard the dogs barking.

"Sure as hell they're going to wake them up," Lara commented. "The scoundrel may take cover. Sciapan, are you sure he's home tonight?"

"Ryhor assured me, swearing on all his saints. He has never once betrayed our trust," the tall man answered. "Don't worry, Larisa Siamionawna, we'll find him snugly in bed with his darling wife and the loving children right beside him."

Stupefied, Mary tried to figure out who the marked victim was. Was he alone or was his family also to be included? Now Lara's words, uttered earlier that night, acquired an ominous meaning.

Shortly Misha and Patapich came back. "All clear," Patapich reported. "No lights anywhere. We didn't approach his house; the dog, you know..."

"That beast," Lara said, "we have to get rid of it first. Any ideas anybody?"

"I'll do it, Larisa Siamionawna," Sciapan volunteered.

"How?"

"Leave it to me," Sciapan asserted. "Wait till my whistle, then you can move."

Anxiously they waited. Clad rather lightly, Mary shivered with cold. Chilly wind swept right through her worn-out quilted coat. The dog barked once near the homestead and just as suddenly ceased altogether. Partisans heard a low whistle.

"On the sleighs fast!" Lara commanded.

She jumped on the front one, grabbed the reins and, fully erect, her legs spread apart, steered the horses toward the homestead. In less than five minutes, they rushed the doors. A tall shadow moved at the front one. "Anything stirring, Sciapan?" Lara inquired.

"Not a thing," the partisan replied.

"Kola and Grisha," Lara instructed in a whisper," you go around and guard the back door just in case. Misha, you mind the windows and we'll start knocking."

Their weapons at the ready, Lara, the two men, and Mary approached the front door. Lara knocked gently, cocked her ear. Someone stirred inside. Lara repeated the knock. A few more seconds elapsed, and then muffled cautious steps from behind the door reached their ears. Someone stopped, listening. Lara knocked again, this time more insistently.

"Who's out there?" the male voice asked.

"Your friends, open up," Patapich responded.

"What friends? The voice doesn't sound familiar. Who

are you?"

"Police from Haradok. We want to see your son right away on a very urgent matter."

A hesitant pause, then the door latch clicked. Immediately Lara forced the door open. The flashlight in her hand blinded the old bearded man who was dressed in his night attire; he helplessly blinked his eyes, undecided what to do.

The narrow light beam searched the nooks and crannies of the wood shed. All kinds of farming implements lined the walls and the earthen floor. A huge gray cat minutely eyed the intruders. Patapich rushed to the back door and opened it, letting Kola and Grisha in.

"Move into the house," Lara prodded the old man.

"Who are you? What do you want with me?" he pleaded.

"Move!"

Kola held the door ajar and they all went in. The beam from Lara's flashlight darted around the room. A large wooden table stood in the comer, the bearded images stared at them from the icons above it. One long bench stood alongside the table, the other one along the wall. Lara was not interested in sturdy, homemade furniture. She darted into the bedroom, ordering on her way: "Blind the windows and make light, boys!"

There were two beds. In one of them a middle-aged woman, her hair tussled, sat blinking her eyes at the light beam. In the other double bed, two small children, apparently boys, uneasily stirred in their sleep.

"All right, where is he?" Lara barked, holding her light straight into woman's eyes.

"Where is who? Who are you? Keep that light away from me!" the woman retorted angrily, shielding her eyes with the palm of her hand.

"You know whom I mean. Your husband." Lara approached the bed and shook the woman vigorously. "Wake up, you bitch."

"He isn't home. Keep your hands away from me!"

"You lying bitch," Lara spat, cursing, "what's his uniform doing on the wall? And who slept here beside you?" With her hand Lara explored the warm bedding beside the now visibly alarmed woman.

The green uniform of the county leader of the Byelorussian Youth Association hung on a hook in the wall. The organization had nothing to do with politics.

The woman looked at the uniform and paled. Suddenly she acted wide awake. The younger boy awoke, rubbing his eyes, on the verge of tears.

"Here I am," the man exclaimed, jumping down from the ceiling. Evidently he had taken refuge between the ceiling and the thatched roof. He stared at Lara.

"Yanka!" exclaimed his wife, visibly perturbed.

"Never mind, Sonia, stay calm," he reassured the woman. Clad in pajamas, wearing sheepskin coat, he was a man about forty. His wide, high-cheekboned face was the face of a man who looked you straight in the eye with confidence and assurance of self-dignity. Now he stared at his wife, his children in the bed and the other partisans, his light blue eyes questioning. Then he closely scrutinized Lara again.

"So apparently you're the one they call a beautiful demon. I dare say you properly fit the definition."

Lara slapped his face hard and prodding him with her automatic, barked: "Out into the living room! We are going to have a talk."

The children were presently wide awake, the younger boy crying. Yanka's wife, hysterical, jumped out of bed and grabbed her husband around the waist as if to shield him from the intruders. A scuffle developed. One of the partisans hit Sonia mercilessly, and she reeled, falling back on the bed.

"All of you, out of the bedroom!" ordered Lara. "Children too!"

They had to drag them out. Yanka stopped in the middle of the living room, angrily appraising the armed people. Mary Karaway stood aside by the door. The old man, Yanka's father, leaned against the table. The children, aged about five and three, tugging fearfully at their mother's hem, looked scared for their lives.

"What do you want from me?" Yanka demanded of Lara. "I take part in no politics, only work with our youth – "

"Spare your breath; we know the nature of your job. First of all you run the Byelorussian fascist youth organization, helping Hitlerites herd the Soviet youth to slave labour camps in Germany. On top of that you're a Gestapo agent!" Lara recited these facts, drilling the youth leader with the eyes of a prosecutor in a military tribunal.

"Soviet youth, my foot!" the youth leader thundered. "Why don't you Moscow hirelings get off our backs? Germans and Russians are blood-thirsty predators in this country, and we Byelorussians want to get rid of both and be masters in our own house. And get this," he pointed his finger straight at Lara, "I'm nobody's agent but my people's. I suppose it's too much to expect you'd understand this."

"Shut up, you filthy fascist; we haven't come here to argue with you!" Lara yelled. "Sciapan!" she barked, motioning Yanka with her eyes.

The tall partisan approached the youth leader. He struck him full-force in the chest with the butt of his sub-machine gun. Yanka reeled, losing balance, panting for breath.

"Rotten rats, Bolshevik jackals!" he yelled scornfully. "You are the devil's paws, unworthy to be called human beings!"

His face filled with scorn, he was menacingly impressive in this outburst of anger.

"Once again!" Lara barked.

The partisan jumped on the youth leader. He kept slugging him until the latter fell on the floor. With a shriek of desperate anguish, his wife rushed to assist him. Unceremoniously, Sciapan pushed her away. Numb and shaking, the old man, the picture of utter helplessness, supported himself by the table edge. The children squealed.

"What's the matter, Lara?" Mary interrupted, her voice bitter. "Can't you do your own dirty work? Show what a heroine you are, you dirty whore. Perhaps you should start with the children, they can't resist..."

Anguish, hate and desperation cut through Mary's voice. The partisans, their attention busy with Yanka's family, now turned to the woman at the door. Her eyes challenging them, she stood there shaking, her eyes filled with menace. Lara turned abruptly to Mary and, as a bloodhound ready to jump its quarry, hissed right into the teacher's ear: "You miserable wretch, can't you be patient enough to wait your turn? I can assure you it won't be long now. Kola," she ordered the young partisan, "come here and keep an eye on her." The partisan took up his position beside Mary.

By now Yanka, his face bruised and bleeding, stood erect and ominously eyed "the beautiful demon". His lips moved slowly, accentuating every word: "You can kill me, you can kill my family, but you can never kill us all. The day of reckoning will come. Our people will kick Russian and German parasites off their backs and render themselves free. You are ignominious vultures, and your days are numbered." He spat blood straight into Lara's face.

As she fired rapidly, other partisans joined her. The proud youth leader, along with his father, wife and children, writhed in agony as the bullets streaked across to the icons in the corner. After the thunder of automatics abruptly stopped, Lara spat venomously: "Fascist dogs!"

At the door, Kola seemed lost in what to do about Mary. She had fainted and was lying on the floor at his feet. They carried her to the sleigh. Then they returned back to the farm to slaughter the livestock. Mary soon recovered. Shivering with cold, scared and exhausted, she crouched on the snow. After the slaughtering humans and animals was done, the partisans paused at the teacher.

"Why all this game of cat-and-mouse with her, Lara?" Sciapan asked, motioning to Mary. "A useless burden... Isn't it better to finish her right off?"

Lara did not answer immediately. She looked at her companions, then at the crouched figure in the snow and pronounced with an undertone of mockery in her voice: "Are you kidding? I have better plans for her. Tomorrow we're going to celebrate the victory, and she'll be our star attraction; like Irina was last month, remember?"

The partisans looked at Lara, then at one another and chuckled with glee. The laugh of beasts about to devour their prey echoed throughout the bleak February night.

"That's our girl, Lara. We'll toss you a dozen times thanks for it!"

"Before that perhaps you should toss a couple of grenades into the house, eh?" Lara laughed, proud of her victory.

The two of them raced to the silent building. A few seconds later, an explosion rocked the wooden house.

As the squad moved away on its heavily loaded sleighs, the fire hungrily licked the dry timber of the farmhouse. It seemed all the dogs in the village were now awake joining in a common chorus of fierce barking. Across the valley, without undue haste, two sleighs loaded with slaughtered domestic animals, with seven people trudging alongside, melted into the darkness.

13

THE DARK ABYSS

They did not disturb her all the next day, but sleep came uneasy. Time and again horrible pictures reappeared in all their vividness. She embraced and cuddled her darling daughter Alenka, kissed her on the nose, on her rosy cheeks, whispering sweet endearments in her ear. Out of nowhere, a man in a police uniform appeared; muscular hands reached out for her little daughter. Mary struggled, held fast, but her physical strength was not enough to stop the beast. Mary gasped for breath.

The nightmare receded, and presently the heavy soldier's boot that mercilessly kicked her child on the floor disappeared. A hideous mask of "the beautiful demon" mocked and taunted her. Venom-filled eyes drilled through her, sadistic lips moved, and a drunken, wavering contralto spat out a threat: "You wretch! You nasty miserable wretch! You stinking Christian! You'll beg for your life, licking my boots..."

She must rid herself of that face! Her hands, propelled by concentrated vengeance, reached out, the fingers clawing into the smooth, soft neck of the "girl... demon". They kept squeezing, choking. Her own breath became heavy, she was suffocating.

With a start, she woke up. Both hands kept clutching the pillow. Horrified, she realized she had almost choked herself to death. She sat up, cold with sweat. It was dark in the dug-out. The two other cots stood empty. One of them belonged to Prudnikava, the other to her thirteen-year-old orphaned niece, who probably right now was helping her aunt with never-ending camp chores.

Mary's head weighed at least double what it should. The uneasy sleep, she realized, failed in the slightest to calm her taut nerves. Quite the contrary – the hideous nightmares had tired her and made her more jittery. She sat there, in the semi-darkness, immobile and broken, making no effort to sort out the chaos in her mind. The dead and the living clamoured for her unreserved attention; with space and time erased, rationality upset. Her own long dead children merged with Yanka's tots, whose slaughter she had witnessed only a few hours ago.

The "girl-demon", her left arm akimbo, the right one clutching an automatic weapon, faced the scared family. "You miserable fascist dog!" she spat at Yanka. Mary wished she could somehow undermine her footing and wrestle the gun from her. She reached out, but the next instant her hands, as if seared by an invisible flame, promptly withdrew. Flames sputtered from guns, the thunderous salvo tearing the insides out of her. As the children and adults were cut down by murderous gunfire and writhed on the floor, the demon's lips spat contemptuously: "You miserable fascist dogs!"

So unbearably painful! Gradually the malevolent countenance receded. Helplessly shaken and alone, Mary pondered yesterday's events. There emerged the bloodied and contemptuous proud face of the defiant youth leader: Rotten rats! Bolshevik jackals! You are unworthy to be called human beings. One day our people will kick Russian and German parasites off their backs and regain freedom!"

Tall and towering, erect and menacing, contemptuous and scornful, this man's tongue mercilessly lashed his executioners. A noble reincarnation of great national heroes from the deep past. The incomparable Kastus Kalinowski must have acted thus, whose voice penetrated the ages: "Fight for your life, my brothers Byelorussians: From under Muscovite gallows I proclaim: then and only then will you regain freedom and fulfillment, when Russian despots rule you no more!"

Deathly silence from the thousands; middle class, workers, and peasants held their breath, their eyes glued to the proud, commanding nobleman facing the executioner's noose. The great son of the soil, saturated with the blood and sweat of his brethren, ascended the pinnacle of their struggle-burdened history. In his sublime glory, he faced the executioners, physically conquered but not alone, for at that very moment he embodied the aspirations of oppressed millions. To them he had revealed the goal and the way; henceforth the oppressors were never able to suppress his people's thirst for complete freedom. Implacable in his scorn of the nation's tormenters, he knew that through his sacrifice other revolutionaries would be born. He was only twenty-six when he faced the gallows. One of the youngest among the great, he must have dwelt on the nature of Providence's endowments.

At those distant times, the executioners still perpetrated their crimes in public with all the theatrical trimmings of the devil's élan. The noisy, terror-inducing drums, the impeccably calculated moves of practitioners of "legal crimes", stony-faced marionettes in military uniforms, their bayonets bared and ready for any emergency, the gawking multitude in the tightly packed square.

Belatedly the masters with bloodied hands realized their practices had misfired. Out of the blood of the martyrs publicly shed grew a new crop of avengers. The perpetrators of genocide dismantled the gallows in public squares, substituted concentration camps and gas chambers for processing the countless men. The leaders were disposed of in strictly guarded compounds. Countless single and mass atrocities of recent wars and periods of uneasy peace defied all former rules and conventions. No human being – sex and age notwithstanding – appeared to be immune from the hands of the executioners.

The youth leader Yanka was probably moulded from the same clay as his great compatriot Kalinowski. Placed in a different historical panorama, he might have grown and led others. Working with youth, he elected to build, not destroy. When cornered by the degenerate girl-demon, he acted a courageous and dignified warrior.

No one except a beaten and broken Mary Karaway witnessed the murder of youth leader Yanka and his family. The man was unaware that another of the girl-demon's hostages was witnessing his execution. His behaviour was neither planned nor premeditated. His malignantly vehement utterances, directed at the despised enemy, were not concocted for public consumption. In the only manner available, he rebuked and castigated his own, his family's, and his country's tormentors.

Reconstructing all the details in her mind the next morning, Mary realized she had witnessed something exceptional. Perhaps, given an opportunity like this, many a despairing soul would come to realize that all was not bad in this world; hope for a better tomorrow need not be irretrievably lost if among the corrupted and morally eroded multitude one encountered a small but glittering star like Yanka. Truly, she had only a brief and meagre glimpse of that star, but the moment of its supreme endurance was when it shone the brightest.

Mary, who loved history, had often speculated on the behaviour of martyrs and revolutionaries when facing their executioners. The teachers and history books invariably projected the past in an official interpretation of the people in power, quite often at variance with the facts. Official versions aside, how did those people really behave? How much was acting and how much was real?

Giant trees, when felled, thunder down, bearing destruction in their path – the maxim is often reasonably well applied to people. What about small and seemingly insignificant ones? Human nature being as feeble and contradictory as it is, one may safely assume there are those, in the majority probably, who if faced by the gallows or the firing squad, would crawl and lick their executioners' boots to spare their lives. But there are others, palpably few, who are courageous, great, and heroic in their unpretentious and natural behaviour. Mary saw one of them and thanked God for the opportunity. She admired and adored Yanka. Mary's faith in her own people was reinforced, and her will to resist the onslaught of evil was thus fortified.

Most remarkable, of course, was that Yanka spoke as if on behalf of all oppressed peoples. Had he solely his own interests in mind, how totally different he would have acted and appeared in Mary's eyes. He spoke for himself and for Mary, for all those millions not then and there present. The interests of his countrymen were paramount in his consideration. It was the awareness of this, no doubt, that so mercilessly stung his tormentors. For in that instance, if only subconsciously, they surely must have realized their own nothingness, vanity, the criminal nature of their actions. Here they were – about to execute a true and loving son of the people who, in his malignant wrath towering above them, castigated them as degenerated scum, the Judahs of their own brethren. His noble outburst, like lightning bolt, pierced their tenderest tissues. Unless totally devoid of human conscience, they surely must have received the message clearly, although no one would have hoped that they would realize their own unworthiness.

Then Mary viewed the medal from the other side. Surely Yanka must have known that these predators understood only the language of lead and fire. Why then had he acted as he did? Mary knew that the officials of the Byelorussian Youth Association carried no weapons. Perhaps Yanka had none. Perhaps even if he had, he realized the battle was lost before it was started. He might have chosen to act on a slim chance to save his family hiding inside the ceiling. Why had not he moved them out of the guerilla-infested zone? Perhaps... There were too many "perhaps" to cope with. One could lose one's own way trying to reason out the probabilities and motivations of a man one never knew. Surely Yanka was no fool and knew that only net results – not actions themselves – counted in this atrocious war. The doubts assaulted her anew.

Way back, before the onslaught of the official Communist regimentation in Red Pioneers and *Kamsamol*, Mary used to pray regularly. Her pious mother diligently observed various religious ethics and endeavoured to keep her daughter in line. She became deeply disappointed when she realized that little Mary lent a responsive ear to the Devil. Many a time she threatened Mary that one day God would exact retribution for her unpardonable sins.

Presently Mary recalled her mother's pleas and warnings. The pressures of the times took their toll: children's loyalties were divided. The Party and the regime – actually one and the same – undertook to break up the family unit. They undermined the authority of the parents over their children; Pawlik Marozow became the national hero. The Leader was the Father and the State – the Mother of one and all. No room was left for religion and what they labelled superstition. These so-called remnants of the bourgeois past had to be promptly uprooted and done away with. "Destroy the old to build the new," went the slogan.

Since the godless regime considered the old generation unfit and unable to accept their unorthodox ideology built on hate and destruction of established values, they concentrated their guns on the youth. The young were coached and goaded, urged and cajoled, to march in the forefront, to form the avant-garde of the regime's destructive forces. Young hands hauled down the crosses from the houses of God; youthful lips uttered sacrilegious parodies on stages in village squares and city clubs, ridiculing the Creator, lashing the believers, prodding everyone to follow Satan. The incessant Communist indoctrination permeated every academic subject in the houses of learning. One received no good marks unless one was versatile in the jargon of Communist ideology. Those who desired to get ahead in this new predatory society were forced to embrace the poisonous serpent and feign adoration.

This then was the stifling atmosphere in which as a teenager, Mary Karaway had to grow up. She came to realize, none too early, that there remained no possible basis of reconciliation between her mother's Christian beliefs and Communist dogma. One totally excluded the other. Mary followed her school educators and claimed adherence to the accepted doctrines. In time she even abandoned prayer.

Presently, in the captivity of the Red guerillas, she considered, rightly or wrongly, her immediate past and present physical and moral ordeals as expiations for the enormous sins of her past. Her mother's pleas and warnings now appeared to her in a different light.

What about this girl Lara? Was not she the embodiment of Satan who demanded of Mary the retribution for her past wrong-doings? Mother told her once that God worked for his people through the people. Is it not at all possible that He selected this beautiful misanthrope as a tool to effect Mary's redemption? If so, how should she proceed to placate the Creator for forgiveness? Long ago her mother also told her that God was forgiving and, boundlessly merciful, ready to receive his errant children into the Father's fold any time they genuinely deserved his favours.

In the semi-darkness of the partisan dug-out, Mary's lips moved uneasily, her face contrite. What was forgotten from early youth had to be substituted. The woman realized she need not necessarily follow the prescribed text. Her own direct talk with the Lord might have just as much effect. Not a mechanical repetition of someone else's words, but a prayer all her own....

Even as she talked to God, fragments of the recent past clamoured for attention. Satan endeavoured to reassert himself. If God was really as merciful as they profess Him to be, why does He allow defenceless infants to be consumed by fire, children and women shot, God-loving people exterminated like vermin? Perhaps this God is that glassy-eyed fellow on the icon in Yanka's house? If He is all-powerful, all-merciful, and forgiving, why does not He come down to earth and re-establish peace, order, and justice? Surely one could not imagine a worse inferno than the one presently consuming this God-forsaken country...

Doubts assaulted her. Nothing made sense. She could discern no landmark on the horizon to guide her through this bottomless abyss of her inner turmoil, while the indomitable conspirator against the Teacher in Heaven hovered nearby on the brink of chaos, poised to strike.

Unable to resolve the inner conflict that fed fuel to her emotional fire, she gave up wearily, crossing herself. Exhausted and perplexed, she buried her head deeply in the hay-filled pillow. She wanted to cry, but no tears came. Immobile she lay, listening to faint noises outside, and to her own heartbeat. How she wished her heart would stop so that she could pass away easily and quietly! Thus, in uneasy slumber, she lay, unaware of the time and place, attempting to shut out the world...

14

THE DEVIL'S FEAST

The rusty hinges screeched, the door opened and closed. Heavy steps approached Mary's cot. A moment's hesitation followed, then the bed covers came off with a sudden jerk. Exposed to the cold, Mary sat up abruptly and looked directly into Sciapan's sombre face. There he stood, the indomitable messenger of the girl-demon, a faintly malicious smile playing on his lips, a bundle tied in gray canvas in his right hand.

Mary wondered about this drab, docile, efficient adjutant of Lara. What kind of man was he really? What went on in that darkhaired, thickly covered head? He spoke little, moved around fast, performed his duties efficiently. Mary was intrigued by his enigmatic, handsome yet life-lacking face. Was this man more than he appeared to be? What was his real relation to that girl? Was he her lover, or just her servant?

As Mary sat shivering, trying to cover herself, Sciapan's hand gripped the bed covers. His eyes ogled the frightened woman, and in a low voice he said: "Take these and pretty yourself up. We are going to a celebration tonight."

Mary looked at the clothing in front of her. At a glance, she could tell the blue dress was of fine quality. The sweater, although worn, was still in good condition. She liked neither the man's voice nor his manners. He stood there in front of her, eyeing her without blinking.

"What do you mean? What celebration?" she asked in a halting tone. The embers in the round iron stove in the comer had long since gone cold, and the dug-out was terribly chilly. Mary wrapped the quilt cover around her and stared questioningly at Sciapan.

"Exactly what I said – we are going to celebrate. Lara's orders. Dress up and pretty your face. You have to look decent."

Mary expected him to continue, but the man kept staring at her silently. Perhaps he belonged to the kind who never unnecessarily wastes his breath, even when he does not need to be laconic. It must be late now, Mary thought. Just enough light trickled through a small window to see one's way around.

"What kind of celebration? Why do I have to pretty myself up?"

"You ask too many questions. We're going to celebrate last night's victory."

So that was it. Some victory to celebrate. Suddenly it all came back and overwhelmed her. Last night... exhausted and completely spent, she lay on the snow. One of partisans wanted to finish her off then and there. Lara intervened and directed that her time had not yet come, that she should be spared for celebration. What was left unsaid but implied was even more significant. Mary presumed she was earmarked for some kind of a scapegoat's star attraction, and shuddered at the sinister idea.

"I'm not going," she said with resolute asperity.

"You what?" Sciapan barked.

"You heard me the first time: I'm not going."

The man grabbed both her arms, and squeezing them shook her violently. "You're hurting me, you brute!" she cried out.

Sciapan released her and said quietly, too quietly: "Listen, I'll expect no trouble from you. If you know what's good for you, you'll do as ordered. Don't tax my patience, it's useless. If you resist, I'll have to take you by force."

Mary stared at this human animal. What use to resist him, if resist him she could not? He could certainly carry her on his shoulders, all the while administering proper punishments.

"And another thing," said Sciapan in a conciliatory tone. "You'll have the honor of meeting our commander there. If I were you, I'd jump at the chance." He sat on the small square stool in the corner, pulled out a pipe, tobacco, proceeded to fill the pipe and light it, all the while watching the woman askance.

Still in bed, Mary donned the dress. She reached for the small mirror in the wall and peered into it. She could hardly see in the gloom. Sciapan, noticing this, lighted the candle on the small table and resumed his seat.

Now Mary looked more intently into the mirror. She could hardly recognize her own face. A lean, blanched countenance, with two deep pits under the eyes, dully stared back at her. She brushed her fingers through her hair, some of which must have turned gray in the last twenty-four hours. "My God!" she exclaimed, "what has become of me!" Then and there she decided the face did not really matter. Perhaps what they called a celebration was destined to be her execution... Tomorrow she might rest under so many feet of dirt.

She jerked at the quilt cover resignedly, pulled the blue dress down, and donned the sweater. The dress was just about her size. The woman could not help wondering what had become of its past owner. She combed her hair, put on the boots and the short quilted coat.

While dressing, she shot glances at Sciapan, but her attempts to make conversation failed. The man did not respond. He sat there puffing on his pipe and ogling her. Mary decided the man was a bore, with little if any human feelings. You might get as much response from the wall.

"Let's go," he said, rising when she was ready.

Mary was hungry. She could not remember when she

had eaten last. Food was scarce in the camp. When she worked in the kitchen or in the hospital, sometimes she had enough to eat. More often than not, she would go hungry. Nobody cared. She was treated as an outcast.

Suddenly a desire to have a hot bowl of soup overwhelmed her. Homemade soup, with a chunk of meat in it, and warm, so warm that it could rekindle life in her. She was exhausted, shivering, and cold. The bowl of soup seemed to be a hopeless dream.

They walked through the camp, encountering many people milling about their duties. The huge bare trees towered majestically against the clear blue winter sky. The fresh cold air made Mary's head dizzy, and she realized now how weak she had become. Outside the camp, Sciapan trudged through deep snow in his big capacious boots, Mary following him.

"Where are we going?" Mary could no longer resist her curiosity.

"You'll see. It won't be long now," Sciapan said. They plodded slowly. About ten minutes later they came upon a house in the clearing. Mary judged it must have been another forest guardian's retreat. It was a fair-sized house with shingled roof, windows boarded on three sides, the lean-to completing the structure. It had an abandoned air. In the distance, across the clearing, Mary saw a small stable, a pair of horses tied up to the wall, covered with blankets, unhurriedly chewing hay.

They approached the door. Sciapan stopped and cocked his ear. At close proximity, Mary noticed the light through the cracks in the boarded windows and heard animated voices inside. Sciapan knocked on the wooden door panel three times three – with short breaks in quick succession. Before any response from inside, a stout, heavily clad, and bearded figure appeared behind the corner.

"Sciapan, is that you?" a friendly voice asked. "Why

don't you go in?"

"I'm supposed to knock."

"Nonsense. The door is open, go right in."

"Everybody here now?"

"You bet they are. And from what I hear, they're not asleep."

Sciapan pushed the door wide open. They crossed one threshold and then opened another door.

The lamp, suspended from the middle beam in the ceiling, blazed brightly. Six people sat around the table, Lara among them. All of them, except one, were participants in last night's victorious undertaking. The one who did not take part sat beside Lara at the head of the table. Mary's gaze slowly wandered across the partisans and paused on the man beside Lara. The conversation broke off as everyone stared at the newcomers.

The aroma of fresh-roasted meat and other food assaulted Mary's nostrils. Hazily, her eyes darted across the food-laden table, a huge glass jug full of gray liquid royally dominating the whole assembly. Mary's own long-unsatiated appetite demanded immediate attention. How hungry she was! Will these mercenaries deign to feed her?

While Sciapan took Mary's coat and sweater, the woman's eyes glued themselves onto the bearded man beside Lara. Her face pale, now more than ever alone and scared, facing this group at the table, she was petrified, unable to take a step. This malevolent bald head, with piercing dark eyes, narrow lips, and grizzled beard belonged to her tormentor, who at one time so assiduously lectured her on the subject of proper education in her own classroom at Shuly. The silence in the room underlined Mary's own hectic heart-beat.

Obviously this man must be the one they called Commander Karpatin, whatever his real name was. She had seen him a couple of times before in the camp from a distance and had not identified him. Attired in his green military uniform, without any marks or insignia, the alluring Lara on his left, he held Mary's dumb struck gaze steady, savouring the suspense to the full. Presently, unaware of her afflicting hunger, Mary had eyes for no one else in the room. What a pair, Karpatin and Lara! What did they have in store for her?

The bearded one moved, and a disparagingly poignant voice said: "Well, well, if it isn't my old acquaintance, my dear little teacher. Aren't we glad to see her, comrades?"

The men around the table chuckled, while the Commander continued: "You, my dear teacher, will of course pardon me for my oversight in not renewing our mutually profitable relationship earlier. The pressure of duties, you know. But tonight, I hope, with ready assistance from this devoted group of friends here, I'll be able to rectify my oversight. Don't you think so, Larisa Siamionawna?" Karpatin slightly tilted his head to the radiant girl on his left.

"Certainly, Alaksiey Piatrovich, certainly," Lara eagerly agreed, looking at Mary with a glint in her eye.

"Since we are acquainted," continued the bearded one, "we mustn't waste much time on preliminaries. Our dear guest is hungry, no doubt, so why don't you comrades invite her to the table. Make room for her right here beside me."

While partisans complied promptly and seated Mary on Karpatin's right, Sciapan placed himself at the foot of the table. The Commander continued in his previous manner, his shallow deceptive front fooling no one. Only today I had the full account of yesterday's expedition to Malyja Luki, where you had to dispose of the fascist dog Yanka Biely. I was told that beside the squad here you also bravely took part. So why, I thought should we leave you out of this modest celebration? You deserve to be present here, don't you think so, my dear teacher?'

Mary was close to the food which tantalized all her senses. Spasms of her stomach made her wonder if despite the proximity of this evil man she should not immediately throw her bare hands on the roasted pork meat in front of her. Karpatin and Lara, with her impish smile, and the others must have presently sensed this, observing the woman from all sides.

Mary scanned the select group. She had but a brief glimpse of them in action yesterday. True to the prevailing custom of the forest boys, most of them had grown beards and probably, as their song goes, everybody promised himself a good thorough shave "after Fritz had been chased out of the country." Kola, next to Lara, the youngest in appearance, had wide wandering eyes, bushy blonde hair yearning for a barber's attention, well-proportioned features. He displayed no trace of villainy so common among the older partisans. Misha had a big square head; he was about forty, balding, vacant of gaze, the mouth too wide and out of proportion with the rest of the face, deeply set eyes; Patapich, darkhaired, bushy-brewed, a malignant look of expectation; Grisha, the big bear with the huge peasant palms, porous mottled face, coveting bloodshot eyes; and contented, solemn, but ever-watchful Sciapan, the big messenger boy. All these men had the air of expectation a theatre audience shows as the curtain has risen and before the action on the stage begins. Flanked by this entourage, her importance enhanced by Karpatin, Lara sat with the detached air of one conscious of a job well done, knowing in advance what was in store, like an experienced hunter trapping his long-sought quarry.

Whatever this group had planned for Mary, Karpatin displayed no urgency in his paternal and disarming approach to the captive. Exchanging knowing glances with Lara, he motioned the huge jug to Kola, and the boy was about to fill the Commander's glass, when Karpatin interceded: "Shouldn't you start with our lately arrived guest? After all, she is our – so to speak – honoured guest tonight. And, if I may be permitted to speak frankly," he said directly to Mary, "that dress is very becoming on you, my dear teacher. It does justice to your otherwise neglected looks. Doesn't it, Larisa Siamionawna?"

"Why, certainly," Lara hastened to reply, "it fits well. Do you like it, Mary?"

The partisans commented approvingly. Mary surmised they were about to play cat-and-mouse with her, so she might as well carry her own ball.

"Why, you knew, of course, that blue is my favourite colour," Mary replied to Lara. "It was so nice of you to give me a blue dress. I'm sure you have a wide selection to choose from, don't you, Lara?"

Lara's queenly alluring face, with a trace of vulgarity on it, grimaced slightly as she tartly replied: "I'm so glad you like it. As for the selection, actually there was no choice. The dress's owner had this one and only this one when she was dispatched... "

"You mustn't really spoil our chat here, Larisa Siamionawna," Karpatin interrupted, "by hints not presently called for. May I suggest that we get down to the business of eating? But first, let me propose a toast to the health of all of you, who successfully completed yesterday's assignment."

The short preamble completed, Karpatin raised his own glass which was filled to the brim, and all the rest, except Mary, followed. "To our health!" the partisans exclaimed.

With their glasses suspended above the table, all eyes turned to the outcast in their midst. Karpatin stared at her questioningly. "Now my dear teacher," said he with forced benignity, "do join us. I'm sure you are hungry and eager to expedite the process of consuming this good drink and tasty food. Or is it possible you don't wish us well?"

Mollified by this eloquent fatherly approach, willy-nilly Mary was on the defensive. "Thank you, you are so kind. But I would rather not. You see. I don't drink."

As if rehearsed beforehand, all hands simultaneously placed their glasses on the table. The shade of incredulous annoyance crossed Karpatin's face, while the others grimaced in mild disbelief. Everyone seemed to play his role well. Mary sat pensively, with a guilty look on her face.

"You what?" Karpatin inquired. "Do you hear, comrades? Is it possible? The teacher says she doesn't drink." This was another cue, and the partisans murmured disapprovingly. Evidently they felt restrained by Karpatin, although they had probably drunk before Mary's arrival.

"Really, Mary," Lara said in the tone of an instructress, "we know the local custom of refusing hospitality for appearance's sake. But isn't it wise to dispense with appearances here?"

"You must drink, my dear girl," Karpatin urged Mary, six pairs of eyes on him. "It's your duty. Now come on, raise the glass. You see everyone is waiting... "

Mary wondered when the viper would project his poisonous fang to strike her. She lowered her eyes and regarded her full glass with trepidation. She could not imagine herself swallowing the repulsive-smelling liquid. It would burn her insides. Her stomach clamoured for food. Is not there any way she could make them understand she had to eat first?

"If only I could have a bite right away, I'm so hungry," she whispered deprecatingly, looking straight into these dark penetrating eyes, searching for a ray of understanding.

"You hear this, comrades? The teacher says she's hungry," Commander's voice mocked Mary. Gleeful smiles transformed the partisans' faces.

"Poor girl," lamented Lara, 'I should have told Prudnikava to take better care of her."

"I'll help you," interceded Karpatin. "We all here are reasonable and well-meaning people, and we understand you. We'll solve this in a democratic way. I'm sure you also subscribe to democracy. What do you say, comrades?"

"Commander is right, we should resolve this together," ventured Patapich with guile. The others unanimously supported him.

"So what do you say, comrades?" Karpatin raised his hand, "should we let our guest eat or drink first?"

"Drink!" the chorus of voices simultaneously exclaimed.

"The vote is unanimous in favour of drink. This settled then, my dear teacher, you must oblige by joining us in the common drink," Karpatin said, his voice falsely sweet.

"I can't. Please understand, I beg you. It'll make me sick," Mary again pleaded in a hardly audible voice.

She would have had the same result appealing to a brick wall.

"Do you mean to say you still want to persist in your unreasonable stubbornness, disregarding the unanimous will of all these fine people here?" the shocked Commander asked.

Mary kept silent.

"Well, well, what are we to do about it, boys? Use some persuasion?"

"She hardly leaves us any choice," Lara suggested.

"Kola," the Commander barked, motioning with his eyes to the wide leather belt with the gun in the holster suspended on the long nail in the wall.

The youngest partisan jumped up, brought the gun, and placed it on the table in front of Karpatin. Presently everybody watched the Commander's sinewy hands. He pulled out the drum and released all the bullets. Holding one in front of Mary, he proceeded to instruct her: "You see, my dear teacher, this bullet. We're going to play a simple and exciting game. I assure you it's lots of fun. Now watch this carefully. The chamber is now empty, see? I'll insert this bullet into it, like this," he spun the chamber with his index finger, "and then keep pulling the trigger. There's one chance out of six that you'll be shot. While I'm doing this, perhaps you'll kindly think about obliging the unanimous will of all our friends here."

Karpatin spun the chamber and aimed the gun directly at Mary's temple. The woman paled. All the partisans, holding their breaths, concentrated on Karpatin's index finger which slowly kept pressing the trigger. The hammer pulled away and clicked. No explosion came. The sigh of relief released the tension around the table.

"This time you were lucky. The next one may hit you," commented the bearded one calmly. "Just remember, any time you change your resolution, grab your glass and drink."

Beside herself with panic, Mary felt her own wildly throbbing heart. From the other side of Karpatin, Lara watched her with detached disdain. Misha kept his mouth open, displaying big brown teeth; Sciapan's face acquired an aura of solemn curiosity; Patapich eyed her with thinly disguised malice; Kola stirred in his seat, shooting furtive glances at the others. Grisha, the mountain of a man, ventured a suggestion: "Comrade Commander, lend me this teacher for a few minutes; I'll make sure she learns her lesson well."

Karpatin shot a reproachful glance at him. "She stays right here. I have to try my method first."

The hammer moved half way again, and Mary, by now thoroughly convinced they meant business, slowly took the glass. She brought *samahonka* to her lips. The gun jerked away from her temple. Her whole exhausted body protested.

As the first swallow went down, it seared her empty insides with phosphorous heat. Her breath completely taken away, she coughed so violently that she was afraid to disgorge her stomach, writhing in spasms of pain. A thunderous laugh rocked the house. When it abated, Karpatin's calm voice said: "You mustn't, my dear girl, stop at all. It's only the first time that gives you any trouble, like a virgin's first time with a man, you know... "

Laughter followed this remark.

"After that, it'll go down smoothly, you'll be surprised. So come again," Karpatin ordered.

Her eyes watery, Mary raised the glass again, and this time she promptly emptied it without a pause. The violent cough rocked her feeble body, deafened by the common resounding mirth.

"Bravo, she did it!" yelled Kola with undisguised delight. Karpatin laid the gun on the table and raised his glass. "So now, to our health," he said. They swallowed the gray liquid in big gulps. "Now eat," Karpatin ordered Mary.

He did not need to urge her. The woman, now oblivious of everybody else, loaded her plate with a huge piece of meat, some sauerkraut, black rye bread, and mashed potatoes; and even as she kept filling the plate she busily devoured the food. Perhaps if she could pack her stomach solid, she could neutralize the fire burning within.

Presently the *samahonka* assaulted her brain, and the first impact made her dizzy. Afraid that they might take her food away, she chewed so fast and fiercely that her gums hurt. The partisans also threw themselves on food like vultures, discarding any table manners they had. Only Lara and Karpatin viewed the commotion around the table with a degree of detached amusement, exchanging knowing glances and chuckling as they ate.

Presently the glasses were being filled by Sciapan, and Mary watched in horror as the liquid from the big jug was poured in a small vortex into her glass. It would certainly kill her. An idea occurred to her that she had the choice of being shot by Karpatin's bullet or being poisoned – she was now firmly convinced of this probability – by the *samahonka*. Only superficially she knew the qualities of this home-made liquor. There were two kinds – the most common kind, distilled only once in a crude homemade still, and the other kind that underwent double process of distillation. This was the second kind.

A strange sensation, new to her, possessed Mary. She consumed the food, mindful of the pack of wolves around her; one of them could intervene at any time and take the plate away. No thought of table manners, not the slightest heed to what others thought or did, she speedily ate. Even the subconscious recollection where the meat came from failed to affect her. The stomach knows no morals, and food meant survival. This paramount idea firmly rooted in her now dulled mind, she missed the word of prompting Karpatin who brought her back to reality with a violent shake of her left shoulder. The fork suspended half way between her plate and her full mouth, she looked questioningly at the Commander and around the table. Quiet and expectant, they held their full glasses.

"Drink!" ordered the bearded one unceremoniously. Swallowing hard, she caught her breath and incredulously stared at the drink in front of her. She could not possibly do away with this one, she thought. Eyeing the gun askance, she decided it would be foolhardy to resist.

"If I may be permitted, I'd like to skip this one," Mary glanced deprecatingly towards Karpatin.

"What, again?" roared Karpatin. "You might as well know that you are expected to drink every glass-full given you, and no more nonsense. So don't tax my patience. Drink!"

Mary glanced around, as if expecting assistance. She

could not possibly demur. These beasts would pour it down her throat if need be. Resigned, she raised the glass, sipped slowly, and her – whole being violently protesting – gulped to the bottom. Watching her closely, all the rest followed.

It hit her with a violent force. Her head span. A blazing inferno burned her intestines. Gasping for breath, she nearly choked. The tears ran down unhindered from her eyes. The thunder of diabolic laughter accompanied her extremely annoying discomfort. Now completely stupefied, she grabbed the fork and resumed eating.

"You are quite an inconsiderate host, my dear Commander," said Lara to Karpatin, giggling. "Can't you see the teacher has had enough?"

"Never you mind," the host retorted, "I'm sure she can accommodate much more of it. The question is: is it necessary to waste good liquor?"

"I should say not," Patapich broke in, "let's start having some real fun, Commander. How about you, Grisha?" he elbowed the bear beside him. "What do you say?"

Kola pulled out his harmonica, wiped his mouth with a wide sweep of his left palm, and seemed undecided what to play.

"I?" Grisha rolled his blood-shot eyes, examined the woman on the right of Karpatin minutely." I say let's have some fun." With these words he gave Patapich a friendly bear-slap on the back, which nearly propelled him out of his seat.

"You son of a bitch, don't hit me like that," the man protested. Oblivious of everybody else, Grisha saw only the woman. He got up, moved around the table and before the others realized what was happening, he swung his arm around Mary and was pulling her out from her seat, "You, c'mon, I'll give you a good time," he panted.

On the verge of delirium, Mary saw the immediate world around her through bizarre eyes. Again and again she tried desperately to figure out what was happening, and who these people around her were, and what had happened to Val, the children, her mother, and what she was doing, and what she must do next, when someone grabbed her from behind. She had not yet decided whether to resist or follow him, she could not think logically, when the grip was released.

Misha jumped on Grisha: "You leave her alone, you bear! I'll have her first."

"No, you won't!" snarled Grisha. He released the woman and jumped on his adversary. While the two men exchanged blows, Kola's harmonica accompanied them with a vivacious polka. The two rolled on the floor.

"Take them apart, boys!" Karpatin ordered. Lara seemed disappointed. "Let them be, Commander, I like to watch. They're both strong and perhaps have too much juice for the poor wretch."

"No," contradicted the Commander heatedly. "I'll see that everybody is satisfied. That means there must be order. Patapich, Sciapan! Take them apart!"

The two wrestlers were separated and stood panting.

"Now let's do this like civilized men. No fighting. Kola, get me some paper and a pencil."

Puzzled, the participants of the feast watched Karpatin expectantly. He tore the sheet of paper into five pieces, wrote the numbers on them, rolled them up and threw them into his round cap.

"Now attention, everybody. There are five men here, excepting myself. I have five tickets in here, marked one to five. Each one of you will draw one ticket and will not open it before the draw is completed. Then, when I order you, you'll unroll your own piece and read to me the number you have. The number one ticket will go with the woman first; number two, second; and so on. The last one, I mean number five, will also have the additional pleasure of disposing of the woman." Karpatin scanned the faces for the impression he had made. "Any objections anybody?"

"I say that's fair enough. Everybody has an even chance and number five has the privilege... " Patapich supported Karpatin.

"What do you say, Lara?" Karpatin asked the girl.

"I say you're a genius. What about you? Don't you want to take part?" Lara said, castigating him with her eyes.

"Should I?" the Commander smiled. "And leave you alone? Oh, no, my dear girl, we're going to have fun together." With this remark, he administered a resounding slap on her behind.

"You hurt me, you brute," exclaimed Lara without any rancour and to the accompaniment of common mirth.

"Good," said Karpatin laughing and hugging Lara. "Now then, draw your tickets." The five men pulled the rolled pieces of paper out of Karpatin 's cap.

"Now for the numbers... Who's got number one?"

"Here," Patapich replied, a satisfied grin on his malignant face and his covetous eyes on Mary.

"Congratulations!" Lara giggled.

Sciapan drew number two; Grisha, three; Misha, four. Pale and calm, Kola stood, his mouth organ in one hand and the piece of paper in the other, his eyes darting from Mary to everyone in the group. He had never executed anybody in his short life; now he wondered about Mary, the poor girl, to whom he had already developed some sympathy.

"Now, my boy," Karpatin approached him, laying his heavy hand on Kola's shoulders, glancing first at Mary and then straight into the young partisan's eyes, lowering his voice, "after you have had your fun, grab my gun and take her to that large pit on the edge of the forest; you know the one I mean?"

"'Yes," Kola answered, trying to hold his composure.

"Shoot and push her down. Understand?"

"Yeah."

"Take someone with you for a witness."

Kola nodded.

"All right then, now everybody is satisfied, I believe." Without any further talk, Patapich approached Mary, grabbed her by the arm, and pulled her behind the curtained doorway of the bedroom. The others followed them with their eyes, undecided about what to do.

"Let's have another drink." Misha proceeded to fill the glasses. Kola sat on the bench, his earlier verve for fun and buoyancy gone. He held the harmonica at his mouth, undecided what to play. Karpatin took his gun from the table, loaded it, and slid it into the holster hanging on the wall. He peered closely at Kola. "What's the matter, junior? Are you by any chance disappointed on your lot?"

"Oh, no, no!" Kola jumped up. "I'm really glad, Comrade Commander." He smiled with an effort.

"I see no reason why you shouldn't be," Karpatin said with finality and followed Lara into the bedroom on the left.

15

THE RAPE

Half-conscious and numb, Mary was dragged to the bed by Patapich. Her will to resist completely gone, she held fast to the swaying bed, relieved that her heavy head could at last rest on a pillow. She made a supreme effort to prevent vomiting.

Her undergarments were ripped off with a savage jerk, and Patapich's rapturous thrust induced waves of tremours along her alcohol-saturated exhausted body. The man clutched her with the powerful grip of a vice and spent himself at least three times in quick succession. The hoarse laughter behind the curtain augmented her agony. With a burning hell in the pit of her stomach, now they were drilling her from the bottom. Wincing and squirming, grinding her teeth, gasping for air, she sank her fingernails deep into the hay-filled mattress. Pangs of pain shot through her side, reminding her of the beast Bergdorf.

Sciapan never came. Grisha made up for all of them. Mary shrank from this bloodshot creature who ground her with a savage ferocity, the alcohol delaying his release. He slapped her hard on both cheeks and cursed. The *Yablachka* tune grated on her nerves like the thrusts of a dull, rusty knife.

The beasts gone, the tune of *Yablachka* stopped. Her body ravaged and soiled, the scents of Grisha and Misha lingering about, she lay there recovering her normal breathing.

Kola came in quietly, like a cat, and nested on the edge of the bed. The narrow beam of light filtering through the gap in the curtains presented a sight that disgusted him.

Although like many others he was driven into the ranks of forest mercenaries by the force of circumstances, he possessed no stomach for unnecessary violence. Once – it now seemed ages ago – he had studied agriculture in the Hory-Horki Academy for two years. A collective farmer's son, he loved life and nature with every fiber in his well-developed body.

Imbued with Marxist indoctrination, he earnestly believed the Kremlin's Red-Starred beacon of light projected the path to follow towards a better future for all the underprivileged. Hitlerism, on the other hand, embodied oppression, darkness, and barbarism. Never in his partisan duties had he wantonly wreaked vengeance or rape.

Karpatin liked him for his succinct wit, joviality, efficiency, and reliability. His whole nature recoiled from the role of an executioner. His keen mind now hectically worked out ways and means by which this woman, whom his degenerate partners had transformed into a miserable wretch, could be saved. How could he do it unless he risked his own life? Thus immersed in conflicting speculation, which offered no clear-cut solution, he heard Mary's weak whisper: "Water." Kola jumped up.

"What's the matter, Kola, you chickened out?" Grisha ridiculed him. "Maybe you want me to do it for you? Or are you still a virgin?"

"You boys made her thirsty," Kola said calmly, fetching water from the pail that stood on the birch-tree stump in the comer.

"Why bother?" Misha said, his tongue now loosened by *samahonka*, "she'll be dead soon anyway."

Kola did not argue and went directly back to Mary. The woman drank and breathed with relief.

"Now listen," the partisan said, "let's rock this bed together so we can fool them while we talk. I want to talk to you, tell you what's coming. I don't know if it'll do you any good but I feel I must... "

The bed squeaked and rattled at the joints. "Hear that? I told you he's no novice at this job," laughed Misha, joined by others. "How about another drink?"

"I heard. I'm to be killed. You?" Mary held her breath.

"Yes."

There came a long silence, interrupted by the bed's noise and the partisans' banter behind the partition.

"Believe me," said Kola haltingly, "I'd give my right arm if I didn't have to do this, I mean... if I could save you."

He looked at her closely. In those dazed misty eyes, he discerned a shade of apathetic resignation, but no enmity. "You had better dress yourself, I can't, I won't... like the others," he whispered.

"You would save me? Why?" Mary inquired.

"I have my reasons," Kola answered modestly. "I can't explain them now, there's so little time. One of them is – I don't believe in wanton killing. God knows, too many innocent people are being killed nowadays for no reason at all... When there's no chance to discriminate, like in battle, that's different, but now... Besides, I think it was all Lara's idea. I think she's a blood thirsty bitch. It has nothing to do with war..."

His compassionate eyes watched the woman closely, and he appeared to Mary as an angel, descended from unexpected quarters. Squeezing her left hand with tenderness and undisguised emotion, he reached out for her sweaty face, gently rubbed her chin and both cheeks.

"What a pity I didn't meet you in a different place and time. You are so lovely. I curse the day that so disastrously brought us together and made me to be your executioner. No, I won't, I can't... " His lips drew tight. "On the other hand, how can I possibly back out? That licentious bitch will consume me alive, meat and bones."

"Kola," Mary stuttered, her wave of unchecked emotions released, engulfing her, choking her voice, "thank you a thousand times." She drew him closer and lightly kissed his hand.

"No, no, you mustn't," he jerked his hand away, completely losing control, afraid he might cry.

"You can hardly imagine what you've done to me," Mary continued. "Your words of solace and understanding are the best present from God. May the all-merciful Lord guard and protect you every hour and day. Thank you, Kola."

Avoiding her moist eyes, the partisan rose abruptly.

"Dress yourself, time to go," he ordered in a totally different, taut voice, then disappeared behind the partition to fetch her clothes. The four partisans, now almost completely drunk, rocked on the benches, unevenly bellowing the popular partisan song of the time:

Oh, you birch-trees, you pine-trees,
Partisans' sisters...

After depositing her sweater and quilted coat on Mary's cot, Kola alighted again and raising his voice above the slurred singing of the partisans, yelled: "Anyone going to help me?"

The gritty melody broke off. They stared at Kola busily pulling out the Commander's gun from the holster on the wall. They stared at one another, trying to recollect what it was all about. Kola scanned each one of them closely, minutely examining Sciapan. Lara's adjutant was also drunk, although Kola knew he was the one to hold his liquor best. Rarely would he abandon himself to the pleasures of the body, throwing caution to the winds.

"Well, c'mon, I must have a witness," Kola insisted.

"Sure, why not," Sciapan said, rising. "I'll help you."

"Me too, dear boy," Grisha woke up, his eyes searching for a point of support. "Aw, c'mon, let's have some more fun," he decided promptly and swayingly proceeded towards the bedroom where Mary was.

"No, you don't! You had your turn with her and now she's all mine," Kola heatedly protested and grabbed the brute by the arm.

Grisha stopped, mutely eyed Kola's gun. "What's the matter, junior, why should you save the fascist bitch? She's to die anyway, isn't she?"

Abruptly he pushed Kola away with such a force that the boy nearly lost his balance. He grabbed Grisha by the arm again and pushed the gun into his stomach. "That's enough from you," he threatened. "I have my job to do and I'll do it even if I have to kill you. Do I make myself clear?"

The message got through. Eyeing the gun, Grisha meekly mumbled: "All right, junior, you can have her, but I'll have another drink," whereupon he hobbled off to the table.

"C'mon, I'll help you," Sciapan laid his hand on Kola's shoulder. Kola looked at Lara's trusted adjutant attentively and wondered whether she instructed him to volunteer. Sciapan looked sober enough to know what he is doing. Not even bothering to don his sheepskin coat, he followed Mary and Kola outside. Kola halted and called the guard: "Maxim, why don't you go in and have a drink? Everybody forgot you, I believe."

The half moon above occasionally peeked from behind the thin clouds. Soft, huge snowflakes fluttered down lazily, covering the nocturnal forest with a silvery pillow.

"That way," Kola pointed across the clearing. Slowly, somewhat hesitatingly glancing over her shoulder, her long tousled hair now covered by silvery flakes, Mary led this strange procession: Kola with the gun in his hand at her heels, and Sciapan, unevenly harrowing soft snow with his capacious felt boots, a score of paces behind.

The fresh winter air had somewhat awakened their senses. Mary turned her face upwards and rubbed it with falling snow. She drew in a deep breath of crispy fresh air, the vital sustenance of life. Her dazed mind now clearly aware of the nature of this trip; her whole being was gripped by the indefatigable will to stay alive.

A thick white wall of trees ominously loomed across the clearing. Huge and calm in its still majesty, the forest resurrected in Mary's memory the fascinating winter wonderland of long ago. A tinge of nostalgia, now prodded by the trepidation of imminent death, presented a cherished picture of the past with unbelievable clarity.

When she was a small tot, her mother fetched her along to the forest to cut Christmas trees. The tiniest details of those trips had lain long dormant in her memory. Now etched by an over-active imagination, they brought back the image of a small girl fascinated by the winter wonders, sights she had rarely imagined. A sense of a child's curiosity examined the snowy trail of the rabbit and partridge, savoured the hammer-sounds of the woodpecker; her eyes darted through the brilliant whirling snowflakes trailing the bronze, heavily furred squirrel gliding from one fir-tree top to another. Above all, she was immensely impressed by the snowclad giant trees.

"Mother, do trees grow in winter?!" she asked.

"No, my little tot, they sleep."

"Look, mother, up there. See that squirrel? Why does she jump? Isn't she cold?"

"No, my dear. She has thick fur to keep her warm. She's busily looking for pine cones."

"Why, mother?"

"She eats the seeds."

The little girl would ponder her mother's answers. Then again, "Mother, what will we do if we come across a wolf? Aunt Nasta one time told me about a wolf who was about to eat a little girl when she was saved... who saved her, mother?"

"It was uncle Ryhor, who was hunting. He shot the beast."

There appeared to be no limit to the child's curiosity. While her mother kept explaining the puzzling vistas of nature to Mary, the child's imagination ran rampant like the squirrel on the tree tops, darting from one branch to another.

Hauling the fair-sized fir-tree home through knee-deep snow was no easy task for a man, less so for her mother. Mary tried to assist as best she could. The little girl herself was a picture of loveliness: the puffy frost-crimsoned cheeks, the runny nose, the sense of accomplishment in her large blue eyes, the quiet joy of anticipation of the Christmas Eve ahead. It was all so vividly carved in her imagination. Happiness once cherished and never forgotten.

Now every step brought her closer to death. Any moment the thunder of Kola's gun would rock the quiet forest. Mysteriously dark in its depths, it held its breath, as if solemnly paying its last respects to the condemned woman on her trek to the grave. Mary whispered prayers.

They were about to reach the edge of the precipice. Kola raised his gun when Mary unexpectedly tripped on a high protruding root and plunged forward. Immediately four shots rang out in quick succession, but the man pulling the trigger never attempted to hit his target, which now fell forward into the huge snow-covered pit. Sciapan immediately levelled with Kola, staring into the abyss below.

"Good work, my friend," he patted Kola's shoulder. "You really must have hit her; she flew down like a bird."

"Poor girl," sighed Kola, careful not to reveal his gratification at his unexpected twist of luck. He was sure he had missed Mary and was quite certain the woman would come out alive, perhaps bruised and scathed, but certainly in one piece.

"Poor woman," repeated Kola, "what a death... And she wanted to stay alive so much."

"Now don't you become a crying sissy for a fascist wretch," Sciapan said, nudging him. "Let's go back."

"I'm certainly not going to," Kola assured his companion, "but I still think we should have given her a decent burial... "

"Why bother? The wolves will have a feast," Sciapan chuckled.

The wolves never approached Mary. With rape and wholesale murder rampant the length and width of the country, the predators were amply supplied with food. Human flesh was to be found in over-abundance everywhere. Those discriminating wolves could choose among roasted women, fried children, and adult males.

Shocked and numbed, Mary lay in the snow, slowly realizing she was still alive. Cautiously she wiggled her toes in turn on each foot, making sure the limbs were intact. She moved her hands and suddenly sat up.

The voices on the hill above her moved away, and deathly stillness descended on the nocturnal forest. The thick snowflakes came down continuously. Preoccupied with herself, Mary did not notice them. First of all, she decided that since the forest was unfamiliar to her, there was no alternative but to wait for daybreak before moving away. Certainly nobody would look for her. Twice she was brutally dispatched to the grave, and both times miraculously saved. Scarred and bruised she was, but still alive. The entries in both the *Schutzpolizei's* and partisans' dossiers would probably mark her as a "liquidated enemy of the people."

The people... What about them? Truly, if she were anybody's enemy, it was not the people's. The two giant predators, warring for her country, victimized all her countrymen, the common people who refused to raise their arms in someone else's war.

Presently a bizarre idea sprouted in her mind: since she was liquidated by both adversaries and would be duly entered into the records as officially dead, perforce she could start life anew among her own people, perhaps under an assumed name in a distant and safe place, provided her endurance would sustain the new beginning. Her health's deterioration, augmented by tonight's bout with alcohol and rape, alarmed her most of all. Warm shelter and good food were indeed imperative for her survival.

Where could she find them? Obviously she could not return to Shuly, the village turned into a heap of rubble. In her somewhat dazed and erratic memory, she searched for an assisting hand, the embrace of a genuine friend, who could and would harbour and feed a beaten, broken, and homeless victim of war.

Her teacher-friend Yustyna from Haradok came to mind. Certainly she was the only one to turn to. Mary reproached herself for forgetting until now her warmest and devoted friend. Was it due to the jitters and anguish she was experiencing? How was Yustyna? She must have heard of her being killed by Bergdorf. What a surprise she would make, suddenly resurrecting on Yustyna's doorstep...

Preoccupied by her own thoughts, Mary was totally impervious to the thick snowflakes, which fell without ceasing. Like a white, lifeless mummy, she sat immobile amidst trees and shrubs, staring straight ahead and seeing nothing. For a while she pondered how she was saved from the partisan's bullets. Was it a protruding root, a tree stump, or the hand of Providence? Was it a lucky predestined accident, or a Will from above? Mary's lips silently moved in grateful prayer to the Almighty. She marvelled at the invisible power of the hand of God, her contrite heart filled with gratitude.

Then her bodily discomfort took over. She felt considerable pain at the back of her right shoulder, apparently bruised by the tree limb which somewhat arrested the impetus of her downward plunge. Otherwise – she decided after closer examination – she had come out unscathed. The soft pillow of snow absorbed the shock of her fall.

Dawn began to thin the snow-clad forest in front of her, and Mary rose to go. Glancing around, she decided to move away from the partisans' camp.

16
THE BULLET HOLE

Late in the afternoon that same day, after the school children left for home, the office of the teachers of the seven-grade school in Haradok heard some hectic arguments. Five teachers were present in all, the youthful and aggressive principal Todar Shpilka, and the home-room teachers of four senior grades.

Yustyna Murashka sat close to the table, and through the hazy tobacco smoke concentrated on the hole in the windowpane. Like the sun's rays in a child's drawing book, almost symmetrical in length, the hole radiated the cracks that shattered but did not totally split the glass. The pane needed a gentle push to fall into splinters. It was probably a stray bullet, she was once told, that found its way through the windowpane and lodged itself in the wall close to the ceiling.

Yustyna mused on the nature of that hole, cocking one ear so as not to miss the principal's words. Like the window-pane pierced by a stray bullet, the mother's heart was hurt today; speculating on the possibility that her young and only joy – a twelve-year-old son – could be taken away from her and dispatched to learn, as the official version went, some useful trade. She could not willingly agree to this atrocity, she decided.

Shpilka's gray probing eyes scanned those present, as he continued: "I cannot, ladies and gentlemen, over-emphasize the importance of this undertaking. You must realize as well as I do that we cannot face the Germans and bluntly tell them that not a single student has volunteered. They would simply refuse to believe us. Mr.

Trakhimovich, the county inspector on education, told me in no uncertain terms that the German commissar of education in the district expects some good results from us. The way Herr Budke envisaged this – and these are his words, not mine – Byelorussian parents should be grateful for the opportunity offered for their children's advancement."

Prompted by the last sentence, ironical smiles crossed the teachers' faces. Yustyna Murashka sniggered at the clever presentation of Herr Budke's alleged remark. It rang a bell in her memory. The self-styled builder of "the new Europe" appeared to be badly mistaken if he harboured illusions that such outworn platitudes could guide the people who had stomached over twenty years of Russian Soviet colonial oppression.

The teachers and general population of colonized Byelorussian territories had heard and properly digested similar ambiguous propaganda missiles before. Year in and year out, time and again, they were told that what they knew as a terrible serfdom was allegedly a paradise on earth; their children should be grateful to comrade Stalin for their happy childhood; they should prostrate themselves before the dictator in boundless gratitude for the straitjacket he put on them.

"The children who shall volunteer to go to trade schools in Germany," Principal Shpilka continued, "will have free lodging, food and the best possible medical care and first-class instruction in trade schools. German authorities have assured Inspector Trakhimovich that there's not the slightest reason for parents to worry. I have told you this yesterday, and I'm stressing this again today. For I cannot but suspect some of you have approached this problem nonchalantly and half-heartedly. I have no choice, there-fore, but to ask you for your fullest and most ardent co-operation. Try to do better tomorrow than you've done today. Children will have spoken with their parents tonight, and let's hope they'll be more receptive to this opportunity tomorrow."

Shpilka paused, his eyes darting across the gathering as if expecting some a rush of denial, but none came. He was visibly perturbed by the silence. What's the matter with these people? Cannot they possibly understand that unless the project succeeds in some measure his own job will be jeopardized?

The Grade Seven teacher, Mikola Runovich, fidgeted in his chair. Wrinkling his high forehead and pulling on the left side of his long brown moustache, he spoke: "Mr. Principal, I for one got the message. I'm puzzled, however. Aren't we putting the cart before the horse? Surely the proper way to go about it, if one must, is to ask the consent of the children's parents. Certainly they should be the ones to decide a matter of such magnitude. To put it in modest terms, I was rather taken aback by the methods suggested. What do the Germans take us for? A bunch of nincompoops? After all, those of us who have children – if we were confronted by a like proposition and learned that our children were being goaded behind our backs to renounce their country and sign away their lives – certainly couldn't remain indifferent. Moreover, some of us would lose confidence in the school authorities. Aren't we overestimating ourselves? After all, ladies and gentlemen, what the Germans are asking us to do – and I'm sure this is not an isolated case, but probably the general method applied throughout Byelorussia – is to become the recruiters of manpower for the German labour machine. How to reconcile this repugnant task with our teachers' ethics, I'm sure I don't know… "

"I was coming to the question of parents," Principal Shpilka explained, blushing. "However, before I expound on it, I'd like to take issue with your remark, Mr. Runovich. From what you have just said it appears you are biased. Nobody – and I repeat – nobody is asking anybody to renounce their country and sign away their lives. Let's view this matter in its proper perspective. I'm certain you all agree that our children deserve the best possible education they can get. Now you know that we have very few secondary schools in this country, trade or others. I'm not going into the question why. You also know that German trade schools are possibly the best that one could wish to find anywhere. Now I ask you: what's wrong with our children taking the opportunity offered and then, later on, benefiting our country and themselves with the skills and trades acquired?

"The German authorities assured our County Education Board and Inspector Trakhimovich that the recruitment of our children for education in German trade schools doesn't constitute the recruitment of labour. Germans are being explicit about this. In no way should this recruitment to schools be misconstrued as an attempt to fill German factories with cheap labour.

"Now about the parents. As I mentioned before, I was coming to that. I was specifically instructed to go about this task exactly as I have. Of course, the German authorities realize the children cannot decide for themselves. What they wanted us to do was to explain the programme in the broadest possible and most attractive terms so as to make the children understand it fully and correctly. That being the case, some of them, especially the bright ones, may willingly jump at the opportunity.

"You must bear with me, ladies and gentlemen, and try to understand how their German minds work: they consider this a great opportunity, perhaps a blessing for the local young population. They are benevolently offering our youngsters a chance to advance themselves in a profitable education, and later both Germany and Byelorussia will benefit. Of course, we'll have to ask the parents' consent; of course, we'll probably have to call a general parents' meeting. This canvassing of children was merely preliminary. You'll pardon my presumption for not enlightening you more broadly on all the aspects of this subject at once, but frankly I myself wanted to see the results of preliminary canvassing before calling on the parents' authority."

And so it went on. Yustyna examined the Principal's lean boney face minutely. Was the man really that naive, a heartless bureaucrat, or a plain common fool? How would he act if his own children were involved?

Shpilka was an old bachelor, a rather experienced and versatile pedagogue. Working alongside him for two years, she found his co-operation and understanding agreeable. He was lame on his left foot and thus escaped the dinosaur of war. Now suddenly she saw him as an inconsiderate agent of the occupational regime. Did he really believe what he said and try to make them believe? Had the fellow forgotten that the bloody war was raging all around? What possible guarantee could the parents have that after graduation from the trade schools – if that's where they really were destined to go – the children would be returned to their parents?

Taking all the uncertainties and risks involved – not to mention parental love and the desire to keep families intact – how could anyone possibly agree to this outrageous proposition? Of course, Germans must act as they do. After all, their own labour resources had dwindled by the insatiable demands of war; they had to look ahead and plan for the future. Provided they were successful in recruitment – God forbid – and after graduating from the schools in some distant future, they decided not to release the youth, who would make them do it?

Yustyna was very sensitive on this subject because her own son was involved. She just could not imagine parting with her dear boy. Who knows how the war would turn out? Perhaps one day the Bolsheviks would come back...

Just consider what would happen then. Just think about it... It's hard to comprehend, indeed! No matter how one hates them, if they come back one simply could not dig one's own grave and nonchalantly jump into it.

What the Germans were, in fact, asking the parents to do was to sign away their rights to their own children, hand over their dearest ones to the occupational authorities on a plate. Outrageous! Have not they burned and bled this country white? With the population decapitated by both predators, the bloody dagger of war was now attempting to open the native vulva! Merciful God! All those sweet assurances, the voice of a wolf in sheep-skin! And she – the mother herself – was she not being asked to sacrifice her own son and to induce and recruit others? Suddenly the bullet hole in the cracked window grew beyond its usual dimensions and penetrated the mother's tender heart.

Uneasy dusk settled on the war-scarred town when they finally left the smoke-filled teachers' room. Feeling quite unnerved and alone, Yustyna kneaded the dirty February slush. Engrossed in the unfortunate twist of fate, she walked mechanically past the ruined and fire-gutted houses, military traffic on the street, two drunken *Schutzpolizei* staggering toward her across the full width of the sidewalk. Miraculously, the school building remained intact. Only last week, the solid brick building was inspected by the local army commandant, probably in view of its possible use for the accommodation of troops.

Yustyna quickened her pace to reach her dwelling before the evening curfew. The clatter and din of traffic around the railway station echoed gloomily in her heart. Uneasiness brought recollections of the frightful past, the people who had disappeared from her life, the husband who perished on the Finnish front, her kin, her closest friends. Mary Karaway stood out among them.

Poor woman. What a noble, life-loving soul, murdered by those beastly partisans together with her mother and children. Her village of Shuly was razed by the Germans last week; the whole population was herded into the school building and perished alive in the fire.

Yustyna was an attractive, easy-going woman who rarely let her emotions take over her reason. She had originally come from the forested country some hundred miles south. Combed and ravaged by two opposing forces, the area had become a barren desert. Her father, a collective farmer, perished in one of the German pacification sweeps that cut a swath of destruction among the peaceful population. Her mother died before the war. Her only older brother was drafted into the Red Army; no news about him since...

She lived with her twelve-year-old son Maxim, renting two rooms from an elderly lady called Agatha, whose small old wooden house on the outskirts of the town had somehow escaped the flames of the war. It was hand-to-mouth existence. The small plot of land, allotted to her by the education authorities, supplied them with vegetables; the meager teacher's salary evaporated in the spiral of war inflation. Underfed and overworked, she dragged her feet from day to day, no promise of better days at all in sight.

Numerous widows in the town had done better, throwing morals to the wind and adjusting to wartime conditions. For favours rendered, they were amply supplied by local police and military personnel with food and clothing. Yustyna received no shortage of offers. At one time or another she entertained the idea of taking a lover. This, she reasoned, would jeopardize her teacher's job; children's parents, among others, would condemn her without a second thought. She decided against it. The patched overcoat, dresses, and boots became the trademark of her hard work. Undernourished and tired, she carried on. Even this miserable existence now appeared threatened. Her only son could be taken away from her. What was she to do? One had to reckon with the possibility that if no children volunteered to those cursed schools in a distant foreign land they might simply take them away by force.

"Ausweis!" barked a voice. Two towering military guards appeared in front of her, scanning her outworn dark coat, the yellow shawl, the Astrakhan hat, the patched boots. Jerked by the master's voice, the woman dipped her hand into her pocket and fished out a small gray identification card. The man in the steel helmet examined the photograph minutely, scrutinized gaunt Yustyna's face, handed the document back, and motioned her to move.

17

THE REUNION

Just as she turned the corner, a block away she sighted her own Maxim, hurrying in her direction.

"What are you up to, Maxim? Don't you know any better? The curfew." She met him with a barrage of questions.

"Mother!" he panted, gulping for breath.

"What is it?" Her perturbed eyes searched his face... Speak up."

"Mother, you'd never guess... We waited and waited for you, and then we were scared something had happened to you, so I ran –"

"What do you mean, 'We waited'? Who is 'we'?'"

"This you won't believe, mother. Cross my heart, you won't believe it," he stood in front of her with an enigmatic expression on his youthful freckled face, the true picture of his late father. Yustyna loved him even more for this resemblance.

"What's this mystery? Has anything happened to Agatha? Come on, out with it!"

"When I came home, I found someone in your bed. I know you'll be surprised, mother, but there she was – Mary Karaway! ... Honest to God, mother!"

It was incredible. If Maxim told her that their house had fallen through the ground, she would have been less sceptical. "Mary?" she exclaimed incredulously. "Am I hearing right?"

"You hear right, mother. Your dear friend Mary Karaway, that's who... " chuckled the boy triumphantly.

"But... but Mary is dead! Do you hear me? She's dead,

Bergdorf told me so himself. What's the matter with you? Are you pulling my leg?"

"No, mother, honest, why should I lie?" the boy's hurt voice retorted. "I'm telling you, Mary Karaway is very much alive and resting in your bed. She came before noon, she told me. I think she's sick, maybe very sick... "

As the boy rattled the big news in a single breath, Yustyna peered deep into his eyes... No trace of falsehood there... now her heartbeat accelerated. She felt as though she was losing her balance, so stunning was the news. Paralyzed, she stared at the youngster, unable to move. Suddenly aware of herself, she grabbed the boy's hand and steered him around. "Let's hurry up, son. If it's really Mary, let's go!"

Confusion receded, and logically she tried to adjust to this most unlikely development. The attempt to rationalize this thunderbolt proved futile. There was no point of focus. A beehive of questions assaulted her brains. Mary, dear Mary, who would have imagined... after her imaginary burial and requiem in the local church, suddenly she appears right in her own house...

The ten-minute walk lasted a century. Her heart throbbing irregularly, Yustyna opened the door hastily and found her hunchbacked, sallow landlady Agatha in her bedroom. The half-burnt candle's feeble flame flickered on the night table beside the bed.

Agatha rose and whispered: "She is resting. A peasant brought her to my door this morning; she, the poor thing, half-frozen, exhausted, begged me to let her in. I had to put her in your bed, you see... "

"It's all right, Auntie, all right... you've done a proper thing, God bless you," Yustyna replied, her anxious eyes glued to the woman in the bed.

She lay covered right to her chin. The white bed covers sharply contrasted with her death-yellow complexion; for a second it appeared to Yustyna that the woman was lifeless. Her eyes remained closed. Yustyna approached the bed on tiptoe, scrutinizing the gaunt face, the large areas of darkness under Mary's eyes, the gray hair. As she stood contemplating the next move, the heavy bluish lids moved, and the haggard eyes stared at her waveringly. Slowly a sign of recognition flickered, and Mary attempted to smile, the futile try withering away in a faint grimace.

"Mary, my darling, is it really you? My dear pigeon, how are you? What have they done to you? Where have you been?" Yustyna grabbed Mary's hand, and choked with emotion hugged and kissed her on the forehead. The head was hot, the pulse irregular.

"Yustyna, my dearest, forgive me," Mary's hoarse voice responded weakly. "I have a cold, I think."

"Oh, my dear girl... forgive you for what?" Yustyna embraced her tenderly, showering her with kisses. The tears appeared in both women's eyes. Locked in a tight embrace, the profundity of feelings engulfing their hearts, they poised suspended in immobility from life itself. The loud heart-throbs and rapt breathing fed fuel to their excruciating emotions. Maxim fidgeted, unable to decide what to do. Agatha sneezed into her handkerchief, ready for tears.

"Now don't exert yourself. Lie down," Yustyna ordered in a soothing voice. While she tucked the blanket around Mary, she turned to Agatha, "Auntie Agatha, could you do me a favour?"

"Yes, dear. What is it?"

"She has a temperature. Please boil some water with lime blossom. She has a bad cold, perhaps pneumonia. Has she eaten anything?"

"I gave her some barley soup with milk, but she wouldn't touch it," Agatha replied.

"Please then."

The landlady left the room. Presently Yustyna, taking

off her coat, said to Maxim: "Why don't you do your homework?"

"Mother, I haven't eaten yet, waiting for you."

"I know, my dear. Go fetch a piece of bread, I'll make supper later."

Alone in the bedroom with Mary, Yustyna again anxiously scanned her sunken face. Had she changed! Yustyna preserved in her memory an earlier image of Mary. Miensk. The graduation party at the Pedagogical Institute. Modest and beautiful, Mary Karaway with her dark-haired, dashing Valodzia. Two young birds, full of life, poised on the springboard just about to plunge into the turbulent waters of the world. Embracing one another, their eyes filled with love. Dreams cherished, hopes to be fulfilled... What a happy couple they will make, everybody said. The bullet hole in the school window came back to Yustyna. Superstition? Was this broken and spent woman in her own bed the same happy girl she had known earlier?

"Mary, please, my precious, tell me," pleaded Yustyna with compunction, "what happened to you, where have you been? I might as well tell you from the start that we had a requiem for you in our church. Oh my God, forgive us... "

Mary looked at her askance. The blue haggard eyes appeared larger than usual. "Thank you, Yustyna," she whispered, "thank you immensely. Don't ask God for any forgiveness. He'll certainly understand. I was killed twice, and yet I'm alive. Perhaps... I hope I'll pull through..."

"You shall, darling, you shall," Yustyna assured her heatedly. A spell of deep coughing rocked the bed. Then she rested peacefully, attempting to catch her breath, and continued: "The first time, Bergdorf shot my family and me-"

"Bergdorf? Why, the son of a bitch!" Yustyna jumped up

angrily. "One day he came back from his partisan raid and spread the news that you and your family were killed and burned by partisans. Of all things!"

"The brew is ready," Agatha announced through the door. Yustyna rose precipitously, and a minute later reappeared with a cupful of deliciously aromatic light green steaming liquid. She propped Mary up in bed.

"Drink, my dear. This is lime blossom, the best medicine for a cold." Yustyna held her cup.

"But why are you nursing me? I can manage myself; thank God, I'm strong enough to hold a cup and in a day or two, after a good rest, I'll be up and around." She managed a languid smile.

"Of course you will, dear. Only there's no need to hurry. You are in good hands among friends, and now your ordeals are over," Yustyna assured her.

Between spasms of violent coughing Mary related her incredible story: both encounters with death, Kolpakoff-Bergdorf; Lara Voynik, Karpatin, Yanka Biely, and the rest.

When she finished, Yustyna sat silent, her face clouded.

"What is it, dear?" Mary inquired.

"Nothing important..."

"Something is bothering you. Tell me," the woman in bed persisted.

"Mary, what happens if Bergdorf learns you're alive and right here under his nose?"

Deep silence followed. Mary drew her lips tight together. "Must he?" she asked.

"No reason at all. Right now only three people know about you. I'll see what I can do... Maxim!" Yustyna called.

"Yes, mother," the boy appeared in the doorway.

"Please fetch Agatha. I want to speak to both of you." When the boy and the landlady reappeared, Yustyna said in a solemn tone: "Please listen carefully, for this is a matter of life and death. Understand?" They nodded. "Don't tell anyone, no one at all, that Mary is here. Understand?"

"Anyone? Why?" Maxim asked.

"I told you this is a question of life and death," Yustyna continued. "Nobody must know that Mary is here, especially Police Sergeant Bergdorf. He shot Mary and her family, then spread the news that they were murdered by partisans. Now, if he finds out Mary is alive, God knows what he might do." She scanned their solemn faces.

"I understand," Agatha said. "God forbid if my tongue ever... "

"Why, the God-damned bastard!" the boy exclaimed vehemently. All three widows turned their eyes on him instantly.

"Maxim, stop!" Yustyna admonished him. "What are you saying? Where did you learn to swear like this?"

"I swore, mother, and I'll do it again," shouted the youngster defiantly. "That lousy rotten murderer, that's what he is. So it's true what some people say that he kills innocent people, isn't it, mother?"

Animated and angry, he faced the three women, malice and chagrin written on his crimson freckled face. In his open defiance and questioning challenge, Yustyna instantly recognized her late husband. He yielded his path to no one.

"He deserves a slug himself, mother," the boy continued. "I swear he does!"

"Maxim!" Yustyna approached the boy, laid her hands on his shoulders, and peered into his eyes. "What's got into you? Hush! Keep quiet, unless someone hears you. People get killed for less nowadays..."

"I won't keep quiet, mother!" he jerked away from her. "Don't shoo-shoo me! You are scared because you are only women, that's why." He eyed them, a flicker of contempt in his eyes. "Well... I'm not scared. If I had a gun, I'd go right into the police station and kill the murderer!"

"Maxim!" Yustyna shrieked, horrified. "I order you to keep quiet! Understand?"

Yustyna had never seen her son like this before. What might happen if... the thought froze her blood veins. Maxim was boisterous and extremely aggressive. Meekness was entirely out of his character.

Reluctant to give any ground, undaunted, the boy continued: "Why, mother, is it right for one scoundrel to go around and kill innocent people and wrong for others to defend themselves? Why, mother? He murdered Aunt Mary's family, didn't he?"

"He did but –"

"But it's wrong to go and shoot him for it. Is that what you're trying to say, mother?"

Hopelessly stunned, Yustyna slumped into her chair. Mary eyed the boy with interest and an appreciation of what she heard; Agatha crossed herself repeatedly with unction, her parched narrow lips whispering a prayer.

"Maxim, please," Yustyna pleaded with the youngster, "my dear son, you are still only a little boy. Think about school, not murders. Please do what I've asked you to..."

He hesitated a moment. "You haven't answered my questions, mother. Now if you don't want to be frank, I'll try to resolve them myself."

"Please, son, none of this foolishness, I beg you."

Suddenly, a stark realization dawned on Yustyna. Children mature so much faster during the war. It appeared to her that while she was busy with her school children, she had neglected her own son. What was he doing out of the house after school hours? Of course she knew the company he kept. He and other town boys criss-crossed the town, knew the local permanent military personnel, probably sampled more life than Yustyna imagined. Apparently the boy's outburst was the product of his war-time experiences.

Suddenly Yustyna felt old. She looked at the boy pleadingly and said: "Son, I don't want to hear any more of your foolish ideas. If you really want to help Mary, I would like you to promise to keep your tongue on the leash. What do you say?"

"All right, mother, if you wish so. But it's against my –"

"Never mind that," Yustyna cut him short. "Now go into the kitchen and I'll be right with you."

Reluctantly Maxim left the bedroom.

"Merciful God, who would have thought... " Yustyna sighed.

"Do you think he'll keep quiet?" Mary asked.

"I'm sure he will. But he scared me so... Tell me, Mary, did anybody you know see you coming into town this morning?"

"No," Mary said, after a thoughtful hesitation. "I tried to be as inconspicuous as possible."

"That's fine. Now tell me how you feel. Perhaps we should call the doctor, though it's risky, and the old man lives on the other side of town."

"Don't worry, Yustyna, I'll be all right. I have a slight fever, but it's hardly anything to worry about. Just let me rest... "

Their eyes met, and they both understood Mary's simple lie.

18

THE RECOVERY

They were about the two worst weeks Yustyna ever experienced. Although Mary stayed in bed as a hard dry cough rocked and convulsed her periodically. Several pros and cons were considered, and the women decided against calling a doctor. There were two elderly civilian doctors in town, maintaining small practices on their own. A shortage of medicine made them practically helpless. The local hospital was filled with military personnel.

The women trusted nobody. What if someone they called in to help let an unguarded word slip? One could not risk losing Mary while trying to assist her. After Mary regained some strength, Yustyna decided, she would take her to see Inspector Trakhimovich, to find her a place of work and a new name. This done, Mary could have a thorough check-up and, if necessary, a cure. Meanwhile, landlady Agatha employed her treasury of knowledge of medicinal herbs, a practice remarkably widespread in this country, and Yustyna kept her fingers crossed.

Well within the second week of her convalescence, the rapidity and frequency of Mary's coughs subsided, and some natural colour reappeared in her cheeks. She seemed to be well on the road to recovery. Yustyna thanked God, for her meager household resources were extremely heavily taxed. She had to borrow money to support her friend and could not imagine how in the world she would be able to repay the loan on her stringent teacher's purse. Yet she was immensely glad. The satisfaction of a helping hand, properly and timely extended, constituted the best reward for trouble and expenses incurred.

Agatha tended the sick woman while Yustyna worked at school. In the evening – obviously to the detriment of her household chores and school homework – Yustyna kept vigil by the bedside. Time passed unnoticed in lengthy chats, both women lingering in their reminiscences on the dark and recent past. Mary talked a lot, inquired about current news. As if by mutual consent, both women endeavoured to bypass the one subject closest to their hearts: children and school.

It was evident to Yustyna that Mary was not the same woman she had known. Often withdrawn, somewhat isolated in a world of her own, her memory erratic, she would listen to Yustyna with rapt attention; then, for no obvious reason, her interest would suddenly wither away; her face tired and haggard, she would lose herself in her thoughts.

Mary's interest in life now seemed superficial. Her self-confidence gone, fear-ridden and completely broken, there remained the overwhelming burden of life itself. Somehow she must carry on, keep alive among the living; she could not possibly spend all her life mourning her family and add to Yustyna's already uneasy existence. What future was there for her? How could she possibly educate and guide school children when she sorely needed guidance herself?

When left alone, Mary pondered her predicament from various angles. Reflections sometime drove her to desperation. At first she would unbridle her emotions, shed tears freely. Then, gradually, apathy set in. Like a drunkard awakened after a short sleep, burdened by a terrible hangover, her mind would wander unchecked, unchained by any comprehensible logic, oblivious of the hardships and trivialities of life.

One day, alone in her bedroom, she looked out the small

window. There must have been a heavy snowfall the previous night. A high wooden fence separated Agatha's orchard in the rear of the house from the neighbour's. No wind disturbed the fresh snow on the bare twigs of the apple-trees. Other houses and sheds appeared in the distance, one chimney still producing pale blue smoke. The sun must have peeked from behind the clouds, for the tilted fence projected a crooked shadow, and the orchard trees cast their wrinkled images on a white blanket of snow. A huge dark crow glided down, perched on the fence, scrutinizing the area. Spreading its wings lazily, it disappeared, while almost instantly some half a dozen sparrows plunged into the snow, warring apparently for a precious morsel of food. Lost in a flurry of snowflakes, each bird heatedly asserting its right with a rough, loud chirping. The eternal battle for existence all around. Birds – the same as people – only more civilized perhaps.

Out of nowhere, the odious countenances of Bergdorf, Karpatin, and Lara reappeared. Subconsciously, Mary shrank from fear. What does one do about people like those? Must one necessarily dwell in the same cage with beasts? An entirely new idea claimed her attention. There was something someone said... What was it? She had to pin it down. A stark picture of the defiant and chagrined boy, Maxim, challenging his mother, appeared: "Why is it right for one scoundrel to go around killing innocent people, and wrong for others to defend themselves? Why, mother, why?"

Coming as it did from this twelve-year-old, this protest in defiance of his mother's authority, it touched the tenderest strings in Mary's heart. The boy's senses were sharpened, and his maturity accelerated by the war. History was being made right in front of his eyes. He demanded a ready-made answer to a question that intrigued human giants from the dawn of history. What does a mother answer?

Indeed, what about the right to defend oneself? Piqued by this unexpected twist of her reflections, Mary abruptly rose in bed, as if this position would facilitate a ready answer. Of course, it was a fact that a number of people – notably the lower levels of society, Bergdorf among them – acted as if they had acquired a licence for summary judgments and executions of others. Of course, she detachedly watched from the sidelines when others were being molested and murdered. Little did she reckon that sooner or later it would happen to her. And it had.

Examining this so-called licence for wanton murder, what, if any possible standards could justify it? War? Perversion and the abuse of power? Lust for innocent blood? Possibly all of these combined. This, however, presented only one side of the coin. Innocent people were being slaughtered for the simple reason that they were defenceless.

One cannot afford to be a defenceless crow among hungry vultures if one cares for one's life. There is no question of a man's right to defend himself. The crux of the problem is that if one takes up arms in defence one is inevitably drawn into the murderous nightmare and cannot possibly avoid killing other innocent bystanders. Yet what other way is there, unless one relinquishes his basic right of protecting his own life?

The mere child, the schoolboy, handed her the ready answer. What about her? Why, after all the agonies suffered, was she left alive? Was it the caprice of fate or the hand of Providence?

If there was civil law in the land, one would try to make the murderer account for his crimes. German civilian authorities, such as there were, looked after matters of taxation, limited education, recruiting manpower to Germany, and protection of local German interests. Their main function was to oversee that disloyal subjects were kept at bay, that people in bondage do their part in feeding the German war machine. There was neither the time nor the will to meddle with civilian judicial matters. Hence the army and its auxiliary units ruled the occupied land as they saw fit.

While Mary recuperated, the murderer of her family kept subduing and exterminating other innocent victims. If there is no recourse to law, what does one do to stop Bergdorf and others like him? There must be a way...

She pondered the new idea thoroughly. If this criminal is to be punished, who could do it except herself? How could she, a poor sick woman, do anything? For a while she toyed with the idea of somehow procuring a weapon, going to the police station, and administering justice to Bergdorf with her own hand. She was not afraid to walk into a lion's den after what she had been through. Another uncertainty intrigued her. Suppose she got hold of a gun, suppose she approached the monster – with her non-existent resources and connections the possibilities seemed extremely remote – what chance would she have to shoot and kill the criminal? God, what wishful thinking! Bergdorf would sit there smugly in front of her just waiting and pleading to be killed...

There were two voices inside her arguing heatedly: one naive and inexperienced, the other, cynical and hardened... she reckoned with the possibility of losing her own life. She was not scared, provided she took Bergdorf with her. No. The idea was nonsense, and Mary promptly scrapped it, making a mental note to reconsider it in the future.

She picked up a small round mirror from the top of the bedside table and examined her face closely. The decrepit sombre reflection stared bleakly back at her. "My God!" she exclaimed. "What have they done to me!"

19
ENDURANCE TEST

School Inspector Vasil Trakhimovich perched on the edge of the chair in his office and pondered the text of the letter neatly typewritten on gray paper. It came from the Viciebsk District Commissariat and concerned recruitment of school youth for trade schools in Germany. Referring to previous instructions in this matter, the letter urged the Inspector to report on the results of recruitment without undue delay.

Behind the door, the monotonous clatter of the typewriter heralded the beginning of new working day. His secretary, Nadzia Kurzova, proved to be a valuable assistant. A local widow in her late forties, she seemed to be worth triple her salary. Right now, Trakhimovich knew, warmly clothed, oblivious of the discomforting cold in the office, she assiduously pecked on the old Remington.

Beside his countless problems in the educational realm, Trakhimovich had to wrangle with local German authorities for firewood supplies. Shortage of transportation vehicles, inaccessible partisan-infested forests, were the usual reasons given for lack of fuel. They had brought a few loads of bricked peat, which proved worthy while it lasted.

Only yesterday, passing by, the inspector enviously eyed a huge snow-covered mountain of peat and firewood in the back yard of the local German army commandant. The proverb "One's own shirt is closer to one's skin" proved to be applicable here. Angrily Trakhimovich eyed a square brick stove built into the wall between his and his secretary's office. It possessed a gluttonous appetite and projected, so little heat. The dingy brick building, so vulnerable to lengthy onslaughts of low temperature, needed extensive repairs.

There were so many other matters Trakhimovich had to look after besides education. Firewood for his own office and schools was one of them. Local Byelorussian county authorities were housed in another decrepit building and fared no better. Germans, occupied with their own war problems, never intended to make life easy for the natives and were irked when reminded of such trivialities as school supplies, accommodation, and fuel. Their chief concern was to squeeze out as much food and other vital material from the local population and land as was humanly possible. They came to harvest, not to sow.

Cold and discomfort momentarily forgotten, Trakhimovich paced briskly across the squeaking, half-rotten wooden floor of his office. He was a lean, well-built man in his late fifties; dressed in a well-cut, home-made gray wool jacket, green gabardine riding breeches – the style that never went out of vogue with the local population – patched calf-hide boots; a short-trimmed, narrow moustache adorned his oval peasant face; round, wide-set eyes peered from under narrow eyebrows; his thick mop of gray hair was combed straight back. Presently he glanced at the open letter on the table and approaching the window, scrutinized intently the ice that had built up on the inside of the window panes.

Two years ago Trakhimovich had come here from Western Byelorussia to tend the matters of education in Haradok County. His wife came along and taught the lower grades in the town school. Rebuilding the educational network left in ruins by the retreating Reds proved to be a Herculean task. A shortage of teaching personnel adequately trained in Byelorussian instruction provided the main obstacle to be overcome. German authorities, while allowing teaching to proceed in Byelorussian, flatly refused, with meager exceptions, to allow the publishing of any school books. Such an arrangement, no doubt, smacked of a sardonically twisted Prussian mind, conceived to discourage the local patriotic educational hotheads; it was obviously in line with other hatched-in-Berlin incongruities as organizing the national military, the Samaakhova units, but supplying no weapons and uniforms, thus perplexing efforts to act independently of the omnipotent master. While some Soviet-published school books could be utilized for teaching mathematics and science, the history of Byelorussia, the language, and numerous other subjects had to be improvised as best as possible by individual teachers. The majority of texts thus had to be copied by students on the verbal dictation of the teacher. Here again one was harassed by the shortage of paper and even pencils.

Realizing all this, Trakhimovich nevertheless took up the tremendous challenge, aptly assisted by the unreserved devotion of his wife. The chance to bring up the young generation in the national spirit, long denied by the country's foreign colonial regime, was not to be missed at any cost. Short-term teachers' seminars were organized; and programs adapted to local conditions with available school facilities were brought to bearable standards.

No sooner, however, had the educational skeleton begun to flesh out, than the adverse war conditions prompted its disintegration. Trakhimovich's small educational domain was being torn apart, eroded, teachers murdered or chased away by Red guerillas, pupils attending school intimidated, partisan repressions hitting the population daily. Out of over four dozen public schools in the county, more than half were swallowed up in flames or closed in partisan-infested areas. The inspector's job turned into an endurance test for Sisyphus, delaying the inevitable end, the total ruin. All his sacrifices and tremendous efforts – it was now abundantly clear – would wind up in nothing.

This particular order for the recruitment of students to German trade schools – official interpretation notwithstanding – might prove to be the last straw. If implemented with any degree of thoroughness, it would scare the remaining students away from the schools; the thinly disguised recruitment of future cheap labour by occupational authorities fooled no one. Trakhimovich gave it only lip service and never earnestly intended to press subordinates to implement it. He kept hoping the Germans would discard this nonsense. The letter on the table irked and frustrated him.

On the spur of the moment, he decided to call his professional colleague in the neighbouring county, provided that the telephone lines were intact. After a considerable lapse of time, the man answered. The preliminary niceties and inquiries about health over, Trakhimovich learned to his immense relief that the recruiting situation in the neighbouring district paralleled his own. The other inspector had received an identical letter, and after a couple of days intended to report back his lack of results. Trakhimovich promised to do the same, come what may.

That afternoon, some two hours before school was out, Yustyna Murashka took inspector Trakhimovich to her house to see Mary. This seemed the only reasonable approach, since Mary found it too risky to venture to the inspector's office. From previous contacts, Trakhimovich knew Mary Karaway well. He scrutinized the pale gaunt woman in Yustyna's room unjustifiably long, as if making doubly sure he was not mistaken. Wrapped up in Yustyna's gray housecoat, oversized for her, small and withdrawn, Mary slumped in the large ancient chair that cried for an upholsterer's attention; she stopped knitting, the sleeve of a gray wool glove dangling on the chair's arm rest.

"My God!" exclaimed Trakhimovich, holding her thin hand and peering deep into blue melancholy eyes, "You've changed so much!"

"Have I?" Mary gulped meager saliva in her throat, "Well, I'm still in one piece, thank God, and that's what counts nowadays... I'm so glad to see you, Mr. Inspector," she greeted the man affably. She half-rose from her armchair, and Trakhimovich squeezed her outstretched hand with more than casual tenderness, as her wane looks sharply contrasted with a genuine warm glow in her attentive blue eyes.

"You can hardly imagine how glad I am to see you, Mrs. Karaway," Trakhimovich voiced his unrestrained delight. "To tell you the truth, my dear friend, you've established a precedent of sorts. You see, up until now, we've always lost teachers; it was a one-way street, so to speak; but now one, the first one – regretfully – has come back. I cannot possibly over-emphasize my joy of welcoming you back among us."

"But please do sit down, Mr. Inspector," Mary invited Trakhimovich. Yustyna took his coat and overshoes and excused herself to attend to the small iron stove. Both Mary and Inspector watched her as she loaded the apple-tree timber into the round stove in the middle of the room. The landlady, unable to get a supply of fuel anywhere, asked the neighbour to cut down and chop her old apple tree to somehow last through the severe frosty winter. The short-cut chunks of damp timber hissed behind the manyholed grill, resisting the fire's repeated attempts to envelop them.

Perching on the edge of a sturdy old wooden chair, his eyes still on Mary, the Inspector asked: "Well, how are you now, Mrs. Karaway ?"

"Much better, thank you. If it weren't for Yustyna and Grandma Agatha, I believe I couldn't have pulled through. They kept stuffing me with all kinds of herbs imaginable. Thank God, I'm in good hands," she gave Yustyna a grateful smile.

"She's exaggerating it, Mr. Inspector," Yustyna retorted. "Of course we boiled and fed her some herbs, but that was the least we could do. I'm quite sure she'd look better now if we had some food, especially some fats and vitamins."

The silence fell. Mary stared at the Inspector expectantly. "Yustyna told me she has related some of my adventures to you, Mr. Trakhimovich."

"Yes, indeed, she has. What a terrible experience. And may I, Mrs. Karaway, offer my heartfelt sympathies for what little comfort they may bring to you."

Mary looked straight into the Inspector's sympathetic eyes and then cast her own eyes down.

"And Bergdorf of all people!" Trakhimovich exclaimed. "Why, he's the one who should protect us. My God, what terrible times; a rotten bunch of moral degenerates doing as they please; scourges on both sides and our defenceless people in between."

"Mr. Trakhimovich, I want to ask your advice," Mary paused, scrutinizing the Inspector's face.

"By all means. I'll do anything I can to help you."

"It's a matter concerning the murder of my family by Bergdorf."

"I see... go ahead."

"Perhaps you could tell me whether there's any way to bring him to account for what he did?"

A puzzled frown wrinkled the Inspector's high forehead, as he avoided the inquisitive stares of both ladies, apparently concentrating. The crochet needles in Mary's fingers paused expectantly as all three stared at the grill of the round black stove, behind which in playful animation the golden flames danced around the apple-tree timber.

Trakhimovich straightened on the edge of the chair and looked straight into Mary's questioning blue eyes.

"First of all I must ask you ladies to consider this talk strictly unofficial. I cannot jeopardize my position, you understand?"

"Of course, we do, " Yustyna hastened to reply. "Don't you trust us, Mr. Trakhirnovich?"

"If I didn't I wouldn't be here. It's the nature of the times, you know, and l thought I better mention this just in case... "

"But of course, Mr. Trakhimovich, you can rely on us completely," Mary assured the Inspector.

"All right, now for your question. I wish I could give you a straight and definite answer. This, I regret to say, I cannot do, all factors considered. I'll attempt to answer it in a roundabout way."

The preamble over, Trakhimovich scanned the women's faces and continued: "Three weeks ago I went to Miensk on official business. I have many friends in the Byelorussian administration, in education mainly. I saw and talked with many people . I hoped both of you remember Reverend Stanislaw Hadlewski, our late General Inspector for Schools in Byelorussia?"

"Yes, of course," both women answered in unison.

"At the time of his disappearance last year," Trakhimovich went on in a subdued voice, "very few people knew what happened. His wasn't exactly a case about which the Germans would allow anyone to shout from the rooftops. As was to be easily predicted, the absence of an official announcement spawned many rumours. As time passed however the chaff was separated from the wheat; bits and pieces of the jigsaw puzzle together into a macabre picture, which should warn anybody who, like Hadlewski, refuses to be the oppressor's hireling."

The women's curiosity pricked, the Inspector broke off, and his now far-away gaze assumed a mysterious air.

"What happened?" Yustyna prodded.

They beat out his brains in the cellar of the Miensk Gestapo." Trakhimovich pronounced slowly for maximum effect.

"God rest his noble soul," Yustyna said, as both women crossed themselves with mournful unction.

"But why, Inspector? What did he do?" Mary inquired.

"What did he do?" the Inspector blurted out, spreading his hands wide, visibly agitated. "I cannot simply say I don't know, can I? Perhaps the best way to answer would be to consider what he was, because what exactly he did to trigger Germans' beastly act will certainly come out later. So consider what he was: one of the most illustrious sons this country ever produced; a great and ardent preacher, a crusader for a Byelorussian National Catholic Church under the Polish yoke, a man of unblemished honesty and outstanding record, a great patriot, a leading politician. Why, he was so widely known and admired in the country that if he had run for President of Byelorussia in free elections, he would have beaten everybody by a hundred kilometers. Naturally a man of his stature, who refused to bend, had to be broken. Apparently the Germans will permit limited Byelorussian administration, Byelorussian instruction in primary schools, perhaps even small military units under German command, but woe to him who has the courage to stand up to them and demand his rights. They tolerate no such nonsense. Either absolute obedience, or else! The proponents of independent Byelorussian thought, especially those popular among the masses, like the late Hadlewski, actually dug their own graves."

Again their eyes concentrated on the crackling flames behind the grill.

"Perhaps some people have unfounded illusions,"

Yustyna broke in, "that the Germans are our benefactors and will eventually reward us with an independent state."

"I knew the late Hadlewski well," Trakhimovich continued. "I knew him in Vilna and also met him in Miensk. A man so downright simple and honest, yet so practical a realist, devoid of any illusions. His dream, his life's ambition, to which he unreservedly devoted all his earthly powers, and for which job he expected Lord's assistance, was – to use his own oft-repeated words – "Our own independent Byelorussian house". He worked and prayed to that end. He maintained we have to do it solely with – our own forces, even – speaking figuratively – if we have to break and bleed every fingernail while clawing out granite blocks from the mountains for its foundation. No Germans, Russians, Poles, or any other devils will do it for us. This, ladies, was his motto, his credo, his ultimate goal. He proceeded methodically and prudently. Many things he did still dwell in the obscurity of history to day. Time will reveal them. Suffice it to say that if history endowed Byelorussians with any recent martyrs for their liberty and happiness, Hadlewski was one, perhaps one of many... "

"What about the murders of the other outstanding Byelorussians in Miensk one hears about?" Yustyna asked.

"Most of them are the work of the Bolshevik underground, there's no doubt about it. I'll skip the names and details. The moral is obvious. We, Byelorussians, are caught right in the midst of the crossfire. Those of us who keep our heads low and voices subdued can perhaps escape with superficial scratches. Neither the Germans nor the Russians will tolerate our right to self-determination. As independent-minded and self-dignified people, we are expendable to both of them; in the Russian and German books, we're only allowed to breathe and supply their wealth as contemptible serfs... "

"Look around, and what do you see? You know the number of schools we had in this county when we started? Around fifty. That's right. How many have we got left now? Less than half that number. There's no use beating one's head against a stone wall. We're battling tremendous odds, and it's only a matter of time, if this outrageous slaughter continues, before we are engulfed by the total madness of wanton destruction and genocide such as this country has never witnessed before. There's your answer, Mrs... Karaway."

"It's a horrible picture, Mr. Trakhimovich. How do I fit in?" Mary inquired with a small voice.

In deep concentration, the Inspector rubbed his cheek, looked askance at the women... Watching the flames in the stove, he continued:

"There's an English proverb, I believe, which says that 'vultures gather where lions feast'. It amply illustrates the case in question. Bergdorf, if anything, is a despicable vulture, who, like Shakespeare's Shylock, came to get his pound of flesh.

"Now if you stretch the imaginative interpretation of this proverb, you may point out that any self-respecting lion would look upon vultures with disdain; his royal highness won't even deign to consider chasing them away. Why should he? In a way it's his royal escort provided by no lesser authority than God himself, the one who created the noble and the base. The predatory king probably realizes that the morsels of food scattered after his repast are being devoured by these abominable creatures because sweeping the area clean after the master is their natural, God-given function so to speak. So it goes that as long as there are lions there'll be vultures around. In our country right now, the two giant bloodthirsty lions are in the midst of their biggest feast. That's why vultures swanned in here in droves so abundant as to eclipse the sun...

"Now to get back to your problem, Mrs. Karaway. What possible reason, if any, have these lions to penalize one of their vultures just to satisfy you or me or any other of their prospective victims? We are expendable, don't you understand? Bergdorf and his kind are helping the lion to colonize these territories. Never forget that both the Eastern and Western predator have earmarked our unfortunate country for their Iebensraum. The plain fact is we have· no rights, none at all... as long as we are weak and cannot stand up against the aggressors. God help us poor souls, for we are doomed... It seems to me God himself has abandoned us and supports, as He always did, the strong and aggressive."

The whole tragic situation was amply illustrated. Gloomy and withdrawn, Trakhimovich himself pictured the man caught between two giant grindstones slated for perdition.

"That's the plain repugnant truth, and there's no other, ladies," whispered the Inspector, horrified at the prospect of what tomorrow might bring.

"It's all so clear, so very clear now, Mr. Trakhimovich," whispered Mary, her voice charged with emotion. "Of course, I imagined as much but couldn't for my life illustrate it so picturesquely. Which means there's nothing I can do to bring this bandit Bergdorf to account. .."

"If you were a man, Mrs. Karaway, I'd not hesitate to advise you to go and shoot this vulture yourself. You could be shot in the process, you know, but one realizes now there's no other way. It's about time we started shooting back for we've not been afforded any choice and we're doomed for extinction."

Small furrows, underlining determination, etched deeply the Inspector's narrow lips.

"It's all idle talk, Mr. Trakhimovich," Mary retorted, "I'm not a man and I've been executed twice. As far as the

Bolsheviks and Nazis are concerned, there's no Mary Karaway any more. What am I to do?"

"That's why I have come. We have to figure something out."

"If I may, Mr. Inspector – " Yustyna broke in.

"Go ahead by all means."

"First of all – Mary and I have already agreed on this – she has to get a new identity, complete with birthplace, age, etc. That means," a smile crossed Yustyna's face as she looked at Mary, "we have to christen you all over again, dear. After all this is completed, you have to get a job and continue teaching, I suppose. You have to go away someplace where this vulture Bergdorf cannot reach you. How do you like this idea, Mr. Trakhimovich?"

"This is a sound idea," the Inspector fidgeted in his chair. "We have to find you a safe spot, Mrs. Karaway. After what you've gone through you need peace to recuperate. I'm concerned about your health too."

Trakhimovich rose, crossed the room over to the window, and mutely stood there, looking outside as if expecting to find assistance there,

"You haven't any documents with you, Mrs. Karaway?"

"I was about to go to bed when this beast came in drunk."

"I see. Never mind. I have someone in mind who should be able to get you an identity card, work certificate, and perhaps a permit to travel by railway. You must be patient and understanding, for I cannot do all these things overnight. You haven't any clothing, have you?"

"Practically none."

"The Byelorussian Mutual Aid has to be contacted. Perhaps we can get you a decent coat. I'll have to talk this over with my wife, and I'm sure she'll be able to do something about clothing. Meanwhile, you have to sit tight here while I go about these things. Have you any names in mind?"

"No, not exactly," hesitated Mary.

"Think it over, and when you have decided, let me know through Mrs. Murashka. How's that?"

"I'll do that. Have you any ideas about a job and place, Mr. Trakhimovich?"

"Well, I have one. Of course, I must call a man and ask him. I have a hunch he can find a spot for you. I'm talking about a good friend of mine, Zarkievich, General Inspector of Schools in Byelorussia. After what happened to Hadlewski, this man is somewhat jittery, but I'm sure he won't refuse to help me. How would you like to teach in Miensk, Mrs. Karaway?"

"Like it? I'd love it. I used to love that city so much." Galvanized by the idea, Mary's brooding eyes came alive.

"When were you there last?"

"Quite some time ago, long before the war, matter of fact... "

"The city is a heap of rubble now, very little of it left intact."

"Of course, I've heard about it. German air attacks... "

"That's half of the story. Retreating Russians had orders to demolish everything; that was even before Stalin issued his infamous "scorched earth" orders, you know."

"Yes, of course."

"So you see, Mrs. Karaway, it's a pile of rubble I'm sending you to. Everything considered, it'll be a safe place for you. The partisans are not closing any schools in Miensk, and there's quite a number of people living and working there."

"God bless you, Mr. Inspector. I'm really so grateful to you," Mary's voice was tinted with emotion.

"Please, your gratitude would be premature." Trakhimovich outstretched his right hand to Mary, as if to ward off the outpouring of gratitude. "So far I haven't done anything to help you, have I?" he smiled benignly.

"Yes, Mr. Inspector!" Mary smiled weakly. "Even talking to you has been a great help to me. And you'll certainly help. I don't know how I'll ever repay you."

"Don't. It's my duty. Now let's summarize: you'll sit tight here until I get the necessary papers, clothing, and a job. Mrs. Murashka, will you kindly – after she has decided, I mean – write down on a piece of paper her name, place, and date of birth, physical features of her face, the size of her dress, and – oh, I almost forgot – the people in the ausweis office will need her picture. You'll have to get one."

"That'll be a problem," Yustyna frowned, looking at Mary.

"Well, you'll have to solve that one yourselves. Now, ladies, I have to be on my way. So if it's all right with you, I'll take my leave. Please keep in touch with me, Mrs. Murashka."

"Certainly. Thank you very much for coming, Mr. Inspector. Too bad we cannot invite you to the table. There's nothing... "

"You don't have to make excuses for anything, Mrs. Murashka. Let's hope there will be better times when we can enjoy our Byelorussian hospitality and visit one another."

"Mr. Inspector, you are an angel. I can't imagine what I'd do without your help," Mary said with a serene face.

After Trakhimovich left, Yustyna, with a look of accomplishment written all over her face, asked Mary: "Well, what do you think?"

"To tell you the truth, I knew him only officially before. He seems to be very understanding and helpful."

"He certainly is. No one has ever said an unfavourable word about him."

"Thank God," Mary sighed.

20

THE RUINS

The twenty-second of June came, sunny and warm, as if made to order. Such days are blessed by country and city folk alike – a barely noticeable breeze and a mild warmth without any discomforting humidity.

The dilapidated Byelorussian capital, like numerous other cities in the German-occupied territories labelled "Ostland", was about to celebrate its designated "Liberation Day". Four years ago in the small pre-dawn hours, guns on the river Bug spewed their initial salvos, thus launching Operation Barbarossa – the ultimate undoing of Hitler's Third Reich. The Drang Nach Osten, temporarily impeded by political considerations – and now resumed, spread panic and devastation from the Baltic to the Black Sea. The day that unleashed a plethora of destruction unknown in recorded history, had to be camouflaged as a milestone of liberty for 'the new Europe', The battle-scarred master, whose ambiguous plans had long ago ceased to puzzle the subdued people, had to have one more try acting the benevolent liberator.

The task was double-pronged: the war-weary muscles had to be flexed to demonstrate publicly their vital resilient strength, and the black-eyed hideous brutal countenance had to be camouflaged by a paternal mask of saintly love and devotion to the unruly subjects.

Twenty-fifth of March Street, the main thoroughfare of Miensk, was designated as the parade route. From early morning, it drew civilians from all corners of the ruined city. On the eastern side of the street, where it gently sloped to Svislach bridge, the newly erected platform stood flanked by two flag poles. A gentle breeze fluttered the Byelorussian flag beside the German Swastika.

Around ten o'clock, the war-weary, mildly curious civilians, clad in their unusual assortment of war-scarce clothing, crowded the sidewalks; piles of bricks and rubble were heaped along the western side of the street. With the agility of a spider, the younger set mounted gaping window holes of the adjacent fire-gutted buildings. A German military brass band was stood expectantly a few paces to the left of the platform.

Presently the eyes of the multitude followed a long green Mercedes convertible, which drew up. The tall, lean, long-necked, stork-like SS/Polizei General von Gotberg, General Commissar of Byelorussia, alighted from the rear seat. With his adjutant keeping a respectful distance, he scanned the assembly, received a report from the garrison commander, and then, supporting himself with a brown cane, carefully hobbled up the steps to the platform. After saluting and shaking hands with the dignitaries present, he placed himself in the center, leaders of the Byelorussian Administration on his left, and the Germans on the right. The almost imperceptible nod from the hook-nosed ruler spun the parade wheels in motion. As the military band struck up Edelweiss, infantry units descended from the hill.

As soon as the helmeted, goose-stepping German SS/Polizei company approached the reviewing stand, it became apparent that the Germans had no intention of flexing their muscles on that day in Miensk. Quite likely those muscles were enduring immense strains endeavoring to plug the holes on the Dniapro River, through which the tide of Soviets poured to the western banks, menacing the heartland of Byelorussia and approaches to Germany.

Following the Germans came troops of the newly created Byelorussian Home Defence, the BKA. No longer able to cope with Red guerillas, the Germans permitted the Byelorussians to organize a limited number of men for self-protection and miscellaneous guard duties on the communications lines. Von Gotberg's decree creating the BKA was issued the previous March. The Germans reserved mandatory rights over the new army and at no time permitted more than a battalion's strength under Byelorussian command.

The draft orders, though ignored by many, swelled the ranks of the BKA to some fifty thousand men. Shortage of weapons and uniforms, along with organizational and training problems, rendered the new army ineffective from the very beginning.

Some Byelorussian patriots, eager not to miss the chance of getting arms so that eventually they could stand up to both adversaries – disappointed and disillusioned though they were – nevertheless decided to give it a try. Right after the Germans took over the country, some Byelorussian military leaders rightly felt that the nation's only chance of achieving some degree of selfrule lay in building up a military might. Although the Germans from time to time lent a sympathetic ear to the Byelorussian demands, they never intended to fully acquiesce until this late hour taxed their own strength beyond endurance. Thus a few poorly trained units of infantry and army engineers, scattered throughout the length and width of the country, constituted the nucleus of the Byelorussians' unrealized dreams. The cadet school, established in Miensk, recruited some four hundred young volunteers, who were soon undergoing their first drills. It was this "cream" of the newly created army that was now approaching von Gotberg's reviewing stand.

Clad in black uniforms (the green ones were not yet available), these sturdy, healthy, peasant boys – the average age was eighteen – pounded the cobblestones with well-mastered steps. The thunderous applause from the civilian crowd drowned the tunes of the military band and echoed among the hollow ruins of the prostrate city. Then something quite unexpected happened.

The captain, leading the cadet column, ordered the school to halt in order to report to his commanding officer on the reviewing stand. In the continuous rain of applause, his order failed to reach the ears of those at the column's rear. As the front halted abruptly, a hail of uneven footsteps rose from the cobblestones in the back. Accompanied by loud boos from the crowd, the blushing officer jerkily saluted, reported to the displeased colonel, and proceeded to the Svislach bridge. The cadets were followed by a company of army engineers and other infantry units, and then came the men's and women's units of the Byelorussian Youth Organization, the sight of which brought unreserved exclamations of approval from the spectators.

Mary Karaway shielded her eyes from the sun's glare, craned her neck, scanning both the passing troops and the civilians around her. Not a single familiar face in sight! She wore a cheap yellow cotton dress, and her hair, rolled in a bun, was covered by a flowered green kerchief. Right at her elbow a tall extremely attractive, lean, dark-haired girl named Alena Maroz commented: "Look at those handsome, lovable, sweet boys! What a bunch to take your pick from!" She giggled and looked at Mary.

"Why don't you join the organization?" retorted Mary sourly. "I'm sure you would have a better chance to make a proper selection."

"Perhaps I should, Vera. Let's do it together, eh?" she winked.

Alena Maroz had met Vera Shulava (formerly Mary Karaway) some four months ago in the school at which she was teaching. The two women, so different in character were drawn to each other like opposites. In a well-to-do Western society, Alena Maroz might have passed for a sophisticated spinster. Light-hearted, well-read, frequently cynical and witty, she treated life lightly and seldom took things seriously.

Improbable as it sounded, she told Mary she grew up in a state children's home. Although the normal development of her character must have been hampered by the strict, inhuman dogmas of a regimented Communist society, she fully spread her wings and blossomed during the war, after the bearded and bald-headed Communist prophets had tumbled down from their precarious pedestals.

At times Mary admired her new friend, for with a few, well-chosen and well-aimed words she could disarm the pompous, strip the bigot, make friends with the shy and modest, and reward the generous. Some well-balanced people, once stung by her acid tongue, even turned around and liked her for it.

With her intellectual and verbal facilities augmented by a measure of prudent self-restraint, she could have become an above-average diplomat. Sometimes Mary, witnessing Alena's sunny disposition and devil-may-care approach to life, suspected it constituted a well constructed shell for the disappointed and secluded soul that dwelt inside. Mary was not sure, for she was never allowed full access to that inner sanctum.

Even if Alena's treatment of life was a well-mastered and painstakingly developed craft, one could profit by learning from it, Mary reasoned. Never before had she viewed life from that angle. The girl often made her laugh when she was about to cry, or disdain and ridicule the others when they abused her.

After a brief acquaintance, Alena invited Mary to move in with her into her modestly furnished flat beyond Niamiha, where some brick dwellings had escaped the all-consuming flames of the war. "Let's put our resources together." Alena suggested. "I'm sure we can economize better together than we could separately."

Mary accepted the invitation eagerly, and in a short time both women realized that the arrangement proved mutually satisfactory. They worked in the same school, cooked together, and shared numerous other interests. The times were not conducive to social life in Miensk. War-time austerity burdened the clerk, the teacher, the merchant, and the worker alike; what little prospects of social and cultural life there remained were quite effectively hampered by the Communist underground.

In the middle of an operatic performance in the local theatre, a time-bomb exploded under the stage. Three actors were killed, and the majority of the cast and some patrons were injured. Clandestine Communist publications hailed this barbaric murder as another victory in the paralyzing of Byelorussia's allegedly bourgeois culture and the rendering of some fascist collaborators harmless. The theatre re-opened after repairs, but many drama and opera lovers preferred to remain in the safety of their homes.

The assassination of numerous Byelorussian and German officials, with General Commissar Wilhelm Kube heading the list, created more fear among the people in administration, theatre, education and publishing. Because of her own nightmarish past, Mary Karaway viewed the bloodshed and struggle with no impartial interest. Alena Maroz, however, carried on as if life were rosy and smoothly normal. Once Mary broached this subject with her roommate.

"Why worry, my dear? Who would want to harm poor wretches like us?" Alena smiled disarmingly. "Even supposing we are killed one day, so what?" Pensively, she continued: "Remember what Maxim Bahdanovich once said? So many illusions in life we pursue, so many dangers we avoid, hurrying, sustained by hope, dazzled by success, or at other times clouded by anguish and disappointment, failure or sorrow. Chasing shadows, substitutes of happiness in vicious circles... And yet when we have finally arrived at the edge of the grave, what do we find there? A slowly crawling worm, that's what... The creature, that never hurried has covered the destination ahead of us, all set and ready to feast on our remains... Brrr ! What an epilogue to the mad scramble someone misnamed life! What a repugnant joke!"

Alena made a disgusted face and an involuntary gesture, as if to ward off the fat black hairy worm of colossal proportions about to devour her. Mary watched her, impressed by her power of penetration and eloquence. At times like these, she wondered if her room-mate had ever taken God seriously.

The gloomy shadow on Alena's smooth face was dissolved by her friendly yet enigmatic smile as she brought the main point home: "When creating this irrational world, God didn't invite its future tenants for consultation, yet we have to live in it. Philosophers to the contrary, we were shortchanged on intellectual powers and cannot fathom the depths of human motives or behaviour. The best we can do then is accommodate, act our own size, make the best of the mess, see the sunny side of life, for no matter how hard we try we cannot change any laws of life or alter the roots of human character."

"I wish I could see it your way," Mary retorted with a tinge of bitterness.

"Why don't you?" Alena shot back.

Mary stared at her as one stares at some insignificant object when concentrating on searching one's own soul and far distant events. Should she answer the challenging question? Can this girl gauge the anguish of a mother twice brought back to life from the grave, and still nursing wounds of irretrievable loss?

Many a time Mary tottered on the brink of relating her

past but somehow checked herself. Had she grown suspicious of people who were beyond redemption? She suspected that Alena never confided in her completely. Her experience with Kolpakoff-Bergdorf left a permanent scar in her heart. She had stretched out her hand to assist a poor man back to life and the hand had been chopped off...

Looking back at it later, but much too late, Mary Karaway realized how lucky she had been that Providence had afforded her the companionship of Alena Maroz. The girl's down-to-earth ethics had such an irresistible influence on her that they acted like a healing balsam on her ailing heart. Alena appeared on the horizon at a highly opportune moment, just when Mary hovered on the brink of total collapse. She did not teach or plead, but guided Mary by her own behaviour. "Here I am, look at me," she seemed to say. "I'm no angel, but I have a formula to escape the pitfalls and ride the dangerous crest of the waves of war. Will you follow me?"

Who knows what Alena's past held. Mary hated to initiate mutual soul-searching. If it was just a live-and-let-others-live ethic that Alena expected of her, Mary was willing to do her part.

After some four months of living with Alena, Mary was a better woman. She learned to smile again and soon refused to admit that life could only be viewed in black colours. Try as she might, Alena failed to arouse Mary's interest in the other sex. She eventually gave up. On the weekends, she disappeared for a night or two. She made no secret of the fact that she slept with someone regularly, and Mary speculated on her possible reaction if she even attempted to imply it was morally wrong to do so. The girl made it quite clear that her sojourns with her lover were guided by purely selfish motives; she saw nothing wrong in receiving presents and on occasions doubling or tripling her contributions to their common kitchen. The arrangement suited Mary fine.

Mary could never blot out the vestiges of her past. Remorse and perplexity constantly gnawed at her precarious emotional equilibrium. Her bottled up feelings were attempting to find an escape valve. Alena mentioned the future she had to look to. What future?

Sometimes, when the girl was out, Mary would bolt the door and in the privacy of her room drench herself in tears. Spent and completely exhausted, experiencing only a mild relief, she would then try to fortify herself for the bleak future ahead, Alena never pried into her past, never interfered with her plunges into depression. Almost too good to be true, she stood by like a guiding angel, ready to help only when summoned.

The ghosts from the past haunted Mary frequently. Even now, as she stood in the crowd watching the tawny, young black-uniformed cadets marching, she seemed to see the fatherly image of Inspector Trakhimovich, his face drawn, his lips narrowed, forcefully asserting: "It's about time we started shooting back!"

A couple of weeks ago, Haradok and Viciebsk were swallowed by Red deluge. The pincer-like operation of the Soviet Army thwarted any attempts at civilian evacuation. What had happened to Inspector Trakhimovich and his wife? Where was Mary's own dearest friend Yustyna and her aggressive son Maxim? Locked up in cattle cars, perhaps on their way to Siberia? Worse yet – Mary shuddered at the thought – perhaps they were executed on the spot as Fascist collaborators? General Inspector Zarkievich, when questioned about her friends, was only able to tell her that no one had been heard from. She never learned about the vulture Kolpakoff-Bergdorf either. Chances were he had escaped alive.

"It's about time we started shooting back," the man asserted. Who was to start shooting back? These young boys, still wet behind their ears, on whose lips their mothers' milk had dried only yesterday?

The long, well-trained column of Byelorussian youth, their heads erect, stepping in unison, brought back to life youth leader Yanka. Did these youngsters realize their organization had produced such an unknown martyr? Bloodied, but still castigating the vile foreign hirelings on the brink of his own downfall, what a man that was! How nicely he would fit into this impressive, well-organized column. His two poor little tots, clutching at their mother's hem, were denied the right to live because their father had struggled for the rights of all.

The impulse to jump out into the middle of the dusty street and stop the column nearly overpowered Mary. She had to stop them and tell them about Yanka: "Listen, all you dear boys and girls! Remember Yanka Biely? He was one of you. I was there when they murdered him and his family. Witnessing it, I've died a thousand times. Please stop! Stop marching into the abyss and listen to me! Throw away the shovels and pencils and books and grab your arms. Don't you see the Red meat-grinder in the distance? It's being fed by the flesh of your fatherland. Act now! Grab your arms! The dikes on the Dniapro fell, and the deluge of blood is fast approaching. Do you want to share Yunka's fate? Go, rush, grab the weapons!"

"No... I have no right... I can't... what am I saying? The all merciful God has forbidden us to take the lives of others; that's why we Byelorussians suffer so... we acted like meek sheep among a pack of wolves. While others were moulding the tools of war and destruction, we continued to build and sow and harvest; in our daily life we stuck to God's commandments; we were too good to others, so we brought on our own doom. My darling children, my little angels, my dear mother! Among the wind-swept ruins of Shuly, your bones lie scattered, while I, homeless, scared and perplexed, find no consolation on the breast of the land that gave me life ... "

A brief glance at her friend made Alena aware Mary was undergoing one of her irregular plunges into depression. She attempted to console her, but no favourable response came. After the parade, Mary Karaway, barely acknowledging her friend's parting remark (she mentioned going to the theatre or some such thing), wandered away. The irrepressible desire to shut out the predatory world, to drench her inconsolable heart in tears, overwhelmed her utterly.

The murky waters of the Svislach moved slowly, penetrating cracks in the low concrete lining of its banks; piles of rubble built up in the water and along the shore. A group of noisy children waded in the water along the opposite bank, splashing and chasing one another.

Mary crossed the bridge. Her moist eyes scanned the bowl-shaped panorama of destruction in front of her. Street cans rattled and squeaked behind her. In the distance the rubble-filled basin reached Kamarowka, where some hunch-backed wooden huts, whose age reached well into the previous century, miraculously escaped the flames of war. Many-storied brick skeletons of what were once huge apartment buildings, lined the Twenty-fifth of March Street. To the west, the round, wedding cake-shaped imposing gray structure of the State Opera and Ballet Theatre dominated this field of desolation. It was huge, magnificent sepulchre among the modest tombstones...

The theatre, almost intact and now empty, sheltered the ghosts of the past. One day – quite soon perhaps – the despots who ordered the sepulchre erected will once again repossess their former colony. Party-inspired, artificial characters will be resurrected on the crowded stage, extolling the modern Nero, haranguing those who dared to think differently from the Party dogma. In marching columns, with hated songs on their parched lips, some hungry Plebes will arrive to the adjacent cemetery to scavenge among the ruins and begin a new chapter in "paradise".

Even now some life appeared here. Tiny, fenced-off patches of green spotted the huge desert of rubble; bizarre scarecrows serenely accommodated sparrows on their shoulders. These small gardens, blooming testimonials of human perseverance, breathed life like oases into the man-made desert.

About nine hundred years ago, the industrious natives who built the city on this site named it Miensk the city of barter trade. Later the conquerors changed the name to Minsk. They should have named it Slaughter City, for that is what it has become.

As Mary sauntered amid the ruins, a bluish, white-streaked wag-tail bird jerked her out of her gloomy meditation. It perched atop a rusty iron bed some distance from a pile of rubble, crackling in alarm. Mary approached the rubble and peeked inside. Four wide-open yellow bills at the end of four craning necks clamoured for food. Evidently no cat had been around here lately. Nature was moving in where man had left off.

Later that afternoon, Mary visited the site of what used to be the State Pedagogical Institute. An irrepressible nostalgia overcame her at the sight of the tall poplars, witnesses of the first admissions of love between herself and Valodzia. The trees had grown considerably since that momentous event in her life; the complex of buildings that once housed and educated hundreds now pictured doom and desolation. Where have the winds of war scattered all those she had befriended here? Certainly a number of them were already dead, others – like herself – were vagabond outcasts in their own land, still others in the grip of the octopus of the blood-thirsty war...

21
THE DISCOVERY

Years later, Mary recalled that memorable afternoon amid the capital's ruins when she was wondering about the purpose of God in sparing her life. She had a third close call during the night bombing of the Vilna railroad station, packed at the time with military personnel and civilian refugees. Her friend Alena Maroz was burned alive under a blazing railway carriage while Mary escaped without a scratch. Then came long wanderings across war-ravaged Europe, fear, hunger, and the deprivation in displaced persons' camps in Germany.

Dodging the tentacles of the awesome Red octopus – Moscow repatriation commissions and their British, American, and French assistants – meant fighting against practically insurmountable odds. When apprehended, refugees cut their veins, shot themselves, jumped to their doom from moving trains and road vehicles, and committed suicide in many other ways to avoid returning to their "forgiving fatherland". Constantly haunted by fear and tired of being chased by these blood-hounds, Mary Karaway renounced her displaced-person status, secured a job as a farmer's maid, and somehow lasted until the storm blew over.

A ray of sunshine appeared on the horizon of Mary's future. Through the International Red Cross, she had found out that her long-forgotten uncle was living in Canada. He had emigrated before the First World War and was now an apparently well-to-do prairie farmer. Her uncle responded favourably to Mary's letters, and after lengthy exertions and some expenses, he brought her over to his adopted land.

In Canada, Mary was overjoyed. She looked up to her Uncle Lavon, and considered him a great benefactor. For food and shelter, she tried hard to repay him with work. Lavon, a good-natured man, treated her with compassion and understanding.

Mary's newly found happiness proved to be of short duration. Not without chagrin she discovered that Lavon's wife Lida, a thoroughly unlikeable creature, was the real master of the house. At first she took to Mary's coming indifferently. As time passed, however, the loquacious lady either tried to ignore the girl or subtly demonstrated her spite toward her. Mary's efforts to gain her favours proved to be an exercise in futility.

The reasons underlining Lida's hostility soon became apparent. It appeared Russian propaganda had eaten away her native peasant horse sense. If it had not been for the loss of her only son in the Normandy campaign, she might have treated the newcomer differently. As it was, since she could not directly reach the Germans – the object of her hate – she did the next most rational thing: she hated those who, according to the Moscow version, helped them. The seeds of Red propaganda took roots in the ignorance of this war-affected farm couple.

Uncle Lavon, who should have known better, ignored or at least never contradicted Lida's bombastic arguments about the alleged paradise under Communist rule in the Old Country. It appeared to Mary that her uncle's wife was an incorrigible bigot who got her views from Canadian Communist publications. Unlike doubting Thomas, she refused to explore the wounds of a living witness, who had suffered under the colonial regime at home.

Lida prided herself on being progressive in the Moscow sense of the word. Propelled by her selfish motives, secure in her dubious righteousness, driven by her hate of

Germans and their collaborators, she now adamantly refused to examine the other side of the coin. Mary appeared on the scene at a highly inopportune moment and found herself a ready target for abuse by an ignorant woman seeking retribution for crimes she had never committed. On every pretext, Lida contemptuously cursed D.P.s – the alleged Fascist collaborators during the war – who, according to Moscow and Lida, should be tried by their own countrymen for their war crimes.

Repeatedly Mary attempted to make Uncle Lavon and Lida see the light. She dwelt at length on the inhuman atrocities of Reds in colonized Byelorussia; to the best of her abilities, she pictured the privations of the oppressed people at home. Sometimes the newcomer had illusions that her message got through. Instead, her well-founded arguments were promptly labelled Fascist-concocted propaganda. Guileless Lavon, attempting to rebuild bridges of coexistence between the two women in the house, nevertheless dipped into his own reminiscences about the so-called hungry thirties. Profit-thirsty war-mongering capitalists and other assorted enemies of the working people lurked behind every bank desk and upholstered office of huge corporations, coveting the sweat and blood of the impoverished proletarians.

Mary promptly realized she might as well talk to the wall. The simpletons were too old to overhaul their biased opinions. The voice of Moscow notwithstanding, whatever compassion they might have harboured for the ill-treated war refugees was dissipated by their own bitter experiences in this country. In the light of this undeserved abuse, Mary could not help wonder why her uncle had brought her over to Canada.

One day, while Mary sat at the kitchen table, Lida placed a small tabloid-size newspaper in front of her. "Here's one of your group," the acrimonious voice explained. "Perhaps someone you know."

Mary glanced at the stocky woman, the paper, and instantly knew that another expostulation of Mary's alleged past sins was forthcoming. Mary looked at the picture in the newspaper and sat petrified. Staring at her were those same eyes filled with desire that once coveted her body in the *lasnichowka*, the same lips that uttered scurrilous curses, the head that popped up and down around her in that terrible, unforgettable war.

Gripping the paper, ignoring her landlady, Mary withdrew to her room and locked the door.

Here we must beg the reader's indulgence to dwell briefly on the origins of the newspaper that caused Mary such intense agitation. This fortnightly newspaper was the organ of the Return to the Homeland Committee, then headed by a Russian M. V .D. General Mikhailov, from his headquarters in East Berlin. Ostensibly set up to entice "unreturnables" home, the Committee in fact had a twofold purpose: to wage a psychological war on political-minded refugees, and to gather and document information on them with a view of its possible utilization for the purpose of blackmail. This could also discredit them in the eyes of the society that had taken them in.

While some genuine, if lesser war criminals, like Kolpakoff-Bergdorf, were being exposed from time to time, the Reds concentrated mainly on bona-fide political, religious, and social leaders of the émigré communities. People in these categories, often advanced in age, unable to take root in a business-minded democratic society, found themselves constantly abused and smeared by the Kremlin's masters. Their only alleged crimes lay in the value of their thorough and extensive knowledge of grim Soviet reality. They constantly warned the free world of the Russian menace, and they organized and led their own emigree communities.

Following its ambitious, aggressive blueprint, Moscow

evidently decided no price was too high to pay to silence these formidable enemies. It is a record of history that some of the most distinguished emigree leaders were assassinated by Moscow agents after the war in various Western countries.

An issue of the Return to the Homeland Committee's Byelorussian-language paper regularly reached Uncle Lavon's prairie home. Although inadequately versed in this language, Lida diligently scanned its pages for proof to substantiate her entrenched beliefs that all refugees with no exceptions were genuine war criminals. One may speculate that one day she hoped to be confronted by Mary's own picture staring at her from the pages of the paper.

Still stunned by the perception of the unusual discovery, Mary perched on the edge of the creaky iron bed. Her heart throbbed with excitement, the picture and the small print whirling in front of her eyes. The ominous-looking face, blurred by a decade, suddenly and vividly reappeared in her imagination. Long dormant painful memories overwhelmed her; the agonizing canvas of war years – Kolpakoff towering above everybody else, Karpatin and Lara hovering in the mist – suddenly and starkly came alive again.

When sufficiently calm and composed, Mary started reading. She learnt that Kolpakoff-Bergdorf was born of Russo-German parents in an obscure provincial town. The benevolent Soviet people's regime – so the unknown author asserted – afforded this monster-to-be every golden opportunity for growth and education. When eligible, Kolpakoff enlisted in the Red Army, and who then could have guessed that in the future he would spread his vulture-like wings in the service of the Berlin bandit?

In this vein, peppering his outbursts with derogatory invectives, the author of the article continued to expose

Kolpakoff's career, about which Mary had learned the hard way. As a sergeant of the auxiliary German police, the deserter Kolpakoff burned numerous villages and murdered a number of peaceful Soviet citizens. The blood-thirsty traitor, the scourge of Haradok County, never discriminated between sexes and ages. A number of names, dates and places appeared, although neither Mary Karaway nor her family were mentioned. Evidently someone had done some thorough research. The people who strayed away from "father" Stalin's murderous grasp were not deemed worthy to be named as victims.

A jolt was delivered at the end of the article. Kolpakoff-Bergdorf, it appeared, now enjoyed the bliss of an affluent life in the Canadian city of Toronto. The street and house number were mentioned with the added suggestion for the benefit of "compatriots" to expose the monster, to ostracize and harass him by any means at their disposal.

Mary required no prompting by the Reds. Some time ago she had interpreted her capricious fate as Providence's will to avenge herself and her murdered kin. Now the devil himself stretched out his helping hand.

The heat of emotion takes away cold reason and logic. Over-whelmed by the possible implications of her unusual discovery, Mary promptly realized that henceforth she would find no peace of mind unless she sought out and destroyed the murderer. This rational idea, however, ran into a road-block when she attempted to construct a rough sketch of the plan to realize her just ambition. As far as she was concerned, Toronto was on the other side of the world. Since landing in this country, she had made meager progress in the unfamiliar language, and her knowledge of the country's laws and its people was pretty well zero. With no material resources of her own, no job or connection of any kind, her attempts to exact vengeance were baffled from the very start.

All through the afternoon and evening, Mary wrestled with the problems presented by the task that now loomed ahead. The one and only treasure that miraculously escaped all the vultures in the war was a small silver cross she wore inside her clothing on her breast. Customarily, Eastern Orthodox children are given such small crosses by their godmothers during christening ceremonies.

The prairie twilight darkened the room while the woman pulled out her small silver cross and examined the worn-out image of the crucifixion on the front, and the legend "Save and Protect" on the other side. Oblivious of the occasional din from the kitchen, where Lida apparently busied herself with household chores, Mary now readied herself to appeal to God, seeking guidance.

She crossed herself with unction, reverently kissed the tiny crucifix, and her lips uttered in the semi-darkness: "My Lord, please listen to me, I beg You. I realize I've been a great sinner in the past, for at one time, blinded and led astray by the Devil, I have even dared to deny Your existence. Please forgive me, O Merciful Lord...

"You have taken away to Your fold my dear children, my loving husband, and my most precious mother; You have expelled me from my own country. For my wrongdoings, You have punished me severely. But they say Your mercy knows no bounds, and that You forgive those who realize their misdeeds and properly repent. May I dare to hope now, my dear Lord, that You will listen to me and perhaps bestow on me Your healing kindness and Your infinite love? Right now I am hopelessly lost... Please show me the way.

"Is it too much to expect that You will deign to pay attention to a miserable wretch who is groping for light in the darkness, banned to dereliction and neglect? I do not really know how to pray to You, how to ask what I want... I hope You will understand. My words are not coming to You from any prayer book. They are the result of the deepest and most profound feelings of my heart...

"Since You have taken away my husband, children, and mother, smitten by Your just and inexorable wrath, I know no peace. You have exiled me to this distant land to dwell among unfriendly people, and today You have made Satan himself point out the refuge of the murderer of my kin.

"As perturbed and worn out as I was, until now I have been trying to forget and forgive, although I am too weak and human to forgive the man who has taken the lives of those closest to my heart. Now, commanded by You, the Devil has pointed a way. Surely You willed it so that that henceforth I cannot help but follow it to avenge my mother and children. I realize that if I stay where I am and do nothing, my life will certainly become one terrible agony, and peace will never dwell in my heart as long as I walk this earth. Please, Merciful Lord, lend me Your guiding hand, rekindle the spark of light in my heart and give me a hint about the direction I should follow.

"You willed it so that we should take no other lives, for no man has the right to set himself up as an arbitrary judge, unless it is done by Your kind will and command. What then was the purpose of revealing the murderer's address? Am I to seek out and destroy him? If that's Your will, Merciful Father, how can I, beaten, depressed, and unworthy of Your generous help, sustain the burden of an immense task ahead? Please, dear Lord, I beg of You, do not penalize me any more. It is peace above all that I want. Please..."

Her ardent prayers, emitted in spurts, convulsed her whole body. Unchecked tears flowed abundantly on her cheeks; her right hand, oblivious of the pain inflicted, spasmodically clutched the small crucifix. Immobile she lay on the bed, then shivers again rocked her body. Her subconscious warned her that if she continued this way she might lose her mind. Jolted by the new revelation, she was unable to find solace in direct prayer.

On the morrow, austere and worn, her eyes crimson and her eyelids puffy, she confronted Uncle Lavon, careful to make certain that Lida was not in sight, and sought his advice. The stooping farmer scratched his silvery, thin-haired head, winced uncomfortably, as if someone had saddled him with a two-ton load. Then, confounded by his niece's intentions, he said: "You better get the idea out of your silly head and stay where you are. You have as much chance of finding him as you have of reaching the moon. Even suppose that you located him, then what? What exactly are you going to do? Kill him? Perhaps he is married, has a wife and children? What about them?"

"I could," Mary stuttered, "go to the authorities. Let them know about him... take the case to the court... "

"Court? What court?" her uncle derided Mary. "For courts you must have sacks of money in this country. How much have you got? So, who will listen to you? You are not even a citizen. What rights have you?"

With this he walked away. Uncle Lavon had confronted her with more questions than she had imagined possible. Her intended revenge now appeared to be almost impossible of execution. Obviously the ageing farmer failed to comprehend either the intensity of Mary's feelings in this matter or her determination to wrestle with the dilemma.

What rights indeed did she have in this country? A worn-out and spent derelict, that is what she was. The labyrinth in which she found herself offered no avenue of escape. Yet she knew it was not in her power to check the forces that propelled her to action.

22

THE UNCLE

One cloudy Sunday morning Mary stood on the back porch of the big prairie farmhouse and wished she could cry. Try as she might, no tears came. Something choked her from inside. What happened had been expected for a long time. This expectation had somehow cushioned her against the oncoming shock. The pill was no sweeter, however, than other ones in the past. The solid ground had disappeared from under her feet. Once again she stood suspended in the void.

Her large blue expressive eyes scanned the horizon, the length and width of the flax field, seemingly unaware of its majestic beauty, undecided where to settle. Other pictures from ages ago came to her mind: the small lovely girl chasing many-coloured butterflies and industrious bees, peering into the fragile, bell-shaped, tiny flowers with absorbing, childish curiosity and anticipation of discovery. The carefree time passed unnoticed; no problems burdened the sunny day. Amid the blooming field, she herself seemed like a flower.

The flax field ended in a straight line to the right, and the wheat field stretched endlessly, its green at the edge of the horizon melting into the pinkish-gray sky. Mary knew what lay beyond. A number of times she had walked there at sundown. A small prairie town with its huge grain elevators dozed in the distance.

Otherwise immobile, the woman was apparently undecided what to do with her hands. Tightly clutching and wringing her fingers, she thus betrayed her inner turmoil. She heard two voices from inside the house, reverberating in a heated argument. The subdued man's voice paused, pleading, undecided how to proceed. The woman's falsetto cut into it with the swiftness of a sharp razor. The exchange continued unabated, while Mary on the rear porch watched Sunday morning come into its own.

From a distance, a church bell tolled. Mary wondered if she should go to town church, and then she promptly discarded the idea. Alien religious rites and a foreign language would be too much to digest at one time.

In her childhood, Mary was always fascinated by church bells in the distant town back home. She attended church services with her mother, immensely impressed by the gigantic and majestic centuries-old stone and brick edifice. Awe-struck and completely overwhelmed by the grandiose splendour around her, she watched the pigeons flying high up inside the heavenly blue cupola. While various angels and saints stared at her from frescoes, her whole tiny being became enraptured by the incomparable tunes of the choir somewhere high up in the choir loft. It seemed to her that those voices originated in heaven when, vibrating in their intensity, they fluttered and in slow waves descended to earth, while the gray-bearded, richly adorned priest chanted in front and behind the high colourful, glittering altar.

Some time later, godless people took power. For reasons the little girl failed to comprehend, they undertook to ridicule God, the churches, and the believers who attended them. One Sunday morning the church bells tolled no more. When Mary inquired of her mother what made the bells stop, she heard the laconic explanation that Satan had taken over and henceforth God found shelter in pious people's hearts. Now the nostalgia of those long gone years again touched the sensitive strings in the woman's heart.

The argument in the house stopped. Apparently, as

many times before the falsetto voice had the better of it. A few minutes elapsed. Heavy steps approached the door, which opened with a thin squeak, and the steps seemed undecided whether to proceed or stand still.

"Mary, I'm sorry," the gruff voice of Uncle Lavon said behind her back. "I tried my best to explain to her your situation. I got nowhere. Lida can't see it my way. You know I have tried hard, don't you? To make matters worse, she puts the question squarely: it's either you or her, she says. You know what that means, don't you?"

Mary did not reply. She did not turn around. She knew that if she tried to look straight into the gray eyes and at the furrowed face of her tall lean uncle, he would not meet her gaze. Somewhere, deep inside that man, a sense of guilt and shame lay buried.

"I don't know what to do," continued Lavon behind Mary's back, the screeching porch floor betraying the immensity of his burden. "I really don't know. I don't want to hurt you after all you've gone through. But things have become unbearable; they can't possibly go on like this... you understand." He trimmed his voice to whisper. "She hates you... "

The voice broke off, and still Mary did not turn around to face the miserable old farmer. Some four decades ago, penniless and eager to make a new start, he had landed in Canada. Today, by any standard, he might be considered wealthy, owning a huge, well-equipped grain farm, and with a fat roll of money in the bank. Yet handicapped by ignorance, he never learned to enjoy the simple blessings of freedom, health and work. His loyalties were divided between his waspy wife and his refugee niece, and Lavon found himself unable to reason with his emotions.

How unequally God divides, Mary mused. One human being finds out the hard way the values of freedom, a full stomach, a well-clothed body, and good health, yet he cannot afford them or is robbed of them by others; the other one is given an abundance of everything, but God makes him blind and dull. Thus both suffer.

Mary's misty eyes wandered far across the rim of the wheat field. Presently the traces of compassion on her smooth sun-tanned face disappeared, the lines around her well-cut lips hardened, and a flicker of contempt sharpened her countenance. As she slowly turned around, staring straight into her uncle's pale-blue vacant eyes, Lavon nervously winked his eyelids and guiltily looked away like a child certain to be admonished for some mischief.

"Don't strain yourself, Uncle," she replied in an even voice. "I understand perfectly. What's more, I expected this to happen for some time now. Still, it hurts terribly... I don't know where to go, or what to do. But really it doesn't matter." She swallowed hard. "I've been kicked around for so long now that I've grown used to it like a homeless dog... "

The bitterness of her predicament, the hurt of her feelings, were amply accentuated in those last words. Unable to continue, she turned around again to stare at the summer scene.

"Mary, my dear, I'll help you," her uncle pleaded, "only you must leave. Do you understand?"

"Yes, Uncle."

Lavon's voice descended to a subdued whisper: "I'll give you some money and the address of a good friend in Toronto. He's a married man with a family. For a time we used to work together. I'm sure he and his wife will put you in touch with other good people in the city, perhaps even find you a job. You'll discover that life in the city is easier for you, I'm sure you will. Perhaps in time you'll find a man, marry, and... "

All this the farmer pronounced in a single breath, as if in a hurry to get it promptly off his chest to experience some relief. "I'll take you to the train tomorrow. You know enough of the language to get by, and with your education I'm sure you'll do well in the long run."

"Do well." Mary echoed her uncle's words. Whatever that means... She never did well in the past. Her cup of bitterness overflowed, enough for several people. There was no one to share it with. Tomorrow she would be adrift again, a lost soul in the vast indifferent world, a storm-lashed vessel yearning for the safety of a calm haven. "God help me!" she whispered hoarsely to the sound of her uncle's retreating steps.

Then another idea which had all the while lurked in the back of her mind forcefully asserted itself. The murderer of her mother and children lived in Toronto. Had God employed Lida to steer Mary on the road to her destiny? Was this new turning an answer to her ardent prayers?

Imbued with anxiety and uncertainty about the risky plunge into the unknown which she was about to take, that whole Sunday Mary moved about nervously. She made sure to avoid the hostile landlady, and packed her meager belongings for the trip the next day.

23

THE COURTROOM

In the morning the police van brought them into the huge inner yard of a massive stone building, and through the heavy side doors they were herded into the wire cage. The jail matron, with a pompous official expression, moved about her routine duties with the efficiency of a well-oiled machine.

Mary looked around the chamber, crowded with various people, a Salvation Army woman on the front bench, men by the tables facing the judge's bench. The sleepless night in jail weighed heavily on her eyelids. A beehive of thoughts, now stirred by the proximity of the arm of the law, accelerated her heartbeat and increased her uneasiness.

Most of the women in the cage had an aura of indifference about them. Some of them whispered and giggled, others just yawned and looked bored, as if it was an act of an insignificant drama which they have viewed many times before and in which they knew how to act and what co-operation, if any, to expect from the others on the crowded stage.

The chamber with its immensely high ceiling looked forbidding. Rows of long benches faced the judge's dais. The yellow light from two separate fixtures somewhat dissipated the gloomy twilight in the chamber, which was dark even on sunny days... The picture of a young, radiant, gracious lady on the wall above the bench clashed with the surroundings. Mary already recognized the young Queen, the crowned head of this country.

It was the last thing in the world Mary expected – by a

capricious twist of fate she would now collide with the law of this country. The fact was now obviously plain that she was taken for a prostitute. The point that a terrible mistake had been made did not amount to much. It was what the Judge would think that mattered. How would she explain to him what had happened, with her tongue-tied by a foreign language? They must have an interpreter, they surely must. She would have to ask for one. Perhaps these people had understanding and mercy in their hearts...

Presently the well-groomed, stout, middle-aged clerk of the court rose and said in an official, well-modulated pitch: "Will everybody please rise. The Magistrate's Court is now in session. Judge Ferguson presiding."

A tall, dark-robed, bleak-faced man appeared from the side door, advanced to the dais, grabbed the gavel, and pounding three times intoned: "The Court is now in session. The Clerk will detail the cases, please."

Judge Ferguson scrutinized the assembly in front of him and the policeman by the door. Then he looked at the wire enclosure, filled with the day's crop of customers. As he proceeded to deal with the cases, his impassive voice and manners testified that he was no novice to this game; some of the people to whom he generously dispensed justice were repeaters familiar to him.

Mary had never seen the inside of a courtroom either in a Communist or a democratic country before. From the books she had read she could only vaguely imagine what the law was like in action. Observing Judge Ferguson at work, she imagined an automaton, totally impervious to the human side of the creatures in front of him, engaging himself not a whit more than officially prescribed and necessary.

When her turn came, Mary lost her will to move, and the matron nudged her gently out of the enclosure. All her soul-searching and emotional preparation notwithstanding, she trembled when confronted by the Judge's penetrating gaze. She felt completely naked; so much in fact that the Counsel, a tall, lean elderly man with an owl's face, had to repeat the question twice to bring her to her senses. Must be how a rabbit feels when trapped in a triangle of advancing hunters.

"On July 20," the Clerk's monotonous voice drummed the charge, "the said Mary Karaway, of no fixed address and no means of support, was duly observed in the vicinity of Dundas and Jarvis Streets, loitering in the area and approaching passers-by. When questioned by John Smith, the Police Constable on duty in the area, she was unable to explain her actions. The said Mary Karaway had therefore been detained and charged with vagrancy."

"How do you plead, Mrs. Karaway?" the counsel asked.

"I... " Mary stuttered, "I don't understand."

"You mean you don't understand English?"

"Yes."

"What language do you speak?"

"Byelorussian, Russian, and German."

"With Your Honor's permission, may we call the interpreter?"

The Judge nodded, and presently a bald-headed, middle-aged, scholarly looking man rose from the bench and approached Mary. "Mr. Sarochka, please ask this woman how she pleads," the Counsel advised.

The interpreter, upon explaining the charge, told Mary to plead guilty or not guilty. Aware of being scrutinized by everybody present, Mary was unable to command her tongue until repeatedly urged to enter a plea.

"I plead not guilty," she said at last.

"Perhaps then, Mrs. Karaway, you would tell us in your own words what happened?" the Counsel asked.

"Your Excellence," Mary began in a halting tone, blushing deeply, " I don't know why I have been arrested. Yesterday morning I came here on a train from the West and wanted to contact my uncle's friend. I didn't find him at the address given; apparently he and his family had moved. I was lost, I didn't know what to do. I figured if I could come across someone who spoke my language perhaps I'd get some advice and help. That's why I approached some people on the street. I had no luck at all. Almost ready to give up, I sat down on a park bench. Two drunks came and sat beside me, and they kept bothering me. I was trying to figure out what they wanted when the policeman came, questioned me, and arrested me. That's exactly what happened to me, Mr. Judge. Honest to God, that's the truth..."

When Mr. Sarochka translated, Mary felt greatly relieved that the story was finally out. It took all her breath away. Anxiously she watched the Judge. It appeared to her that a shade of slight amusement crossed his face. As he spoke to her, his voice seemed less stern than before.

"You say, Mrs. Karaway, you have come from the West?"

"Yes."

"How long have you been in this country, and where do you come from originally?"

"I've been in this country for about two years and I come from Byelorussia."

The Judge asked the Clerk for documents.

"Hmm," he muttered, supporting his sagging chin with the palm of his left hand, examining her immigrant's passport. "What was the purpose of your coming to Toronto, Mrs. Karaway?" he inquired.

"My uncle's wife is a Communist, Mr. Judge. She was making my life miserable all the time I stayed with them, and she finally made my uncle, who is a gentle, meek, and misguided person, kick me out of the house. I had no choice but to come here, hoping the people whose address my uncle gave me would help me to find a job and a place to stay. These people apparently moved, so I landed right on the street, Mr. Judge... "

Mary caught her breath and swallowed hard. "I beg you, please help me, Mr. Judge. I want to find a job and live like other decent people do. I don't want to be a burden on anybody."

The Judge looked at her, a small pathetic figure of a woman in trouble. He seemed to be visibly concerned.

"Your case, Mrs. Karaway, is not at all unusual to our city," he cleared his throat," except that some women come here looking for an easy living." He hesitated. Pleadingly, Mary looked at this powerful person on whom her immediate future depended. "I must make sure that you did not."

The arresting police constable was questioned, and Mary watched them all anxiously trying to guess what went on. Finally the Judge spoke directly to Mary: "It's quite obvious that a mistake has been made, Mrs. Karaway. I hope you understand it and will pardon us for the inconvenience caused. However, you yourself have admitted that you are a newcomer to Toronto without any means of support and accommodation. It's my duty then to rectify our mistake and properly assist you as you have asked us to do... "

Mary heard this through the court interpreter, and her anguished spirits rose. Instead of administering her an undeserved kick, this man, who seemed so impassive at first, was now promising to help her. Breathing a sigh of relief, she looked at the gracious lady in the portrait with gratitude overflowing her long suffering heart. Never in her wildest dreams had she envisaged the impersonal law offering her a hand of assistance just at the time when she so sorely needed it.

The judge beckoned to the lady from the Salvation Army, leaned over his dais, and exchanged a few words with her. The woman then withdrew, and the Judge again addressed Mary: "You don't know the English language,

Mrs. Karaway, and have no one in the city who can assist you. We intend to contact a church of your ethnic group and ask them to lend you their assistance. That may take some time. Meanwhile, Mrs. Findlay here, who is an officer of the Salvation Army, has offered to help you. You will go with her. You will find food and shelter until such time as the officials of your church have been contacted. Does that satisfy you, Mrs. Karaway?"

The bleak face now acquired the features of the benevolent gentleness of a father. Mary was ready to leap at the official in the dark robe and smother his hands with kisses of gratitude.

"Yes, Mr. Judge, thank you. May God bless you... "

The gloom in the Court Chamber was lifted. Judge Ferguson nodded at Mrs. Findlay, who approached Mary and took her arm: "Come my dear, follow me."

Late in the evening, secure in her belief that a benevolent Providence had manipulated these people to stretch out their hands in assistance to a wretched derelict from a distant land, Mary took a bath and prepared for bed. Before falling asleep between the clean linen sheets, she warmly thanked the Lord for His generous help.

24

THE MURDERER'S TRAIL

Mary got off the streetcar and slowly proceeded down a narrow street in the East End, looking for the house number, which, together with that hated name, haunted her since she had first found it in the Communist newspaper. Forebodings of a risky adventure – totally unlike anything she had experienced – kept her nerves taut.

Behind her solid determination to locate Kolpakoff-Bergdorf lurked only a vague idea of what to do after she found him. Her feelings were like those of a hunter who, after a hazardous chase, was about to corner a predatory beast in its lair, only to discover that he had neglected to bring ammunition for his gun. Mary's intentions were rather modest – she came just to find out if Bergdorf really lived here – but the premonition of some unknown danger persisted. What would she do, for instance, if she found herself facing him at his front door?

She contemplated this possibility a number of times when washing dishes in a huge hospital kitchen. She had held the job for three weeks now. It was not much of a job, but there was hardly any choice. The people from a local Byelorussian Eastern Orthodox parish, mostly newcomers, toiled in sweat-shops. Saddled with huge mortgages and various other debts, they worked hard to make ends meet. Most originated from peasant stock in the old country. The immensity of the various problems of adaptation to Canadian life presented a man-sized challenge to each and every one of them. Adjusting to urban life was perhaps the easiest.

Mary was grateful to them for the understanding of her plight, their warmth of brotherly feeling, and their eagerness to assist her. In due course, she reasoned, she would be able to look around, learn the language properly, and perhaps attend a night school to master a new trade. For now it was enough to belong somewhere, instead of being a derelict no one cared about.

Some of her newly befriended countrymen told her that when they first arrived in Toronto they too were totally confused, helpless, and alone. Unlike displaced persons of various other nationalities, who were ably assisted by their long-established and prosperous national churches and social organizations, Byelorussians were on their own from their first step on Canadian soil. No national churches or organizations existed here; they had to start from scratch themselves.

The previous wave of Byelorussian immigration, oppressed and because of oppression ignorant at home, easily fell into traps set for them here by their unsolicited "guardians", Russians and Poles. These two "older brothers", who had partitioned and colonized Byelorussia, except for some lip service totally disregarded the present trends of emancipation. They stuck unabashedly to their outdated political mottoes, which maintained that Byelorussians, for one, had not yet reached the maturity needed for self-determination; perforce they should be used as fertilizer for the growth and blossoming of their Russian and Polish masters.

The labels and tactics of oppression in the New World had to be overhauled. Whereas at home captive Byelorussians were ordered around and penalized for insubordination, in Canada – the country of their choice – where everybody who was somebody professed to subscribe to the right of self-expression, the homeland serfs had to be lured by a newly concocted bait. Ignorance and loneliness came in handy.

Eastern Orthodoxy and Roman Catholicism, so much abused at home, were given a generous coat of fresh paint. The old lie which held that all Roman Catholics should be Poles came to be unblushingly advertised among ignorant Byelorussian Catholics, urging them to join Polish parishes. At the same time, Eastern Orthodoxy, the veritable vehicle of Russian imperialistic interests, was being presented as the "loving mother" of all Eastern Orthodox Slavs.

Both fraudulent ideas still held a magic spell over so numerous ignorant and nationally unconscious Byelorussians. Polish and Russian priests in Canada, following in the footsteps of their professional counterparts from across the ocean, generously dispensed the poison of assimilation among Byelorussians. To make this vicious circle complete, Communism made considerable inroads among those who stayed away from their churches. Ignorance spawns poverty, and vice versa. The ill-fated hungry thirties afforded leftist elements ample opportunities to utilize economic depression for swelling their ranks.

Thus the post-war Byelorussian immigrants upon their arrival in Canada – to their immense chagrin and disappointment – found the previous Byelorussian immigration completely swallowed up by Russian and Polish churches, social organizations, and Communist clubs. Some old immigrants were so assimilated that, although they still spoke their mother tongue at home, they often denied their true origin.

In Toronto, numerous newcomers tried to contact the old immigrants but were promptly rebuked for their alleged fascist and nationalist beliefs. Mary heard a string of stories about some foolhardy souls who ventured into the local "wasp nests" of the Reds, naively assuming they could somehow undo in a month what Moscow's agents had accomplished in over a decade: pull the "made in

Moscow" blindfolds off their ignorant compatriots' eyes and enable them to see the light.

Mary's own bitter experience with Lida and Uncle Lavon has been etched into her memory as if by a white-hot branding iron. If ignorance tinted by an alien ideology and fueled by raw emotion could trigger fireworks among close blood relatives and get them to jump at each other's throats, what then could one expect from people who traded their national identity and dignity for dubious, "pie-in-the-sky" promises of foreign hirelings?

Mary doubly appreciated the help given her by members of her parish, for by now she had thoroughly realized how hard their own first steps in this country were. The government, among other things, discouraged "old country quarrels", did not care who assimilated whom, as long as all newcomers paid their share of the various taxes and did not swell the ranks of native criminals.

Now Mary walked along a narrow paved street, shaded by sparse maple trees, lined by rows of semi-detached houses in what appeared to be a lower class district. The evening was now well advanced. The oppressive heat of summer had subsided with the descending sun, all living creatures welcomed the cool relief. It appeared that everyone crawled out of his hole to stretch his muscles and catch his breath. Children swarmed on sidewalks, creating a terrific noise; they darted across the street from between parked cars, triggering shrill honking of horns from passing motorists.

As Mary neared the house numbered seventy-three across the street, her legs grew heavy with dread and her anxiety increased. Now there it was, right opposite her, with the front door ajar. A stocky, lightly clad, flaxen-haired woman comfortably slumped in the spacious verandah chair, keeping an eye on a chubby youngster pushing toy cars on the concrete walk. The small patch of green lawn was getting its rain from a water-sprinkler. The house was part of a red-brick row, and it looked freshly painted and well-kept. On Mary's side, a man was busily mending a small lawn fence. Glancing absent-mindedly at the man, Mary slowed down, undecided what to do.

"Hot day, wasn't it?" the man spoke. Evidently eager to strike up a conversation, he appeared friendly. For all Mary knew, he might be that rare exception among aloof urbanites, and might well prove to be the helping hand she needed.

"Certainly was," she smiled. Since landing a job at the hospital, she had devoted most of her time to learning English and made enough progress to sustain a limited conversation.

"Another record broken. Ninety-three, the radio said," the man continued. "Looking for someone?"

"Yes," Mary hastened to answer. "Now that I'm here I'm not quite sure I've come to the right place. Perhaps you can help me... I hate to bother the wrong party."

"Glad to help if I can," the man responded, his eyes examining the damage to the fence and then rapidly shifting to look at Mary. "These kids... a nuisance," he grumbled and spat out a thick stream of tobacco juice. Had Mary known Canadian lumberjacks – a rugged, tough, weather-beaten and straightforward lot – she would, no doubt, have placed this man in that category. He seemed to be out of place in a bustling, noisy city.

"All the damage they do," commented the man. He looked big and strong, with a face of a simpleton, bushy dark hair, no more than thirty-five. As he regarded the woman with a question in his narrow brown eyes, his chest and arm muscles relaxed under an evenly sun-tanned skin.

"Perhaps you know who lives at number seventy-three?" Mary inquired, lowering her voice and staring at the man, her back turned on the house in question. "You see," she added, "I'm looking for someone but I don't believe it's the lady on the verandah."

"Well, I'll tell you," he shifted on his feet. "These people rent the house. I don't know their last names. They've moved in shortly after the New Year. Who is it you're looking for?"

"A man named Bergdorf, a German. This is the address I got. Do you know him?"

"Sure do. That's his house all right, only he don't live here. He lives someplace in West Toronto, I heard. Why don't you go and ask that lady, she might help you."

"I sure will. Thank you very much."

Abruptly Mary turned around to cross the street. For an instant she wondered if the woman she was about to approach would accord her a hearing as favourable as the tobacco-chewing man's.

Before she reached the verandah, another lucky turn made her trip easier. The child playing with his toy-cars, no more than two, evidently quite absorbed by the intricacies of transportation, crawled within reach of the water-sprinkler. Generously sprayed with cold water, he responded with a loud shriek of surprise, which immediately brought the plump woman, some two hundred pounds of her, to the youngster's rescue. As she bent down and pulled the boy away, her lips emitted one long continuous chain of motherly admonition, all of it in flawless German, a language Mary commanded well.

The woman wiped the boy's hair and face with the hem of her flowered skirt, and in a soothing voice tried to allay his chagrin. With his calm restored, he immediately proceeded with his game, whereupon the woman, straightening herself, confronted Mary with a question in her dark green eyes.

"It appears the little fellow doesn't like a shower," Mary said in German, smiling.

"I've warned him so many times to keep away from the water, but he always forgets," the woman smiled back at Mary. "No matter. Water on a day like this won't harm anybody... Say, do you live around here? I don't recall seeing you before. Are you German? You don't sound like one." The fast-talking woman came up with her own answers.

Mary said: "You guessed it. I don't live around here and I'm not German but I've been in Germany. I wonder if you could possibly help me?"

"Be glad to if I can."

"I'm looking for a man named Bergdorf. A friend of mine gave me this address."

"Johan Bergdorf? You a friend of his?"

"Yes, a close friend. I knew Johan Bergdorf in Germany," Mary hastened to reply.

"I see," the woman appraised Mary from head to toe. "Mr. Bergdorf is our landlord. I can give you his address. Would you mind waiting here a minute? I'll write it down for you," the woman looked at the youngster, now totally absorbed with his toys, and went into the house. Mary wondered if she had the least inkling the kind of man her landlord really was.

The woman presently returned from the house and handed Mary an address scribbled on a small piece of paper, then resumed conversation, inquiring how long Mary had been in Germany, where and when, how long she had been in Canada, whether she liked the country and shared her own observations.

Out of this conversation Mary learned that Bergdorf was now happily married, had an attractive young wife, two children – a boy and a girl – and worked in real estate. Content that she now had a great deal more than she hoped for on her initial reconnaissance trip, Mary amiably thanked the lady and left.

25

ONE JUMP AHEAD

Late in the afternoon three days later, Mary paused in her work unpacking her belongings in the middle of a spacious, well-furnished second-floor front room of a house in West Toronto, and minutely surveyed her new surroundings. The rug on the floor, the furniture, the room itself, did not conform to her idea of modest living. She could ill-afford the rent, which was double what she had paid for her small nook in the old section of the city close to her place of work. The rent, however, was inconsequential, considering that her front window and balcony provided an excellent vantage point from which to observe a house and the people in it across the street.

She stood there and chuckled; the idea that at long last she was one jump ahead of Bergdorf made her bitter life so much sweeter. Perhaps this would prove to be the break she had so eagerly sought.

For speculation's sake, she attempted to place herself in Bergdorf's shoes. Apparently well-to-do, a contented father of a family, leading the life of a complacent suburbanite, he probably considered the war years as being far away, himself now partaking of the bliss of material affluence in a democratic country. His middle-class neighbours, no doubt sometimes rubbing shoulders with this new citizen, probably never suspected the man was not what he appeared to be. Perhaps Kolpakoff-Bergdorf had long ago buried Mary Karaway in his other memories of the war. The nature of his war exploits was not the kind to reminisce about with an amiable soul over a cup of tea. Would he ever jump if somehow he found out that the village teacher who had nursed him back to life and whose family he had so bestially slaughtered was not dead, but right now lived across the street from his own house.

Bergdorf's spacious gray bungalow, with a private drive and an attached double-garage, stood on a large lot with a well-developed front lawn. Now the garage was closed and a maroon-coloured Buick was parked in front of it. Mary examined Bergdorf's property and decided everything appeared perfect. The adjacent properties, though built in a variety of styles, apparently expressing their owners' ideas of architectural tastes and reflecting their material resources, fitted well into a single price range. There was no room for an ordinary working man here, only the petty bourgeois who made good. No "room for rent" signs on his doors or windows.

The house in which Mary had rented her room belonged to two pious spinster pensioners, well advanced in age. The house appeared to be rather old and was probably built long before the population from the city's core spilled over into the surrounding countryside. People of means apparently considered this area exclusive enough to build their luxury nests here. To Mary's knowledge the suburb housed at least one exclusive vulture.

She again surveyed her room, speculating on how long she would have to stay here until her work was completed. Then she proceeded with the unpacking, putting her meager clothing into a closet and a wardrobe. She had moved in here only an hour ago, and now she was ready to do some preliminary observation. No matter what step she would later decide to take, some detective work was a prerequisite for the ultimate success of her undertaking.

She closed the screen door behind her and stretched out in a large upholstered comfortable chair on the balcony. She looked to the left, where some distance away the street joined a well-tended park, which gently sloped into the Humber River. Mary had never heard of Hurricane Hazel and could not have possibly imagined that, except for it, debris and rubble would still be littering the spacious, undeveloped river banks. Only after vicious Hazel prompted Humber's calm waters to rise and swell and cause millions of dollars in damage in the immediate vicinity, did the reluctant city administrators decide to curb the river's possible future excesses. The results, to put it in modest terms, appeared rewarding.

Newly planted trees took root, freshly mowed grass smiled at the sun, people rested on benches., youngsters pursued their never-ending games.

The balcony, with a protective cover overhead, presented a perfect view. To the south, along the lakeshore, smaller dwellings were crowded by apartment buildings along the highway. The rays of the descending sun showered gold into the azure waters of Lake Ontario. The white sails of tiny boats appeared from this point like immobile, gentle feathers glued to the water's surface. Farther to the east little planes buzzed around the Island Airport. The abundance of green on Toronto's islands seemed to challenge the skyscrapers downtown, daring them to come over the busy stretch of water.

Mary was overwhelmed by this sight. No wonder the old spinster landlady, showing her the room, properly emphasized the existence of this balcony, from which Mary could view the surrounding city and lake to her heart's content. Indeed, Mary thought, this was a place where a poet would love to dwell and – soothed by a beautiful view, nurturing gently the fragile seeds of inspiration – spawn all kinds of nonsense in his fertile imagination.

Mary sighed. Curbing her fanciful thoughts, she rapidly descended to the life-and-death struggle that brought her to this place. Neither yesterday nor today had she glimpsed anyone around the house across the street. In the back of her mind the gnawing fear persisted that the German lady who gave her the address might have led her astray. One could assume Bergdorf had heard about Moscow's interest in him and could have taken precautions. One of them would logically involve detouring any information-seekers at the door of that old house whose address was mentioned in the paper. The possibility remained, however, that Bergdorf felt entirely safe, for unlike some others he had not even changed his name.

Mary wished she could somehow penetrate the rich brocade curtains in the front windows of that expensive bungalow and see what was going on inside. She could, of course, have asked her landladies but she prudently decided not to stir their inquisitive minds, for upon her inquiry about the room two days ago she had been showered with an abundance of questions, mainly pertaining to her social and marital status. There was no point in letting them in any way suspect she was interested in a particular neighbour across the street.

At long last things began to happen. Mary's watchfulness galvanized her nerves into a wild spin, and she rose from her chair uneasily, as a man alighted from the side door of Bergdorf's house. He hesitated on the small step, his back turned to Mary, said something to someone inside the door, then turned around looking at the Buick. A woman, two little children, and a tiny white poodle immediately followed. Mary recognized the man instantly. Her heart leaped with a mixture of exhilaration and fear. At long last she could leisurely examine her man while he was totally unaware of her.

The man appeared to be stocky and did not move with his familiar agility. A small brush moustache adorned his upper lip; he wore a brown hat, and his apparently expensive brown suit failed to conceal the extra pounds in his expanded middle. With his looks he could well fit into the stereotyped image of a prosperous businessman. Even from a distance, Mary noticed his full, chubby face and his sagging chin.

Well, well... Herr Bergdorf must have properly adjusted himself to the new conditions and lived well. Realistic man, no dreamer he. He had probably hewn out the cornerstone for this luxurious nest in that other country, which he pillaged and raped so assiduously.

His wife (who else could it be?) appeared small and fragile alongside of him, her adolescent face more properly fitting a girl of fifteen than a mother of two. Bergdorf opened the car door and slowly slid in behind the steering wheel. As the motor purred contentedly, he eased the car out of the driveway. The woman and her children stood waving goodbye. Truly an idyllic suburbanite picture that sets one's heart aglow: hard-working husband departing into the cruel world to earn some more dollars, his spouse and precious offsprings saying goodbye to the head of the family. All so touching.

Bergdorf swung into the street and roared away. The woman, clad in white shorts and polka-dot blouse, handed the dog's leash to the little girl, and the trio unhurriedly proceeded to the park. The girl tussled with the toy poodle, which entangled the leash around her legs. Her mother coached her, finally fetched the dog into her arms. The boy carried a big red plastic ball.

This was an opportunity not to be missed, Mary decided. She got out of her chair, hurried into the room, took off her everyday blue dress and donned the pink one she had bought the other day at a sale with the money from the first paycheque she had received.

The low wages she earned called for frugal living. She again wondered if the money she spent at a beauty salon was invested wisely. It occurred to her that if she were to face Bergdorf, some form of disguise would augment her chances of success in the job she had to do. The choice perplexed her: either she could make herself appear as an old, beaten woman, or as a young, sprightly vivacious widow. Upon considering the various technical details involved – the expediency of the disguise being the guiding consideration – she came out in favour of the young-widow version. If Bergdorf possessed a keen memory, her appearance would resurrect in his mind a picture from the past. It would be prudent to assume that a young look would afford Mary a better camouflage. What would confuse him more than the image of a person he had long considered dead suddenly confronting him in all her former glory? The man would simply be flabbergasted and lost for an explanation, not trusting his senses...

The hairdresser had done quite a job. The shoulder-length, wavy auburn hair accentuated her natural beauty. One could hardly erase the tiny duck's feet around her eyes; yet considering her turbulent past, Mary marvelled at the durability of the youthful looks she still possessed.

Making faces, she minutely scrutinized herself in a large wardrobe mirror and decided she could do nothing about her round blue expressive eyes. A deep, apathetic hardness came in place of what used to be an innocent, buoyant, wondering girlish look. Those were the eyes that had repeatedly viewed the abyss of death, fathomed the ultimate agony of her heart, and partook of the bitter cup of human degradation. Remarkably enough, the hurt in her eyes persisted only when she appeared gloomy, pensive, or brooding. It became less pronounced, barely noticeable, in fact, when her face turned cheerful, calm, unclouded; the inner dormant sparks then fully restored the brisk vitality of her wholesome, sturdy peasant nature.

Mary put on her old but well-kept shoes, fetched the old handbag and a book she had borrowed last Sunday from the Byelorussian community library. She descended the carpeted stairs and went out through the side door.

In the park she looked around and chose an empty bench close to the Bergdorfs'. They were busy tossing the ball, the toy poodle assisting them with his merry frolics. Absorbed in the pursuit of this simple game, they appeared relaxed and happy. The girl, about four, and the boy, about five, were both dark-haired like their mother. Mary was not surprised to hear that they spoke German.

She opened the book and tried to concentrate on her reading, but the meaning of the words escaped her. Again and again she discreetly observed the Bergdorf woman, speculating on what possible device she could employ to make her acquaintance. The ball precipitated the solution of her problem. The little girl missed the ball, and Mary saw it rolling toward her, and just as she stooped to pick it up, the poodle and the girl, her hands outstretched, were right beside her.

"Hello," smiled Mary, "what's your name?"

The girl hesitated, her eyes shifting from the red ball that Mary held firmly in her hands to the face of this lady who spoke her tongue.

"Erna," the little girl said, her hands still outstretched.

"Hello, Erna," Mary said sweetly, handing the ball over. She lifted her head, and her eyes confronted Mrs. Bergdorf, two steps away, staring at her.

"What lovely children you have," Mary said in a mellow voice, her motherly eyes caressing the children and smiling at Mrs. Bergdorf.

"You are very kind, thank you," Bergdorf's wife smiled back. Her face was one of those, Mary noticed instantly, that never outgrow its adolescent allurement. Her small nose projected just a hint of perkiness. Her soft dark eyes appraised Mary unhurriedly, and her small well-cut lips moved: "Are you German?"

"No, I'm not," Mary replied, still appraising the woman

in front of her. Despite her small size she made an impression of wholesome compactness. Mary imagined her in a German kitchen with an apron, helping her mother. Then, of course, she would make a plain, if not typical, hardworking *Mädchen*. Here, in a different setting, her smooth looks, enhanced by a degree of self-assurance, fitted well a prosperous suburban housewife.

"But I've been in Germany for a few years," Mary continued. "I couldn't help overhearing you talking in German so I thought this would be a good occasion to brush up on mine. Are you German or Austrian?"

"German," Mrs. Bergdorf answered curtly. She turned to her children: "You go and play." She patted Erna on the head. "Erna, Eric, you go ahead, have fun, I'll be right here with this lady."

"Come on, Erna," the boy urged his sister, and they resumed tossing the ball, while their mother sat beside Mary. "Do you live around here? I don't recall seeing you before."

The preliminaries seemed to be on the right track.

"I've just moved in at number thirty-six with the two ladies," Mary said.

"You don't say... then we are close neighbours. The Bentley sisters live right across the street from us."

"Is that so? "Mary smiled. "In that case let's get acquainted. My name is Alena Maroz." Later Mary wondered why on the spur of the moment had she picked her dead friend's name.

"Miss or Mrs.?" the Bergdorf woman asked.

"Mrs. I'm a widow."

"Mine is Mrs. Erna Bergdorf. I'm glad to make your acquaintance, Mrs. Maroz and may I welcome you to our neighbourhood." The frank openness in her eyes suited her youthful looks. Mary could not help liking her.

"Thank you kindly, Mrs. Bergdorf. I don't know anybody around here, but it seems to be a nice community."

"It is and I'm glad you like it. And now you know me. What nationality are you, Mrs. Maroz?"

"I'm Byelo –" Mary bit her tongue, but it was too late. "I'm Byelorussian, lived under Polish occupation."

"I see. Why do you say you have lived under Polish occupation? Didn't you like the Poles?"

"It's more complicated than a question of liking some people. When you settle in some country voluntarily, well, you may like it or not, but it would be your choice. When others broke down the doors of your own house and run your life, why, that's a different matter."

"Well, I know nothing about Byelorussians, and you're the first one I've just met. It's all so interesting. Where do you work, Mrs. Maroz?"

"In the hospital."

"A nurse?"

"Yes."

Preliminaries over, they chatted about Germany, the weather, the children, Mrs. Bergdorf all the time keeping her eye on hers. She asked Mary to join them in the children's play. Some half an hour later they walked home together. Both kids seemed to like Mary too. When Mrs. Bergdorf invited Mary to her house, she could hardly refuse, although she appeared to hesitate.

"Come in, please," Erna Bergdorf took her hand. "After all, I've said I'm glad you moved into our neighbourhood, so let me welcome you with a cup of tea, like English people do."

They sat around the coffee table in the huge living room. While Mrs. Bergdorf chatted almost continuously, Mary admired the expensive modern furniture, carpets, redwood panelling, pictures on the walls. Mary displayed a mild curiosity when the woman devoted some attention to her loving husband Johan Bergdorf. Yet behind her enthusiastic façade, she detected a false note. It sounded as if the lady tried to convince herself of her husband's love and devotion.

Mary learned that Bergdorf was in real estate, had made a success of his job, although there were late and irregular hours to put up with. When Mrs. Bergdorf mentioned this, a note of disappointment and regret crept into her smooth voice. She often had to spend her evenings alone.

Mary had other ideas about Bergdorf's irregular hours, especially late at night. This young woman facing her from across the round, shiny coffee table, saddled with two children, provided with an abundant domestic comforts, sounded starved for human companionship. Mary's alert mind calculated quickly. All she would have to do was to cultivate Erna Bergdorf's friendship. And then… why, this would be the best way to get through the thick skin of that elusive vulture.

26
LOVE'S BEGINNING

After the church service on Sunday, Mikola Hlak approached Mary in the church hall and rather pointedly demanded to know why and where she had moved. Was she trying to hide from him? What had prompted her move?

Mikola was a handsome bachelor in his mid-thirties. He had a well-developed muscular body, was above-average in height, had bushy dark hair with graying temples, a sweet, open smile, and a straight no-nonsense approach. All these things, as well as his correct behaviour, Mary had observed since they had become acquainted about three weeks ago. The woman suspected Mikola was not impartial in his feelings toward her.

Men far outnumbered women among the recent Byelorussian immigrants. Mary had better-than-average chances of being courted. Had she been unencumbered by what she now came to think of as her "mission", she would have more rapidly responded to Mikola's overtures. She needed complete freedom and couldn't afford to be tied down or dependent on anyone. The time for eventual romance would come later, she decided, after disposing of her "mission".

She was flattered by Mikola's attentions and found it hard to remain indifferent. She hated to rudely reject his advances. There was no need, she decided, and tried to turn her moving into a neat joke.

"You see, Mikola, if I knew you cared, I'd have sent you a telegram, asking you to rush to my assistance and help me move all the riches I've collected during my short stay here."

It did not sound like a joke to Mikola. The answer precipitated something she tried to avoid.

"I do care, Mary," Mikola said seriously, caressing Mary with his attentive eyes. Mary looked into his eyes deeply, recognized the symptoms of love, and blushed. The sweet feeling that someone really cared about her, and who freely, almost publicly, admitted it filled her heart with a sense of belonging. Perhaps it was the awareness of a new beginning. The man's simple declaration touched her deeply. They stood among the crowd, looking at each other as only two people could who have suddenly discovered their friendship was growing into a stronger bond.

"I'm flattered," Mary swallowed hard. "That is, if you mean what you say."

"I do mean it, Mary." He took her hand, squeezing it gently. Mary scanned the faces around them. She gently withdrew her hand, saying: "Look, Mikola, I don't know what to say."

"Don't say anything, Mary, not here anyway. Let's take a walk."

Mikola was the one who had helped her find her hospital job, and he never missed an opportunity to inquire about her various problems of settling and adjusting to city life. The familiarity came naturally between them. Both knew little of each other, yet both sensed they had just reached a stage in their relations where – even for a continuation of their friendship such as it was until now – some mutual digging into their backgrounds was necessary. This idea firmly rooted itself in Mary's mind as they left the church hall, crossed the street, and proceeded into the park.

The day was warm and cloudy. At this hour few people were in the park. Some children enjoyed themselves on swings and slides in the playground. Mikola chose a secluded bench under a huge maple-tree. He wiped the bench with his handkerchief and invited Mary to sit down. She complied, stretching her legs, attentively examining her brown shoes as if seeing them for the first time. For a while they sat silently, just staring ahead, both absorbed in their own thoughts after their conversation in the church hall.

"Mary, I meant every word of what I said to you in there." Mikola turned his head sharply to her and sought her eyes while she kept staring ahead. "I do care about you. I don't really know when I realized this for the first time... It must have been when I tried to contact you at your old address. When I heard you were gone, I had a feeling I had lost something irretrievably. Then, in a flash, it came to me that you weren't just a casual acquaintance like the others before you. It's true I've known you only for a very short time, but even so I've come to realize you are the one with whom I hit the right note from the start."

"When you moved away and left no forwarding address, and nobody I asked was able to tell me where you had gone, a fear gnawed at my heart that perhaps you had decided to leave town and move elsewhere, never to be seen again. Indeed, Mary," continued Mikola with a tremor in his voice, "I've never been so completely unbalanced as I was during these last few days. I kept repeating to myself over and over that it couldn't have possibly happened, that you couldn't do this to me. And then suddenly I realized that you owed me nothing, that our friendship had hardly sprouted and taken root. I knew, with no 'ifs' or 'buts' that I was involved. I waited for this Sunday, counting the hours, for I realized that eventually you'd show up in church. The possibility that you wouldn't upset me so that I tried to dismiss it from my mind. That's why I was so glad, to put it mildly, when I saw you in the church today. And now that we are here .."

He stopped and looked around anxiously as if unable to

continue without assistance. "Mary, please, if there's anything I can do, let me help you. Will you? I don't know whether what I feel is love or not; I don't want to be selfish and intrude on your life unnecessarily. All I'm sure of is that I cannot afford to lose you, that I want to stay near you. Will you allow me this liberty, Mary? Is it too much to hope that you'll consider how I feel?"

Mikola took her hand, tried to look into her eyes, but the woman still stared ahead and Mikola was afraid she did not even hear all he had said. Her limp hand lay in his big palm, and he fidgeted on the bench, unsure of what to do next.

Mary turned her face to him slowly, and Mikola was shocked by what he saw in her blue, expressive eyes. There was hurt, disappointment, compassion, and understanding, all mixed in one. A premonition of unknown dangers and unfathomable uncertainties was reflected in her gloomy face, tightly closed lips, and wavering stare. A much-abused middle-aged woman and a child in need of assistance were looking back at him.

Mikola was a reasonably well-educated man who worked as an accountant, and there were a number of women in his past. Hard-bitten and incorrigible, a bachelor not easily caught. But never before did he have an experience of this nature. The woman affected him in some way nobody else had before. She both attracted and intrigued, pained and delighted him. She generated in his being exactly those forces that reap their love's reward through a measure of sweet pain and suffering.

"Mikola, you are galloping too fast," she said, stressing the word "galloping". The voice seemed to be aloof and unbearably impersonal. It made the man wonder whether Mary had any feelings. "Did it ever occur to you that I might not be ready for any association of a romantic nature?" she asked pointedly. "I am flattered by your attentions... but let me ask you, what do you know about me?"

"I don't – " Mikola cut in.

"No, no, don't interrupt me," she stretched out her hand. "Let me have my word. You know that I wasn't born yesterday. You should also know that I cannot divorce myself from my past, nobody can... To make my long story short, there was a reason behind my moving; there's more in my past than you could possibly imagine. All I can say now, if that will comfort you at all, is that it's not the kind of colourful past some girls often have. It's something of an entirely different nature. If and when I'm ready, I'll tell you. I don't think I should now."

"Please, Mary, tell me. Whatever it is, even the worst, perhaps I can help you," he pleaded.

"No, Mikola, you can't. Oh, I don't know," her voice trailed off. "Look, Mikola, you make me so confused. Please, stop asking questions. Don't you see I'm not ready for revealing my soul?"

Now she seemed piqued. Mikola looked closely into her eyes, the shifting expressions of her lovely face, and he knew there was a tremendous struggle going on inside her. She pretended to act calmly, but – if he knew people at all – this girl was on the verge of tears. There was something churning inside her, and yet she was not ready to share her experience with him. He did not want to trigger a premature explosion.

"Look, Mary, could you promise me one thing?" he took her hand.

"What is it?"

"If you need help, any help at all, you'll call me?"

"Yes, I will," she answered after a short hesitation.

"That's settled then. Now, will you let me take you out for dinner?"

"I think I'd love that," she smiled, but the smile was forced.

Mikola took her to his car and drove two blocks to a

restaurant where for a reasonable price one could get a fine old-country meal. They ate unhurriedly, sharing bits of small talk. Mikola observed her every move, trying to see through the mask of indifference and outward calm on her lovely face. Whatever it was she was trying to camouflage, he must get through to her, be a part of her life, for now he knew without a doubt he was deeply involved.

After dinner Mikola suggested a trip to Centre Island, but she flatly refused, insisting on going home. Perhaps it was for the better. After all, if they were to spend some more time together today, an inadvertent word or a clumsy move might produce the fireworks which Mikola so scrupulously tried to avoid.

They were both silent on the way to Mary's home. Parking his two-year-old green Chevy sedan in front of Bentley's, Mikola duly noted the street's name and house number.

"Will you be kind enough to give me your telephone number, Mary?"

"There's no telephone in the house," she lied. "The two ladies I live with are either thrifty or old-fashioned, I don't know which."

It sounded like a lie, but Mikola said: "O.K., then here's mine," and he took a small white card from his wallet. "Call me whenever you feel like it."

"All right, Mikola," she answered in a small voice, avoiding his eyes. "And I want to apologize for being such a miserable company for you today."

"Forget it." He got out of the car, opened the door for her, and watched her go inside the house.

There was hardly a soul to be seen on the street. As he slowly pulled away, Mikola scanned both sides of the street, and it occurred to him that Mary must have had a good reason to move here, where rents would certainly be higher than downtown where she used to live. If he knew

the woman at all – and he figured he did – she was not the
kind to unnecessarily squander hard-earned money. Why
then had she moved? He became more puzzled than ever.

27

UNEASY ENCOUNTER

Mary hardly realized how long she kept pacing up and down in her room, so absorbed had she become in her problem. It was not at all as simple as she had imagined only yesterday. If she had not met Mikola, it might have been. Now she knew for sure that she was in for a rough time.

She liked the man tremendously. It required a Herculean effort on her part to keep calm in the park today. Fortunately he stopped when he did, for she certainly hovered on the brink of a breakdown. She needed help terribly, and yet could not embrace the helping hand of a man whom she knew was already in love with her. Why had she done so? Would it not be easier to confide in him fully, call for his assistance, now that the target was within her sights?

No, and again no. The enjoyment of the fruits of vengeance must be hers, and hers completely. Now that the bitter-sweet cup appeared within reach, she must fetch it herself and not share it with anyone. Then and only then, she felt, would she have done her duty as a mother and daughter. There was no other way.

Yet now, just before reaching for that fateful cup, the biggest stumbling block loomed ahead of her. How was she to go over it? She had no feasible plan.

Her Christian ethics confused the issue. She felt she had the right to dispose of the criminal, but what right, if any, did she have to kill a husband and a father? Perhaps she should see a lawyer or a priest? If nothing else, they would help her in pointing out her exact position. Her own conscience was the prime consideration, the supreme judge, and the driving force to reckon with. And one's conscience comes from God...

The soft carpet muffled her steps, and she was in no way distracted by anything in her soul-searching. A number of times she peeked through the screen door. The house across the street appeared deserted. They must have gone to the beach or someplace, for their maroon Buick was nowhere in sight.

Mary wished she could operate with the indifference and precision of a gangster. To be able to go out and kill with a happy smile on one's face. After all, the agony of her later years was caused by this blood-thirsty vulture. So why the qualms of conscience?

Deep down inside, she felt she would be unable to make the final reckoning. There was God, there was her own conscience, both stern and ultimate judges, who would call her to account. What if she could not present the proper justification for her action, what if she was amiss in her life? If justice is to be dispensed arbitrarily, one must do it from an unshakable position.

She went into a long fit of crying. Miss Bentley's pillows had probably never absorbed so many tears in their uneventful lives. It was the cry of the damned and rejected. Mary realized that no matter what she would do, life had already jumped well ahead of her. The vulture now was not one being, but four. How do you split him away from the organism of his family without damaging the blood artery? How do you pacify the desperate anguish of her heart, the ghosts of her children and mother haunting her?

She calmed and collected herself, and in the late afternoon went out to the park. She strolled along the river bank, watched the children at play, tried to concentrate on reading her novel. The earlier eruption of emotions had now subsided, and she appeared numb and somewhat detached from her surroundings when she walked home at sunset. That was when she met Bergdorf.

She must have been totally absorbed in herself, for she did not see the Bergdorf family, and was about to cross the street when a soft female voice called her: "Mrs. Maroz!" It was Erna Bergdorf.

Mary stopped, turned, and saw them all. They stood by the car in their own driveway in the midst of unloading various paraphernalia they had brought from the beach or some such outing. The car's trunk was open, and Bergdorf was pulling a plastic boat and a mattress. All, except the head of the family, were dressed in shorts. The man wore long trousers. The picnic basket and various other items rested on the concrete walk. The children were hugging their toys and tussling with the white poodle.

"Please come here, Mrs. Maroz," Erna continued with a charming smile. Then to her husband: "Johan, this is the lady I told you about. She lives with the Bentley sisters. Her name is Mrs. Maroz."

Mary approached them slowly. Strangely enough, no element of surprise was there, just a simple curiosity. It was the curiosity of an undaunted hunter who had long ago accustomed himself to the idea that one day he would face the predator he had long sought to trap. Approaching the animal, there would remain the ticklish fascination of observing him alive at close quarters, all the time remembering to keep a safe distance.

Without a single sound, Mary stopped and stared at Bergdorf, almost forgetting Erna. The man, displaying his masculine, gray haired chest and hairy hands under his white T-shirt, straightened himself and, as if stung by an invisible fang, opened his mouth, unable to produce a sound.

Mary looked at the gray probing eyes, recognizing that brutal streak in them, at the thin lips, the small brown moustache, violet-coloured complexion, sagging chin, flabby belly, and challenged the murderer with a steady unwavering gaze of her own. His eyes were the same and yet so different. Now they were lit by a streak of incredulity and surprise, as if their owner had glimpsed a ghost.

This confrontation of eyes lasted a little too long and puzzled Erna. Her charming smile waning, her eyes darted from one to the other. "Johan, this is Mrs. Maroz, a nurse, our neighbour," she repeated, her voice unsteady. She certainly had a premonition of something beyond her comprehension taking place, and seemed to be unable to pin down whatever it was.

"Oh, Mrs. Maroz... glad to meet you," Bergdorf found his tongue at last. His hoarse voice seemed to emerge from his throat almost against the wishes of its owner. Then, with old-time bravado that Mary knew so well, he exclaimed: "I'll be damned!"

This resounding exclamation seemed to be so out of place to Erna that she stood stunned, staring fixedly at her husband, who had never appeared to her like this before. "What is it you are saying, Johan?" she inquired, perturbed.

Jolted back to reality, Bergdorf regarded his wife as if he were seeing her for the first time and mumbled incoherently: "I dunno... I mean... oh, never mind, it can't be... "

"What can't be? What are you saying? What's the matter with you?"

"Nothing, nothing... just forget about it."

He took some time composing himself, then faced Mary again.

"Where are you from, Mrs. Maroz?"

"Byelorussia," Mary answered calmly, now throwing a glance at Erna, enjoying the effect of her husband's unorthodox behaviour. Her young face remained puzzled. When Mary again turned to Bergdorf, her own face displayed a clearly discernible shadow of amusement. It would not have escaped Erna's attention had she not been so confused. Here she had brought two strangers together, and the way they behaved was entirely beyond her comprehension. Perhaps she was too much of a simpleton to recognize the spark of something much deeper inside the two.

"What place?" Bergdorf went on.

"Navahradak," Mary answered calmly. "Have you been there by any chance, Mr. Bergdorf?"

"Yes, passing by... " Now he seemed relieved and yet lost for what to do next. He looked at his wife, as if expecting her assistance.

Mary came to their aid: "Have you been to a picnic some place?"

"Not exactly. We went to the park at Lake Simcoe. It's a lovely park. You must see it to appreciate it. And the water's so warm, the beach so lovely. You should go with us one day, Mrs. Maroz. Have you been working today?" Erna asked.

"No, not today. But I went to church."

Bergdorf opened the side door of his house, all the time ogling Mary, and proceeded to take his things inside.

"Would you come inside with us, Mrs. Maroz? We can have a chat and a bite to eat. Please come," Erna urged Mary.

"I don't think I should intrude on you."

"Nonsense, what intrusion... It's our pleasure to have you." Erna's manner was so disarming that Mary found it impossible to resist. "All right," she said.

"Please, come in," Erna opened the door for her.

"If you'd like me to," Mary said in the kitchen, "I'll play with the children while you put things in order after your trip."

"By all means." Mrs. Bergdorf called her daughter,

"Erna, show this lady your books and toys, will you?" The little girl needed no urging. Accompanied by her mother's smile, she tugged at Mary's dress and led her into the playroom.

Still dwelling on her encounter with Bergdorf, Mary found herself confronted by an abundance of toys and games. There was even a TV set in the corner. Bergdorf must have opened his purse wide to stock his children's world. There was a wide assortment of dolls, little red-dressed Penny and big blonde Dolly included; there was a big shiny riding horse, small writing blackboard, a number of children's picture books, everything in such blessed disarray as only busy, carefree children were able to accomplish. The guns, tanks, planes, warships, and toy soldiers on one side evidently belonged to Eric.

Little Erna introduced Mary to her dolls' world. She was a lovely child, and Mary liked her. She chirped like a lively sparrow and giggled at her own dream world, delighting in presenting it to this friendly lady. Eric busied himself rearranging marching columns of toy soldiers. The white poodle viewed these proceedings from the corner with calm indifference.

"You seem to like children very much, Mrs. Maroz," Erna Bergdorf said, watching them from the doorway. Mary hadn't noticed her enter.

"Yes, I do. Your children are such darlings, Mrs. Bergdorf," Mary replied.

"Thank you, Mrs. Maroz."

"Please call me Alena," Mary said.

"O.K, Alena. Call me Erna," said Mrs. Bergdorf, smiling. "Now will you come to the living room, Alena? Erna and Eric, come over to the kitchen. I have some ice cream for you. Come on."

They sat around the huge coffee table in the living room, ate Danish pastries, and drank tea. After comments on the weather and children, Bergdorf resumed, as Mary expected he would, the interrogation.

"So you are from Navahradak, Mrs. Maroz?"

Sprawled in an easy chair, pulling at leisure on his fancy pipe, tobacco aroma permeating the room, he looked every inch the contented head of the house.

"That's what I said," Mary regarded him, keeping on guard. "And you've been there all the time during the war?"

"Yes, I worked in the hospital."

"I spent a couple of years in your country during the war. I was in Navahradak, Barysau, Miensk, Viciebsk, Homiel, Slucak... wonderful country, very nice people."

"Were you in the army there?"

"Yes. Ours was a special unit fighting against Red partisans. At times the going was rough, but on the whole I can't complain. I never got a scratch, although I was in situations where I had no hope of getting out alive... "

"It must have been really hard on you," Mary said.

"The war is never easy on anybody," Bergdorf puffed his pipe with relish. She regarded him with a suspicious curiosity. There was a constant watchfulness in his eyes, not the kind of shock he displayed when he saw her first, but the perceptive cautiousness of a suspicious dog.

"What happened to your husband, Mrs. Maroz?" Erna asked.

"He was drafted into the Red Army in 1941, when the war broke out. Later I received notice he was lost in action."

Presently Bergdorf's children came in from the kitchen. Erna sat on her mother's lap, and Eric proceeded into the playroom. Bergdorf got up. "Where are you going, Johan?" Erna inquired.

"I think we should have something stronger than this stuff. Don't you, Erna?"

"I don't mind," she said. She turned to Mary. "I was wondering, Alena, perhaps if you have time, you could sit with our children next Thursday. I'd like to go to the theatre; there's a play my husband wants to see."

"Let me see," Mary thought aloud. "There's nothing... I think I can sit with your children, Erna."

"Johan," Erna exclaimed when Bergdorf came in with a tray loaded with glasses, drinks, and mixes, "we can go and see the play you wanted to. Alena just agreed to sit with our children."

"Why, that'll be nice, Alena," Bergdorf grimaced. "You'll be doing us a favour. Baby-sitters are hard to come by in this city. I don't know why."

He placed the tray on the table and said, "What will you, ladies, have?"

"My usual," Erna said.

"What do you prefer, Mrs. Maroz?"

"I don't drink, thank you."

"Oh, come on, Alena," Erna butted in. "We should have a drink for our acquaintance, shouldn't we?"

"All right, perhaps a small one."

"Cherry liqueur? A ladies' drink," Bergdorf suggested.

"All right," Mary agreed.

"Make it the same for me," Erna said.

As he filled the glasses, Mary watched Bergdorf's hands. They handled liquor with decades of experience. That same finger, on which he now wore a topaz ring used to be adorned at one time with a silver skull and cross-bones. The other finger pulled the trigger that night in Shuly.

Mary got her glass filled with blood-red cherry liqueur and stared at the alcohol-saturated, repugnant face, the thin lips solemnly declaring: "Here's to our acquaintance." Her hand itched to throw the blood-red liqueur into the face of the murderer. It was too early.

28
SEARCH FOR JUSTICE

At dusk Mary got off the streetcar and unhurriedly proceeded up a residential street to see the pastor of her parish, who lived two blocks away. She had an appointment with him. As she passed by, she stared at some people watering their lawns, heard the noise of children dashing around busy at their hide-and-seek games – the last spell of their daily activities – before prudent mothers would drive them to bed.

Mary's mind wasn't on the slowing pulse of the busy city preparing itself for a well-deserved night's rest. Again and again her memory journeyed over the words of the lawyer she had seen that day after work. He gave her about five dollars' worth of advice: "You really have no case, Mrs. Karaway, I'm sorry to say. No Canadian court would touch it with a ten-foot pole. Take it from me, the purported crime, as you maintain, was committed by this man – what's his name – during the war. It happened outside of Canadian territory. You have no witnesses. Canadian courts would review only cases involving Canadian citizens at the time of the crime..."

That was it. Certainly Bergdorf must have learned where the Canadian law stood regarding his past activities. This land of opportunity constituted a haven for some criminals. Mary heard about the cases, where the Soviet authorities made trials in absentia for some so-called war criminals presently residing in Canada, after repeated extradition attempts had failed. The Canadian government usually maintained that the wanted person had been cleared by its immigration authorities, was a

Canadian citizen of good repute, and closed the book, ignoring all Soviet overtures and attacks. The Canadians were right, of course. No self-respecting democratic country would allow its citizens to be tried by the dictatorial regime of another country.

Mary considered her own case in a special category. First of all, no agents of the Moscow colonial regime in Byelorussia should have any claim on Bergdorf. To quote Inspector Trakhimovich, "This vulture scavenged the remains of the bleeding Byelorussian organism on which the two predators feasted," the predators being Hitlerite Germans and Stalinist Russians. To amend justice, the Byelorussian people had a divine right to place both the predators and their vultures, such as Bergdorf, on the bench of the accused. But because Mary's much-abused people were again under Moscow's colonial whip, such an idea of course was merely a pipe dream.

But Mary, the victim, and Bergdorf, the criminal, were now both within the realm of a democratic country's law where, in theory at least, the huge apparatus of justice was serving all its citizens. And yet the lawyer was explicitly clear on that point. Bergdorf was out of her reach. A situation much to be regretted, but true.

Uncle Lavon's admonishing words came back into her mind: "You want to bring this man to court? What court? You are not even a citizen of this country. What rights have you? Who will listen to you?" How right her uncle was. Even assuming that various judicial kinks were removed and the man was placed in the dock, how would she cope with the case with no money to back her up? If that was the case, why, she had certain God-given rights... or had she?

Pastor Paval welcomed her at the door and invited the woman into his living room. About sixty years of age, bald-headed, with a small silvery beard, he was obese and slow. The priest was a widower with no children and occupied three rooms of the main floor of the small house. His parish was small and called for frugal living. His combined living room-study was furnished modestly, and an enormous collection of books, chiefly Byelorussiana, lined one wall. The reading lamp projected a gloomy shadow from the small corner table. An open book, with a pair of spectacles reposing on it, lay on the couch beside the lamp.

"I've been expecting you, Mrs. Karaway," he said quietly. "Please come in and make yourself at home." He motioned toward a soft chair opposite the couch, and deposited his two-hundred-odd pounds beside the open book. His wrinkled face appeared flabby and almost lifeless; only his small dark eyes were alert and keen.

A number of times Mary had considered the fact that this old man had so little in common with the stereotyped image of an Eastern Orthodox priest. To her, the standard image should resemble a number of silvery long-bearded saints adorning so many of the walls of various Eastern Orthodox churches she had visited at one time or another: a saintly Byzantine stare, detached from the earth. All you had to do was add wings for locomotion, and speedily a God-loving subject would depart to an embrace of a Heavenly Master.

Mary knew Pastor Paval's forbidding appearance misled many. Besides a noble heart, a keen mind, and a character modest and unassuming, he possessed that often-sought and most-treasured gift, a tool so indispensable in his calling: the gift of language. His well-rounded, amply substantiated, and passionately delivered sermons constituted the living pulse of the otherwise dull Sunday church service-ritual. Usually he would start in a low key, and subtly lead his parishioners to the deeper waters of God's teaching. His mastery of delivery usually made his message land on receptive ears. He constantly strove to reach the younger generation and, by any yardstick, succeeded remarkably well.

As Mary sat down, Pastor Paval's keen eyes regarded her expectantly.

"Father Paval, I have a problem, quite a big problem." She paused, not quite knowing how to proceed.

"Take your time, my child, I'm at your service."

"I don't really know where to begin... you see, Father, my problem, to put it briefly, is a man presently residing in this city, and what I should do about him."

Mary's opening words evidently misled the old pastor, for a hardly discernible twitch of a forbearing smile enlivened his indifferent face. Obviously content he had fathomed the visitor's problem from her opening remark, the clergyman regarded the woman with a condescending detachment, no doubt ready to lend his receptive ear to a story of a love affair that was on the rocks.

"You see, Father Paval," Mary's quiet voice proceeded, "this man murdered my mother and two small children in Byelorussia during the war. Miraculously I escaped death myself."

"Great God Almighty!" exclaimed the priest, his serene face contorted by something akin to a deep pain inside of him. "Did I hear you right, Mrs. Karaway? Would you mind repeating what you just said?"

"You heard me right, Father Paval. The man I'm talking about murdered my two small children and my mother in Byelorussia during the war. Now I've found him. He lives right here in this city."

"Phew," a swishing sound emerged from the pastor's mouth. "Frankly, Mrs. Karaway, when you mentioned a man and a problem I imprudently assumed something of an entirely different nature. Oh Lord, forgive me my unpardonable presumption."

Now it was Mary's turn to be puzzled, appraising the priest's repentant expression. She smiled bitterly, understanding Father Paval's embarrassment. To dispel the awkward silence that followed, he cleared his throat: "Suppose you tell me everything from the beginning, without the most painful details, if you so desire... "

Mary began her story from before the war, when they had drafted her Valodzia into the army. She dwelled at length on how she and her mother saved Kolpakoff-Bergdorf's life, nursing him back to health and sheltering him from the Germans. Then she recounted his infamous activities in the German police. As she proceeded, Pastor Paval's expression gave way to a sympathetic understanding. A few times he interrupted her smooth narration to clear up a point or verify a fact.

With an effort, Mary checked her tears as she described Bergdorf's murder of her family and then her own agonies at the hands of the partisans. She then proceeded to cover her odyssey through war-ravaged Europe and Canada, the chance discovering of Bergdorf's whereabouts, and her present predicament. She stopped exhausted, regarding the Pastor's face which seemed immersed in deep concentration.

"This is obviously a criminal case and as such should be brought to court, Mrs. Karaway," the priest ventured a suggestion.

"I should have told you at once, Father Paval," Mary hastened to reply, "that I've been to a lawyer today. He told me there's no chance any Canadian lawyer – and these are his exact words – would touch it with a ten-foot pole."

"Is that so?" Pastor Paval was visibly moved. "Did he tell you why?"

"He gave me a number of reasons, the main one being that the crime was committed in another country during the war, and that those implicated were not Canadian citizens. Barring that, he said I wouldn't have a chance to prove my case for lack of witnesses."

"I should have known better," the pastor said, absentmindedly reaching for his glasses and examining them. Mary observed him pensively.

"I've never heard of any cases of this sort being tried in Canada for a number of years. It doesn't follow, Mrs. Karaway, that only you, out of all those thousands of Europeans who went through the war and suffering, have had such a singularly ghastly experience. There probably is, there must be, more New Canadians, who could point their finger at some criminals who have settled here and prove their guilt. And yet we haven't heard of one such case being aired in a Canadian court of justice. Regrettable... But that, I suppose, no matter how regrettable it is, it denies you any legal avenue to right the wrong... In fact there's no way... "

"This is precisely the reason that prompted me to visit you, Father Paval," Mary countered, "and ask for your advice."

The priest regarded the woman with a shade of suspicion in his alert eyes. "What precisely do you mean, Mrs. Karaway? What kind of advice do you want from me?"

"What can I do about this man?" Mary stressed the "I".

This prompted Pastor Paval to put his glasses on, and search the woman's face attentively, and then, taking the glasses off, say: "My dear child, if you are contemplating what I suspect you are, God forbid you! How can you?"

Her voice sounded clear and resolute as she said: "Father Paval, may I ask you to bear with me. Over a decade has passed since this beast committed the crime. During all this time I've tried to find a spiritual complacency, to reach for solace in God... Let Him be my witness right here and now, Father Paval, that all my efforts were genuine. I was unable to find peace no matter how hard I've tried. Finally, I've realized that no peace would ever dwell in my heart or soul as long as I live. They've cut my roots, murdered my closest kin, made me a derelict in the prime of my life. The fact that I'm probably not the only one doesn't make my spiritual and emotional burden any easier.

"I've tried to accustom myself to the idea that there's no way of effecting retribution. Then one day I learned that this vulture was alive and within my reach. I've located him. It seemed to me then that God Almighty had erected a road sign, employing the Satan for his purposes in a round-about way. From then on, I've kept thanking the Lord, knowing that He wanted me to go, seek out and destroy the vulture. I kept hoping it could be done legally. I was bitterly disappointed when I learned there's no chance of that. What am I to do, Father Paval? There must be a way... "

Visibly affected by the woman's plight, Pastor Paval rose slowly, reached for a black, leather-bound book on his desk by the window, and pensively leafed through it.

"Mrs. Karaway, I don't suppose I need to tell you that I am deeply and profoundly moved by your terrible personal tragedy," the Pastor replied in a low voice. "As you spoke about it to me, I did my best to imagine all the horrible suffering of your soul and heart. What you want from me, however, are not expressions of my condolences. You want to find a justification, on the authority of God if possible, for the step you must have been contemplating. Yet I suspect you knew the answer even before coming here to seek my advice. You must be a deeply religious woman, Mrs. Karaway, for if you were not, you certainly wouldn't have come to me. That's why I hate so much to disappoint you."

The pastor stood some distance from her, the half-open Bible in one hand, examining the effect his words were producing on his visitor. She looked small and miserable, with her eyes averted, and disappointment and anguish clouding her lovely face.

"In His commandments," continued the priest, "God explicitly forbade one man to kill another. All through His teachings, our Lord Jesus Christ stressed love as the springboard of all human life and behaviour. Love and peace among men on earth – that was the motto, the foundation of all our actions, the fertile soil on which we have to sow and harvest and seek a place in paradise."

"What love are you talking about, Father Paval?" Mary interrupted the pastor hysterically. "Didn't I tell you in detail how my mother and I saved this man's life? What do you think we were motivated by? Hate? Did God reward us for observing His teachings by killing everybody through this vulture's hands, sparing only myself? What is love, Father Paval?"

Violent sobbing convulsed her body. Unnerved, the priest approached her, laid his heavy hand on her shoulder, comforting her: "Please, my child, try to calm yourself... "

Both spoke about love, unable to find a common meaning for the word. The abysmal space between two different concepts seemed to be unbridgeable.

Pastor Paval slumped on his couch resignedly, regarding the sobbing woman in silence. With an effort she checked herself and wiped her moist face with a handkerchief. Gradually a serene calmness spread across her face; she looked at the priest with a newly-found self-assurance.

He did not like the change in the large, blue, hardened eyes. They appeared to be the eyes of a person suddenly and irrevocably reaching an unpleasant decision, a point of no return. When she spoke, her voice and manner were void of her recent uncertainty, the helplessness of an abandoned child reaching for a hand in a tumultuous, indifferent world.

"Father Paval," she said in a voice as hard as a rock, "once in my life I had reneged on God. Frankly, it was the time of my ignorant youth, school years, you know... We were being bombarded every day by anti-religious Bolshevist propaganda. One could use the argument that I, one among many to whom the truth had been denied, was justified in digesting the poison. Yet I felt guilty because I did it in spite of my mother's frequent admonitions. She was a pious, God-loving woman, God bless her soul. She repeatedly kept warning me that one day I'd find it hard to expire my great sins. She was right. I have tried, Father Paval, I have really tried. It wasn't easy.

"Eventually God must have heard my prayers, for I found a new source of strength in Him, although my soul was still occasionally rocked by doubts and recriminations. In the darkest moments of my spiritual depression, on the brink of my own grave, mourning the death of my mother and two small children, I have endeavoured to find strength in God. I came to believe that He would provide answers to all my problems, including that of vengeance on the man to whom we had given so much and who had taken everything I possessed. Father Paval, to say that I've grown disappointed lately, would certainly be a major understatement."

Her face flushed, she rose and looked the priest directly in the eyes.

"It's more than a disappointment, Father Paval! I should be grateful to you for not trying to brush me off with that standard answer I've heard other priests employ in such situations: 'it's not for us sinners to penetrate the mysterious and intricate workings of God.' That, I must admit, doesn't explain anything to me. What's the good of God's teaching if it's inapplicable in practical life?

"I am an ordinary mortal, Father Paval, and I need ordinary, down-to-earth explanations. Right in front of our eyes, life has played the dirtiest tricks imaginable. So what do we do to find our own way in this man-made Golgotha? We reach for the Bible, the fountain of God's wisdom, the source of faith and strength for man who was created by God in His own image. And what do we find in there? Not only are we baffled by the absence of answers to so many of the practical problems of life, but – on the contrary – we witness the immense growth of the forces of evil and destruction all around us.

"Who was it that said – Voltaire or Napoleon? – that God always supports the strong? What are the weak ones to make of it? Look at our country, our people, Father Paval. What do you see? The nation has been under the heel of civilized barbarians for about two centuries. And yet can you possibly maintain that the average Byelorussian is more sinful than the Muscovite colonizer who bleeds him white?

"You know how good and God-loving our people are, Father Paval. You can probably remember the scenes many of us witnessed in our country, time and again during the war: a battle-weary enemy soldier – Russian, German or Polish, it didn't matter – would knock on the poor peasant's door asking for food. A woman would open the door and share with him perhaps the last morsel of food in the house. Just imagine a German housewife doing that to their own men. We've been around and we know...

"Just considering this makes one wonder: is it at all possible, Father Paval, that our people, impoverished and decimated by their so-called Christian brothers, are too good to live among the murderers and civilized barbarians? Or is it perhaps possible that the Almighty proposes to ship them all directly into paradise? What is the explanation, Father Paval? Nothing makes sense, nothing."

As Mary, visibly exhausted by discharging her innermost thoughts, retreated to the door, the priest rose, faced her calmly, and said: "Mrs. Karaway, I assume it was your emotion that spoke perhaps against your better judgment. Let me caution you, however, that it's highly imprudent for us, small and insignificant as we are, given the limited horizons afforded us by God, to comprehend the whole of the universe and question the ways and means of the Master's hand."

Mary regarded the priest with detached resignation and left the house.

29
THE CHALLENGE

Two weeks later Erna Bergdorf invited Mary to her daughter's birthday party. "You must come, Alena," she said with that disarming smile of hers while they sat on the Bergdorfs' back lawn. She had little Erna on her lap, while Eric was flying on the swing nearby. Bergdorf was still away, presumably working. "Erna insists," Mrs. Bergdorf continued. "Don't you, Erna? Tell the lady you'd like her to come to your birthday party."

"Please come, Mrs. Alena, will you?" the little girl said, hugging her newest Penny doll.

"All right, Erna," Mary said, patting the girl on her rosy cheek. "How can I refuse such a nice invitation. And whom did you invite besides me?"

The girl pondered the question and then said: "Jean will come, Mary and Irene... and who else, Mom?" She looked at her mother, puzzled.

"Well, I guess that makes it a full party. Now you can count Mrs. Alena too, Erna."

"I'm glad you'll come," the girl smiled at Mary.

"It will be my pleasure," Mary smiled back. "So how old are you going to be, Erna?"

"I'll be five," the girl replied instantly.

"My, my, you are a big lovely girl now, Erna. Next fall you'll have to go to kindergarten. Did your mother tell you what presents you're going to get for your birthday?"

"No, she didn't, but I told her what I want."

"And what is it you want? Or is it a secret?"

"She wants a houseful of dollies," Mrs. Bergdorf smiled. "Say, Erna, perhaps you should go visit Irene and see what she is doing?"

"She isn't home, Mom."

"Where is she, do you know?"

"I don't know. Nobody is home, maybe they are out on the lake."

"All right then, go and play with Eric on the swing. Come on," Mrs. Bergdorf slapped her gently on the back, and the girl ran to join her brother on the swing in the corner of the backyard.

Erna's birthday party was scheduled for late Thursday afternoon. Mary knew that both Bergdorf children and their mother liked her. Since that memorable visit to Pastor Paval, she sat with them twice, when the Bergdorfs were having a night out at the theatre.

Mary could not help wondering how she had grown so attached to these two children in so short a time. During her first sitting she had contemplated giving Bergdorf some of his own medicine. So obsessed had she become with the idea, that on her trip to the bedroom she suddenly discovered she was tightly clutching a large kitchen knife in her right hand. A sudden realization of the horrible thing she was contemplating jolted her back to reality.

Yet the reality itself was confusing. Rankled by the position she was in, unable to extricate herself from the labyrinth of her conflicting emotions, she often viewed her present dilemma as an added penalty from God. Within striking distance of the murderer, she was unable to deliver a final, decisive blow. She felt constrained by both human and divine law.

Mary often speculated if Bergdorf knew about this protective shield. Either he did or he did not care, which made it much worse for her. Had she found him living alone, the expedition of vengeance would have been swift and merciless. Erna and the children made all the difference. Mikola augmented the confusion with his aggressive courtship. She became nervous and absent-minded. The other day in the hospital kitchen, she was so engrossed with her own problem that she became overly careless and broke a few dishes, prompting a warning from the kitchen supervisor that another offence like this would bring her instant dismissal.

Mary discovered Mikola was quite serious about her and could not for the world understand what made her so cool and indifferent to him. This made him all the more aggressive. Mary hated to reject him for she liked him immensely and yet could not share her burden with him.

Since the completion of her "mission" had stalled in a mire of conflicting emotions, doubts, and self-recriminations, she had no choice but to resignedly wait for a chance to see "the mysterious and intricate workings of the hand of God."

The breakthrough came on Thursday afternoon.

Little Erna's birthday party turned out well. Johan Bergdorf must have considerably loosened his purse strings for after a happy birthday song in both German and English, blowing out the candles, and sharing the birthday cake, little Erna's eyes opened wide as she unwrapped the presents and found all her extravagant wishes satisfied. Her little face was aglow with joy and she chirped with mirthful exclamations, showing proudly her newly acquired treasures to her three honoured guests. Mary's gift was a children's picture book, and she could not help blushing as little Erna unwrapped the package. She gave a superficial look at what she considered the most ordinary of gifts. Nevertheless, prompted by her mother, she rewarded Mary with a generous hug and a "thank you".

The hectic activity of unpacking and examining all the birthday presents subsided and the children moved with the new toys into the playroom. Erna brought in the roast turkey and other delicacies, while a beaming fatherly

Bergdorf solemnly filled the glasses and raised a toast for little Erna's health and bright future. Another round swiftly followed. The Bergdorfs drank, but Mary barely touched hers.

As often happens after a generous meal, especially one accompanied by drink, the people around the table begin to dwell on matters temporal and eternal. Family celebrations, as a rule, tend to channel everyone's attention into domestic stock-taking. The Bergdorfs proved to be no exception to the rule. Relaxed and happy, Erna Bergdorf unwittingly provided an opening that triggered, although in a roundabout way, Mary's accomplishment of her "mission."

"Children are fun," Erna said all aglow, with the contentment of a mother who had fulfilled her duty. "They bring so much joy and happiness."

Bergdorf acknowledged his wife's remark with a warm if somewhat modest grin, while Mary stared sullenly ahead of her. But then the alcohol-flushed face of the murderer across the table jolted her out of her momentary forgetfulness. She sat on live coals, frustrated, making a supreme effort to keep her mask intact. Then Erna turned, directly to her: "Alena, didn't you once mention to me that you had children? What happened to them?"

The ignorant woman provided the spark which ignited the long dormant fuse in Mary's heart. "Yes, Erna," Mary responded readily. "I had two: a boy about the age of your Eric and a baby girl about six months old."

"Go on. What happened to them?" Erna urged.

Mary held her breath. It seemed to her she glimpsed a nervous twitch on Bergdorf's outwardly complacent face. He shifted in his comfortable chair, his gray, alcohol-dulled eyes visibly puzzled for maximum effect, Mary decided it would have the most impact if she told them all at once.

"Both my children and my mother were murdered during the war by a man whose life we had saved. All four of us were shot by a drunken beast. Only a twist of fate brought me back to life from a certain grave."

Erna's impulsive exclamation of shocked surprise cut through the subdued voices of the children in the next room. She froze, staring at Mary in profound disbelief. Bergdorf's hand reaching for the liqueur bottle poised suspended over the edge of the table. At Mary's opening words, an evil light appeared in his eyes which seemed to find themselves uncomfortably crowded in their sockets. Yet the man controlled himself.

"I'm sorry, Alena, I didn't realize... I shouldn't have asked," Erna mumbled apologetically. "If you forgive me, I mean if you find it too hard, we don't have to talk about it." Mrs. Bergdorf shot a glance at her husband, yet she appeared to be so vexed by this unexpected discovery that she failed to note any change in him.

"Not at all," Mary answered, "I can tell you." She emptied her glass to the bottom to fortify herself.

"My God, it must be quite a story," Erna regarded Mary with sympathetic eyes. "Go on."

"As I told you before, my husband was drafted into the army shortly before the outbreak of the war. I was left alone with my mother and my five-year-old son Valodzia. Shortly after that Alenka was born. My husband never saw the adorable baby. I lived in a village and worked for a community health dispensary. My salary was meagre but somehow we managed... Then the war broke out, and the Germans pushed into Byelorussia. Our village stood close to the main highway. The Soviet Army was in full rout, the highway was a sea of panicking humanity.

"The day was sunny and the German fighters made the most of it. The slaughter was terrible. It was like a huge butcher's knife cutting a path through the moving columns. Late that night, just as I was preparing the children for bed, my mother and I heard a faint knocking on the outside door and shortly thereafter a resounding thud – as if a bag of potatoes had been dumped on our verandah. Cautiously we opened the door and found in the darkness a wounded, bleeding Soviet soldier. We took him in, brought what local medical help we could, and decided to shelter the poor man from the Germans. The man was young, handsome, and said he was from Leningrad. His name was Pisareff."

Mary started with an effort, but as she proceeded her small, emotion-charged voice was steady, though at times hesitant. Despite her deep emotional involvement, her ever-present prudence suggested saving her trump card till later. She decided that a complete expose of Bergdorf to his wife at present would do Erna and her children irreparable harm. She liked the woman, and suspected Mrs. Bergdorf was ignorant of the fact that her husband had strewn his war-time road with bones and spilled innocent blood wantonly. This consideration made her substitute fictional names for the real ones.

While Bergdorf shifted in his chair uncomfortably and shot murderous glances at Mary, Erna was listening attentively. "What happened then?" she asked, her curiosity aroused.

"Sheltering an enemy soldier imperiled the lives of our whole family. The penalty, had we been caught, would have been death. Despite this, my mother and I kept nursing the man back to health, not knowing we were saving our future murderer. He was wounded badly in the stomach but some gentle, continuous care and the healthy air of the forest healed the wound. We kept him in an abandoned game-keeper's hut for the whole summer."

"And you fed him and looked after him all that time?" Erna wanted to make sure.

"Yes. It wasn't easy, I must tell you. The fear of being

discovered sometimes made us go without sleep for days. Yet we continued, taking food to him late in the evening to avoid prying eyes. I presume some neighbours suspected or even knew about it but never reported it to the Germans. There is this quality of character in our people that we have always tended to support the underdog even at the risk of our own lives. It is perhaps because we've been in bondage so long and hate all foreign masters yet are too weak to cast off the chains ourselves... "

"I can see that," Erna nodded. "What then?"

"The man recovered sooner than I expected. He grew robust and healthy. To confound my own precarious situation, he started making sexual advances on me."

"You don't say," Erna smiled. Mary regarded her detachedly, glanced at Johan's pale face, and continued: "Once I decided to visit him in the daytime to ascertain what his condition really was. I found the hut empty but he must have been close by, and came back while I was still inside. That time he apparently decided to take me by force. I had to fight for my life."

"What a beast," Ema made a wry face, her eyes intent on Mary, forgetting all about her dear Johan.

"I escaped, telling him I didn't want to see him any more."

"Apparently he was in a good condition, all healed up and well," Ema could not help chuckling.

"You bet he was," Mary agreed. "Well, the next day I found he was gone. My mother and I thanked God for assisting us. It wasn't easy to look after him, you know, with a small child of my own and such a demanding job."

"You still worked at the dispensary?" Erna inquired.

"No. I taught at the village school. I had some education in that line before the war. They offered me a job in the hospital far away from home, but I decided to stay in the village. There was a shortage of teachers so I taught four grades."

"What about that Pisareff?"

"To make it easy for you to understand what happened next and why, I'll have to digress slightly. During the war our country was like hell itself. Stalin dumped his trained operatives in partisan warfare behind the front line; these in turn gathered deserters and forcibly recruited the local manfolk into their units. The cruel repressive measures of the Germans increased the rapid growth of Red partisan units. Germans tried to hold out in towns and cities and protect their communication lines to the front, but the task was self-defeating, as you may say. As they grew weak they sought the help of local elements. Disloyal and distrustful as Byelorussians were, very few volunteered to join the German Schutz-Polizei. But all kinds of riff-raff welcomed the opportunity.

"It soon appeared that they hindered the occupational forces as much as they helped them. In the chaos of war, this riff-raff considered their uniforms as licences for murdering, raping and pillaging the local peaceful, defenceless population. Hundreds of villages went up in smoke, their inhabitants burned alive. One couldn't be loyal to both masters, especially if one lived in the so-called fringe zones where authorities overlapped one another. People were often targets for repression from both sides."

"My God, it must have been horrible," Erna whispered.

"Late next summer, the man named Schwartz became widely known throughout our area; it inspired a deadly fear in people's hearts. We heard that this fellow, whose police unit operated in the region, proved to be remarkably adept at raping, pillaging and burning alive the civilian population. Then one winter night I met him myself... "

Mary paused and regarded Bergdorf with a challenging stare. He averted his eyes and filled his glass as if afraid to confront Mary's accusing stare. He appeared calm.

"Johan," Erna turned to him, "fill my glass. I feel this story is going to be too much for me. You want another drink, Alena?"

Mary passed her glass over. Would not he like to fill it up with poison, if he possibly could, she thought. The vulture controlled himself remarkably well, and Erna still did not notice anything out of the ordinary. She passed the liqueur and a bowl with ice to Mary and said: "What happened that night?"

"It was one of those moonlit winter nights when you could see for a distance. My mother went outside to gather some firewood. She saw two sleighs full of people approaching the village. She naturally assumed they were partisans so she ran inside the house to warn me. My little Alenka was sick and I was nursing her in my arms in the bedroom. Soon we heard loud footsteps on our verandah and the door opened with a bang. Three men came in. The one in front was Pisareff in his *Schutzpolizei* uniform."

"My God!" Erna exclaimed.

Mary paused to let that sink in and sipped her drink, her eyes cutting through Johan over the rim of her glass.

"You should have seen how glad my mother was to welcome the man who had been a part of our life. She rushed to him, ready to embrace him. The man had a submachine gun slung over his right shoulder and acted like a dispenser of life and death. He wasn't sober. Brusquely, he brushed my mother aside and barked in answer to her endearing words: 'I'm not your Ivan Pisareff, you silly old wench! My name is Schwartz.'

"This unexpected revelation brought pangs of terror to our hearts. We didn't know what to do. My mother still attempted to build a bridge across the time that divided us from last seeing this omnipotent monster. But he pushed her aside rudely again, and in a hoarse voice demanded to know – I think his words were – 'Where is that lovely, elusive daughter of yours?'

"I was behind the partition, holding the baby in my arms, and his words chilled my blood to my bones. I recalled his sexual advances and my unceremonious refusal. He proceeded to the bedroom, saw me, and immediately grabbed me. I fought with all my powers, my mother rushing to my assistance. He tore my darling girl from my arms, threw her on the floor, and mercilessly kicked her away. My world collapsed. In that instant, with my baby-girl shrieking on the floor, I must have been close to a complete mental breakdown. I had no chance to fight him. The thunder of the submachine-gun cut me down like lightning, plunging me into darkness."

Mary stopped to catch her breath. She wondered if she could carry on to the conclusion of her story or suddenly lose control of herself and jump at the man across the table. Erna looked at Johan and, noticing his strange behaviour, asked anxiously: "Anything wrong, Johan? Are you allergic to stories like this?" And then in a soothing voice: "You've been in the war, my dear, must have seen dead people... Is there anything wrong with you, Johan?"

"N-no, nothing, nothing," Bergdorf cleared his throat with an effort, staring at Erna guiltily. "I'll be all right."

"Well, how did you survive?" Erna turned to Mary, anxious to hear the conclusion.

"I woke up in a partisan hospital. I must have been unconscious for some time, for they had pulled two bullets out of me and I lost much blood. Apparently Schwartz's unit was ambushed, but the monster had escaped. They told me my mother and both my children were dead, the house burned down."

A long silence followed. In the adjoining playroom, the children giggled at their uncomplicated amusements. Bergdorf proceeded to fill and light his pipe.

"How did you get away from the partisans? Did you hear about this Schwartz or see him later?" Erna asked.

"It's rather a long story to relate – how I got away from the partisans after I got well. I didn't see Pisareff-Schwartz any more. I heard he escaped the advancing Soviet forces and was seen safe, sound and healthy in Germany."

"God Almighty!" Erna exclaimed. "What a beast of a man. Perhaps he's still alive somewhere."

Mary decided this was a heaven-sent opportunity to deliver the stab. Erna, the good naive girl, would twist the knife. She said meditatively, looking straight into Bergdorf's eyes: "No reason why he shouldn't be. Perhaps he's even married and has children."

"Come to think of it," Erna mused, "he might be married, have a lovely wife, a couple of dear youngsters like ours, all the time carefully preserving an image of a God-fearing, benevolent father; his children and his wife being ignorant of the fact that their family was spawned by a monster only fit to be strung up on the gallows... "

My dear girl, you did it excellently, Mary thought. One should applaud you, if one could. Now it is your turn, Mr. Bergdorf.

"Shut up, you!" Bergdorf roared, rising to his feet, full of wrath, ready to jump at his wife like a wounded bear.

"Johan," Erna gasped. "What's the matter with you?" She appeared so dumbfounded by her husband's unexpected outburst that she must have wondered about the state of his health. "Are you really not well?" she inquired in a motherly tone.

Bergdorf's outburst brought the children from the playroom, and they stood hesitantly in the doorway unable to comprehend the reason for their father's outburst.

Realizing not a second too soon that he had almost given himself away, Bergdorf mumbled something incoherently, collected himself with an effort, and withdrew to the kitchen. Erna's eyes followed him anxiously.

"I'm sorry, Erna," Mary said to Mrs. Bergdorf. "I didn't realize your husband was so sensitive. I shouldn't have –"

"Sometimes I wonder," Erna mused, "he must have been through hell in the war. If you only knew how good, gentle, and kind he is. He wouldn't hurt a fly... that war must have done something to him.. usually he avoids talking about it... "

30

DEATH RIDE

The hospital's kitchen staff had to rise early, and Mary usually covered the two blocks to the bus stop shortly before five. The night following Erna's birthday party she slept uneasily, tossing in bed, plagued bad dreams. The alarm instantly jolted her out of her uneasy slumber; she threw off the blanket and slammed the clock's release button.

There was a slight drizzle outside. She hesitated as she reached the sidewalk, deliberating whether to run back in and fetch an umbrella, then decided she could do without it. Later, as she recollected every possible detail of that fateful morning, she wondered why, at the time, she did not attach any significance to the fact that Bergdorf's garage stood open and empty.

Obsessed by the idea that she must not miss the bus – at this time they ran in fifteen-minute intervals – she walked with brisk steps, various speculations about the possible effects of yesterday's events again crowding her thoughts again. Why did she challenge the wolf? Was it the right thing to do? Would he react now that he became had become aware of his imminent danger?

The house on the corner stood some distance away from the street, and its owner evidently liked some measure of seclusion, for an assortment of trees and thickly grown lilacs lined the high metal fence. This obstructed the view of the side street almost completely.

Just as Mary reached the corner and was about to cross the street, looking straight in front of her, the car at the curb on her right spurted into sudden motion and its brakes screeched right in front of her. Just five feet away from her, the door of the maroon-coloured Buick suddenly swung open and Bergdorf jumped out. It all happened so suddenly that Mary was completely taken by surprise. Terror-struck by the man's menacing appearance, especially his red swollen eyes, she stood completely immobilized.

"Get in, Mary!" His voice was hoarse and brisk and even as he barked at her he pushed her violently past the steering wheel into the front seat. Now realizing fully what was happening, Mary frantically reached for the handle of the door on her right, but a convulsive grip pulled her away from it immediately, and she was met with a swift, violent blow to her left cheek, and a threatening hiss: "You try that once more and I'll fix you for good!"

The car jerked into motion and roared down the street. Recovering from the blow, Mary looked at Bergdorf. His flushed red face spelled m-u-r-d-e-r. The Buick roared through a quiet residential area. Its streets, except for an occasional early riser, were deserted at this hour. Bergdorf proceeded west and in fifteen minutes or so he turned north on the highway. Rush hour was about two hours away and the road was practically empty. Still dazed by this unexpected turn of events, Mary racked her brains trying to figure out what to do, the Buick's speedometer needle approached fifty. The drizzle increased, and the windshield wipers worked furiously clearing away the thick stream of raindrops.

"Where are you taking me?" Mary asked.

"Somewhere. You won't need a return ticket!" His harsh voice jarred Mary's taut nerves. "The first time I saw you around my house, I knew there was something fishy about you. I couldn't believe my eyes; I thought I had disposed of you long ago... You see, my girl," an ugly grimace contorted his murderous face, "you were smart enough to find me but not that smart to accomplish what you've set out to do. This time, I'll make sure that you stay gone for good."

The thick raindrops whizzed past as he kept the car at a safe fifty. Even now, taking his victim some place distant from civilization, the man appeared to be unnervingly composed.

Precious seconds, minutes, ticked away. Mary saw little if anything ahead as her mind, facing a life-or-death situation, groped for an escape. Rankled by remorse that she had been so close to her goal and by impulsively telling her story, she had muddled all chances of realizing it, she came to the sudden conclusion that if she was certainly to die this time, the least she could do was try to take him with her. Now that she had made her fateful decision, her mind seemed to work faster. The weapon would be the car...

The highway grew into four lanes and the huge concrete overpass of a newly built super-highway loomed some distance ahead. Mary gripped the seat with her right hand and swung hard to the side, and with her left delivered a vicious blow on Bergdorf's right foot. It came off the gas accelerator and Mary pressed hard. The car suddenly jumped ahead. Obviously taken off balance, Bergdorf tried to regain control of the car, his hands and legs going into disorganized motions. With her left hand, Mary grabbed the steering wheel, as Bergdorf struck her savagely, trying to knock her foot off the gas pedal. Even as the car went wildly zig-zagging across the width of the highway she desperately tried to maintain her grip on the steering wheel. Suddenly a tremendous metal-tearing, ear-splitting impact sent Mary Karaway spiraling once again into darkness.

31
BACK TO LIFE

Her third time coming back to life seemed to be less arduous than the former two, possibly because it was tempered by the sweet relief that the man who had inflicted so much harm on her was finally gone. She woke up in the hospital where she had washed dishes only yesterday. Her left leg was in a heavy cast up to her thigh, and she was bandaged in several other spots. Besides a fractured foot and tibia, she suffered minor abrasions and acute shock. With God's grace, they assured her, she would be on her feet again in a couple of months.

Apparently the foot, which propelled the Buick to the final solution of her "mission", got stuck under the gas pedal, next to Bergdorf's lifeless body. She was told they had quite a job extricating her as she lay there unconscious. It was lucky that she happened to be on the safer side when the Buick struck the bridge abutment with the left front of the car. Her head, except for shock, escaped severe injury.

Through the window, Mary glimpsed the ash-gray waters of Lake Ontario, took a note of four other patients in the room, and realized that this durable if somewhat scarred and tarnished world still kept turning around its axis and was humming with the tempo of life as much as ever. Only one girl named Mary Karaway was for a time taken out of circulation.

The first visitor to see her wore a police uniform. No one could be less welcome to talk to than a policeman. Mary was so intensely afraid of uniforms that it took the man some painstaking digging before he could get a statement from her. Apparently a gun was found on the dead Bergdorf's body, and the authorities seemed eager to know if she had been kidnapped and whether a struggle had taken place in the car that might have caused the accident. To all those questions, Mary replied with a flat no, for she remembered that the least she could do for Erna was to spare her and her children.

Mrs. Bergdorf came the next day. She appeared shaken but composed. Mary was taken aback by Erna's involuntary exclamation of surprise.

"Alena! You?" She stopped petrified by Mary's bed, unable to decide on the next move in the light of this newest development.

"Yes, Erna," Mary said quietly, "coming up here you've been probably wondering who this Mary Karaway was... that's my real name."

"But why, Alena... I mean Mary? I don't understand."

"I'll explain. But first of all, pull up a chair and sit down."

When Erna sat close to her bed, Mary reached for her hand and stared deeply in her dark eyes, so burdened by her singular misfortune. Now they were expectant and puzzled.

"Hold my hand, Erna, and summon your courage... You'll have to take another bitter pill, for you've asked for an explanation. As God is my witness, I never wanted to hurt you or your lovely children. First of all, take my word for it that I'm sorry for you, though I cannot be sorry for your husband."

"What do you mean?"

"Be patient, Erna, I asked you to be brave, for this is going to be quite a shock to you."

Mary caught her breath, looked directly into Erna's youthful, grieving face, and proceeded: "At your little girl's birthday party, I told you about the man named Pisareff-Schwartz, the murderer. I don't really know why I did it right then and there, perhaps because you urged me to. Anyway, I didn't tell you one very important fact: the man who murdered my mother and children had been wounded not in the stomach but in his left leg. Large areas of his flesh below the left thigh were badly burned. That's why it took all summer to heal... I also happened to notice at the time that above his kneecap he had a sizable, egg-shaped birthmark. His name was –"

"Johan Bergdorf!" Erna exclaimed with in a hollow voice and collapsed in her chair, her hand quivering in Mary's grasp. "My God!" she whispered as tears streamed down her face. The moment passed quickly, perhaps because the woman was exhausted by the previous shock of the sudden loss of her husband. She took a handkerchief from her handbag, wiped her moist face, and with an effort looked up at Mary. Fear appeared in her eyes. She rose to her feet and walked to the window. She stood motionless, scanning the horizon beyond Lake Ontario. In the distance, a freighter, probably bound for Hamilton, emitted a cloud of smoke. Caught in a crossfire of conflicting emotions, she hardly noticed the distant ship.

That morning, back in Germany, after the war on the farm, Johan Bergdorf, haggard and exhausted, had appeared on their doorsteps. Her mother, so religious, a widow, sheltered and fed him. An act of Christian kindness. Bergdorf stayed for some time, tending the farm. Male help was scarce and those who were marriageable were almost non-existent. That is why Johan seemed a godsend to Erna's mother. Here was a husband for Erna, the man to tend the farm. Everything was coming up roses. Erna and Johan married and her future seemed assured.

To upset the balance of their idyll, the Allies decided to shift their borders of occupation, and the Russians were to take over their area. Upon hearing this, Johan Bergdorf panicked. There was simply no question of him remaining under the Reds. They had to move. For some time, they stayed with relatives in Western Germany, where her mother passed away. Immigration to Canada seemed an answer to their problems.

The beginnings were difficult, but Johan proved very resourceful man. Life seemed to run smooth for Erna and Johan until their children were born. Then her Johan became a different man. His irregular hours of work seemed suspiciously long. People talked, and Erna was almost certain that her husband was seeing another woman.

How naive she was in those days! Her husband was not a hero but a beast, with innocent blood on his hands. What was it she had said at little Erna's birthday party that prompted his explosion? She searched her memory. Yes, here it is: "His wife is ignorant of the fact that their family was spawned by a monster only fit to be strung up on the gallows." No wonder he had acted as he had. And all through these years she, Erna Bergdorf, so obedient, so properly raised, a farmer's daughter, had embraced this monster. Revulsion and hate choked her. Then suddenly her wrath turned towards this woman on the hospital bed.

Why the hell had she come and disrupted their life? No matter what that life was, it would have certainly been better than a widow's lot. Blissful ignorance is sweeter than the bitter truth. What is she going to do now, alone and helpless? Now that her bread-winner was dead, who was to support her? Who would bring up the children? The children… my God! Erna gasped.

She turned, her face ashen-gray. She approached Mary. Now the realization that this woman had spared her children overwhelmed everything else, pushed Erna's spark of hate for Mary into the background. Simple soul, she was so grateful, almost ready to kiss Mary Karaway's hand. This thought alone prevailed and became a guiding light in her confused mind.

"Alena, I mean Mary... You've been after my husband and you sat with our children... You could have –"

"Yes, Erna, I could have done to his children what he did to mine. Who knows, perhaps I would have been justified. One thing prevented me."

"What was that?"

"My belief in God and my deep attachment to you, Erna. You are a good girl. Bergdorf didn't deserve to have you. Coming from me, who had suffered so much at the hands of the Germans, who had seen so many of our people perish by their lead and fire, that's saying a lot... "

"Thank you, Mary, thank you," Erna attempted to kiss Mary's hand, which she speedily withdrew.

"There's no need for that, Erna. I know how you feel. My sympathies are with you. Don't blame for what I did. I'm still unable to figure out how it turned out the way it did. You see, in the morning, as I was walking to work, he jumped at me on the corner, pushed me into his car, and told me he was going to make sure that this time I would be put away permanently... "

Erna did not utter a sound. She raised her eyes and stared at Mary, her emotional exhaustion evidently keeping her feelings at a low ebb.

Four other patients in the room were obviously frustrated by their inability to understand German, for the behaviour of the two women intrigued them. Of course, they heard about the car accident in which Mary was involved and later questioned her about it. But this confrontation of the two characters of the drama that was spawned in hell on the other side of the ocean was inaccessible to them.

"He would do that... he would do that... My God, my God!" Erna whispered.

The two women exchanged stares more eloquent than any words could be.

"It's a cruel world, Erna," Mary said. "If that'll make it

any easier for you, I want to tell you I understand exactly how you feel. But time will heal your wounds. I'm glad I found you as you are – good and simple. This made me check myself, realize that I had no right to harm you and your children... "

Mary lay quietly, her whole being warmed by the realization that she had been able to do some good in the midst of her misery.

"Tell me, Mary, did the police talk to you? You know they've found a gun on him?"

"Yes, I know. The policeman came here, asked me if I was kidnapped, and if a struggle took place in the car. I said no. There's one other thing you're probably wondering about, Erna."

"Yes, about the children."

"I promise you, Erna, they'll never learn from me that their father was not what he appeared to them to be," Mary squeezed the woman's hand.

"You are an angel, Mary. I am so deeply indebted to you. I can't imagine how he could have done to you all that he did. You and your mother saved his life... It's simply terrible just to think of it. And he was the father of my children... "

"You knew another man, Erna. Perhaps you never even suspected him."

"I had second thoughts, but I certainly suspected nothing like this. Now his outburst at Erna's birthday party makes sense. Well, Mary, right now I can't say anything more, when he's not even buried yet. The less said the better it is. Do you agree?"

"Yes, I understand," Mary replied.

"Thank you again, Mary," Erna bent down and kissed Mary's forehead. Then she hesitated, abruptly turning around. "I'll visit you again, Mary, after the funeral. Take care and get well soon," she said as she went out.

Mikola came in half an hour later. Counting the three

from the kitchen downstairs, he was Mary's sixth visitor that day, and the woman was really tired. She made an effort to accord him a warm hearing and explain in detail what had happened and why.

The man sat by the bedside deeply troubled, even though Mary told her story modestly, it made a tremendous impression on him. Suddenly he realized her reasons for discouraging his attempts to approach her earlier. Remarkably enough, shocked as he was, he found enough resolve to cheer the woman with his warm smile.

"Don't worry, Mary," he said just before departing. "If you'll let me, I'll help you all I can. I'll look after you." Whereupon he blushed, realizing his modest promise was, in truth, a confession of love.

Late that night Mary lay wide-awake, her hazy mind travelling again and again over all that happened. Strangely enough, now that her "mission" was accomplished, she felt utterly exhausted and empty. After all, she had not started living yet. She was still a derelict, her roots cut from the land that bore her.

Pastor Paval's words came to her: "It is highly imprudent for us – small, insignificant creatures – to presume we can comprehend the whole of the universe or question the means of the Master's hand.

THE END